Retrouvailles

Retrouvailles

RYAN MALDEN

MMXVI

This novel is a work of fiction. All of the names, characters, groups, and events illustrated in this novel are fictitious or products of the author's imagination. Any resemblance to actual persons, living or dead, is entirely coincidental.

ISBN: 978-1534916197

Printed in the United States of America

Acknowledgements

My thanks go to the following people for their invaluable advice and contributions to this novel:

Kathleen Horeczky, Jonathan Malden, Diane Malden, and Lorraine Malden

For Auntie Maureen,
Thank you for all the prayers, blessings, and love you have given me.

"He will always be attracted to the woman who reflects his deepest vision of himself, the woman whose surrender permits him to experience a sense of self-esteem. The man who is proudly certain of his own value, will want the highest type of woman he can find, the woman he admires, the strongest, the hardest to conquer—because only the possession of a heroine will give him the sense of an achievement."

—Ayn Rand, *Atlas Shrugged*

• 1 •

In 1644, a beautiful, baby boy was born into humble circumstances in the seaside town of Brighton, England. The cool waves rolling on the shore's stones were a continuous lullaby for this little boy. His parents were overjoyed when they looked upon their lovely son and knew he must be destined for wonderful things. The boy grew up quickly and was the apple of his parents' eyes, and the entire town began to notice him. When he smiled, the boy's bright blue eyes were warm with passion. His laugh exuded pure charisma and joy.

As he grew, his parents knew that he was bound for grand adventures. He would regularly run off into the fields and go far aw from the town in search of new treasures and secrets. He excelled at learning from experience, as all boys do. He would fall down, get scratched, and rise back up. Nothing seemed to deter his ambition for exploration.

The years went by and he learned how to fish and bring home food for the dinner table; he learned how to garden and till the land; he learned how to ride a horse, fix fences, and thatch roofs. The young boy was truly talented and he was beginning to think that his town of Brighton was much too small for him. He needed to expand and grow; he was a dreamer; he knew more must exist. He was on a mission to seek out and shed light on all the corners in the abyss that he could not yet see.

One afternoon while working in his parents' vegetable garden, he saw a girl who would change his life forever. He stared at her, mesmerized. He could not stop gazing. His body was paralyzed. He was like the statue of David, forever holding his pose, wanting desperately to move, but not being able.

As he stood motionless, the young, attractive girl walked past. Her long, brown hair flowed elegantly in the breeze. Although she was too far aw for the boy to be certain, he definitely thought he smelled wisps of roses gracing the air. She walked with the utmost finesse and she moved so delicately. If the boy had not seen her, he would never have heard her. She crossed the field and was suddenly out of sight.

The boy started breathing again and could feel his heart racing as he slipped his hand under his shirt to ensure he was still alive. He caught his breath and promised himself that he would meet that girl and she would one day be his wife. He and she would go on adventures together, and he would get to share all of the treasures he found with her and her treasures with him. He would wake up each morning to her smile, and look into her eyes each night before drifting off to sleep. They would dream together and weave their memories into an eternal blanket, which would cover them in the blissfulness of love. She would be his sun and his moon, his yesterday and his tomorrow. She would be his forever.

Unfortunately, to the dismay of the boy, only days after seeing the breathtaking girl, his father sent him away to become an apprentice to the Great Merchant at the docks before he had a chance to introduce himself to his dream girl.

With his new promising apprenticeship and father's encouragement, the boy worked his hardest to become a savvy, clever businessman. He enjoyed the thrill of bartering and scheming. He listened to and learned the techniques from the Great Merchant on how to get the best prices for goods and influence a conversation to ones advantage. He also liked working on the docks and in the shipyard and amongst the tough, seafaring men. The work was continuously giving him new information and each person he met or spoke with seemed to have captivating stories from far away lands around the world. The boy would regularly look at the horizon and dream about what was on the other side. He thought to himself that one day he would chase the sun across the sky and follow it to the ocean's edge where it disappears every night.

Nevertheless, despite his new position and promising apprenticeship with the Great Merchant, he never forgot about the girl. Thus, upon the end of each day when he was released from his work duties, he would run from the docks to the field where he last saw her. Then he would perch himself on the hilltop of the open field, so that he had the best vantage point, which would make impossible to miss her if she walked across the field again. His eyes would endlessly scour the field below until darkness prevented him from doing so.

After one year of continuing the same routine, he finally spotted her as she floated amongst the summer tulips. He jumped up quickly from his dutiful lookout hill and rushed down the slope toward her. He was sprinting faster downhill than his excited legs could carry him, which caused him to tumble uncontrollably. He ended up rolling half way down the hill before stopping. Unfazed, he was determined not to let her out of his sight. The boy popped onto his feet as if nothing had happened and began his pursuit again.

When he finally reached her—close enough to be heard—he called out, "Hi ya."

The young girl turned around bewildered to hear someone's voice. As she assessed her new company, she wondered why a scruffy-looking boy with dirt and grass marks on his clothing and sweat dripping down his forehead would be shouting at her. She looked at him quizzically as he slowly approached, clearly apprehensive. The boy looked at the girl and smiled at her, hoping to receive a smile in kind; the girl did not offer such a compliment. Unnerved, the boy ran his hand through his hair and wiped away the sweat from his forehead using the back of his hand.

He then did his best to stand tall and he stuck out a hand and said, "Hi, my name's Archie and I would like you to be my wife."

The girl said nothing; she stood there and stared at Archie, for what seemed, in Archie's opinion, like an eternity.

He offered again, "Hi, name's Archie. I would like you to be my wife."

His hand hung outstretched in-between them, and he began to think he should withdraw it from its awkward position.

"Hi," the girl spoke softly.

She said it just above a whisper, as if she was unsure how to proceed with this boy and his preposterous idea of marriage.

"Well, it's a start," Archie said, removing his hand from between them. He smiled as he spoke knowing that conversation was just around the corner. "I am sorry if I startled you, and apologize for my appearance. I have been waiting each evening on top of the hill over there for over a year in order to say hello to you. And here you are. I didn't want to miss you again because I think you are the loveliest thing I have ever set eyes on."

The girl was speechless as she looked into Archie's blue eyes and listened to him.

When she did not speak, Archie understood that he should continue his explanation: "Last year when I was doing some yard work for my father, then I spotted you from afar and knew I must meet you. However, I have been working in the town and at the docks with the Great Merchant, so I never knew when I might see you again. Thus after work, I would wait till dusk and watch, hoping you would come along."

This time the girl spoke, "You have been waiting every day for a year on that hill to say hello to me?"

"Yes I have," replied Archie, proud of his sheer persistence and dedication.

"Why on Earth would you do that? What if I never took this path across the field again?"

"Because I want you to be my wife one day. I needed to wait on the off chance you did, so that I would finally get to meet you."

Archie stood there gleaming, simply because he was finally speaking with his dream girl. She looked at him sternly not sure what to make of Archie.

To break the silence, Archie offered once more, "May I start over? My name is Archie, and I would like to spend time with you. Get to know ya."

He ventured his hand outward again.

This time the girl raised her hand and gently placed it within his and said, "My name is Olivia and I would like that. You're lucky I didn't switch routes. I take this path twice a summer. I see my grandmother in the country and bring her flowers and some sweet biscuits."

"I reckon Fate and Fortune are on my side," Archie said smiling from ear to ear.

Olivia and Archie leisurely walked across the field together, not saying anything more, and enjoying each other's company as the summer night began to consume them.

When they were about to part ways at the main road and go to their respective homes, Archie quietly said, "May I see you tomorrow?"

"Yes," Olivia responded, as she pointed across the field, "but you must wait on top of the hill, just like you have been."

Archie looked at the hill disappointingly, "Why must I wait there? You won't cross the field tomorrow."

"Because you love me," Olivia said playfully as she turned with a smile. Archie stood there and watched as she walked down the main road until she disappeared behind a bend.

Archie gazed up into the rapidly appearing starry, night sky. As he stared, he wondered how many stars had he wished upon over the last year that this night would finally materialize and he would meet the girl—Olivia. He smiled to himself and glanced over his shoulder back toward the empty road in which Olivia had disappeared. Until tomorrow, Archie whispered to himself. He let the joy and excitement of love flow through his veins.

Over the next eight years, Olivia and Archie spent a myriad of precious moments together and grew incredibly close with each passing day. During the days and evenings, they went on little adventures throughout the town and along the shore. They talked about their dreams, their fears, and what they wanted to do with their lives when they were older. As teenagers they dreamed of grandeur, fortune, and opulence that could only be matched by the gods and goddesses sitting on Mount Olympus. They dreamed of the world they wanted to build together.

Furthermore, Olivia was a talented artist and an eloquent writer. During the long Sunday afternoons in the summer, she would read Archie her poems as the waves crashed against the pebbles and the breeze gentle brushed across their faces. Archie would close his eyes as he listened. Each verse she sang gentle nestled into the soft spots of his heart. He could not help himself but fall deeper and deeper in love with her.

They spent days lazily giggling with each other and playfully bantering back and forth. It was natural, authentic, and special. It was theirs. The two of them felt comfortable to be themselves and share their most inner secrets and emotions. Together they were safe; together there was not any worry of judgment or fearful anxiety. It seemed as nothing could possibly go wrong or separate them from a destiny together.

One autumn day on Archie's way home from the Great Merchant's office, he was walking past the local school in town when he heard a girl screech out, which was then followed by several boy's boisterous laughs. He turned his head toward the noise and instantly recognized the girl. Without a second's thought, he sprinted toward the three teenage boys standing around Olivia. Before any of the boys could react, Archie came flying into the fray and threw a right fisted punch at the nearest boy, which sent the boy sprawling to the ground.

Archie slid to a stop and shook his hand vigorously as the pain seared through his hand and knuckles. The two boys stood still momentarily and assessed the intruder. Then one of the boys spoke, "You're in the wrong place mate. Get outta here before we lick you." The teenager who spoke first was a heavyset lad, definitely twice Archie's weight and significantly taller.

"Git him Edward. Teach him a lesson he won't never forget," the other boy said menacingly.

Archie looked at Edward with stone cold eyes as the adrenaline began to coarse through his veins. He raised his fists ready to fight. Edward cracked his knuckles and advanced toward Archie. Within seconds, Archie and the boy were trading punches and neither boy could effectively parry the other's blows. Eventually, the size difference began to take its toll on Archie as he began stumbling backwards with each new and brutal punch.

Archie successfully dodge a big right hook and landed a quick jab on Edward's nose. Blood erupted from his nostrils and began streaming down his face. Edward let out a shriek of pain and closed his eyes as they immediately began to water. He stumbled backwards and fell to his knees as he grabbed his face. Upon seeing their leader stumble and exit the fight, the other two boys did not hesitate and both sprang on Archie simultaneously. During their rapid advance, Archie yelled out, "Run, Olivia, run!"

Olivia frantically picked up her things, which had been knocked out of her hand during the original assault and sprinted away from the fight.

Exhausted, Archie was no match for the newest double assault. He was knocked to the cobblestone and mercilessly kicked by both boys. Archie bellowed out in agony as one particularly powerful kick landed in his side and broke one of his ribs. Then all of a sudden the fierce beating ended. The kicks vanished and were replaced by the boys frenzied voices: "Let's git outta here Langston. That's a copper comin'!"

"C'mon Edward. Git up mate! Stop whimpering 'bout your bloody nose."

In the distance, but approaching fast, Archie could hear a piercing whistle and loud footsteps. The three boys scrambled away desperately and ran down a back alley as the policeman finally reached Archie.

The policeman crouched down next to Archie, "You alright lad?"

Archie looked up at the copper and nodded his head, although his body was aching from his shoulders to his toes. He sat up and let out an excruciating yell as the pain in his ribs nearly made him faint. Black spots formed in front of his eyes as the policeman help Archie to his feet. Each and every breath made Archie cringe in agony. As he stood there and the policeman asked him questions, he noticed Olivia, standing shyly and quietly behind the police officer. Archie's body was throbbing and pain gripped at every muscle, but he bit his tongue and tried to absorb all the hurt to stay strong in front of his love.

Archie glanced up at the policeman, "I will be fine Sir. Thank you for coming to my aid."

"You shouldn't be thanking me lad," the policeman said as he indicated toward Olivia. "Your friend here found me patrolling and brought me." The policeman watched as Archie and Olivia locked eyes and he could feel the instant spark between them. "Well, as long as you are fine lad, I am going to continue on my patrol. I will keep my eye out for those lads and teach them a thing or two about respecting their peers."

"Thank you Sir," Archie mustered softly through half breaths.

The policeman took his leave down the alley way in the same direction that the three boys fled; while, Archie and Olivia started walking down the cobblestone street out of town toward the main dirt road, which would take them to their respective homes.

As they walked, Olivia took hold of Archie's hand and interlaced her fingers within his. She gave his hand a squeeze and spoke softly, "Thank you Archie. Are you ok?"

"I'll live. Those bastards shouldn't have been picking on you like that," Archie said. The adrenaline was wearing off and Archie was beginning to notice how incredibly sore he was going to be for the next week.

Olivia nodded in agreement, "I'm really glad you found me. I was petrified. I didn't know what I was going to do."

"Me too. I couldn't have anything happen to you." Archie smiled and gave Olivia a peck on the cheek. "I'll see you tomorrow. How's a stroll down the beach sound?"

"Sounds lovely. See you tomorrow."

Olivia and Archie parted ways and continued their journeys home alone. As she strolled home, Olivia knew that Archie would always protect her. He would always be there for her; he would be her knight in shining armor, her guardian, protector, and provider. Likewise on his slow walk, Archie knew he would always be there for Olivia. He would be her champion forever; he would be the man who held her close and kept her warm on cold nights; and he would never let her go. This is the girl he would go to the end of the world for. She had permanently captured his heart. Cupid's arrow had flown true, landed, and firmly lodged itself deep inside him.

As the years moved onward, Olivia became more stunning and beautiful. She started to attract increased attention from established businessmen in Brighton. At twenty-one, she was a premier candidate as the future wife of many eager bachelors.

Archie could not help but notice the countless gentlemen who started to inquire into Olivia's situation. Unfortunately, at only twenty-three years old with no real property or savings amassed of his own yet, Archie was hardly the ideal suitor for Olivia. He still knew she was the woman he wanted to marry, so he tried not let it bother him too much. More importantly, Archie and Olivia were inseparable and the path of lifelong happiness and partnership seemed imminent.

• 2 •

Archie looked at the Great Merchant and then glanced down at the table where all the Great Merchant's maps, compasses, and other nautical instrumentations were placed strategically.

"Archie, my boy," the Great Merchant bellowed, "we have the adventure of a lifetime in the palm of our hands. This is the one you have been asking, or rather I dare say, begging for since you arrived as my protégé. Your father told me you wanted to experience the world, well son, now we can."

Archie was standing beside the Great Merchant studying the hand-drawn map of the World spread out on the desk. Archie was excited, he truly was, but in the back of his mind he was thinking about Olivia. He did not want to leave her. Why did he have to go on this business expedition across the world?

Archie's wondering mind was interrupted when the Merchant repeatedly asked, "Did you hear me, my boy? Did you hear me?"

"What's that Sir?" Archie replied still dazed at the Great Merchant's proposed journey.

"I said, we leave at first light in a month's time. We set sail for the West Indies, so go tell your parents and the young lady I've seen you with. Go, go, my boy. I have other matters to attend to, to prepare the *Charlotte* for her voyage across the world."

Archie obeyed and left the room. Before going home, he walked slowly along the docks looking at the horizon where the sun was slowing lowering itself into the dark blue ocean. Archie could not believe his luck and misfortune. The bittersweet emotions toyed with Archie's thoughts. He finally was leaving and getting to see the world, experience one of the grandest adventures he had always fantasized about. At the same time, he knew this adventure might be the undoing of his relationship with Olivia, and this greatly troubled him.

He arrived home and walked toward the kitchen where he heard his mother, Joy, preparing dinner. She glanced up from mashing the potatoes, and said, "Learn anything new today my little merchant?"

"I am going on an adventure to the New World with the Great Merchant. I must leave in a moth's time."

"Oh my! How long is this adventure of yours going to take?" Joy asked worrying for the safety of her baby boy.

"The Great Merchant said my service would be two years, but most likely longer. He said it all depends on how prosperous we can be in the New World. The more prosperous, the more he foresees expansion and the ability to bring business back home. Otherwise, we are there until we can pay for the return trip if it's not as good as promised," Archie concluded, as his father, Richard, entered the room.

"Hi dear, and how's it going Arch?" asked Richard.

"Hi father," responded Archie. "It's going good…"

"Well. It's going well," Richard said correcting Archie.

"It's going well, but I am off to the New World with the Great Merchant next month. We are headed to the West Indies because the Merchant says he has finally received a business proposition there that he cannot possibly turn down."

"Sounds like the journey you have always been waiting for. You must be excited," encouraged Richard.

"I am," Archie hesitated. "But it means I must be gone for such a long time. I will miss you and mum and Olivia so much. What will happen when I am away?" Archie began to feel his chest tighten and the fear settling over him.

The voyage across the ocean was a treacherous one. He had heard many daunting stories from sailors at the docks. He knew it had become safer over the last century, but there were still perilous dangers that took the souls of sailors each day. When he first became the Great Merchant's apprentice, he sought out the most menacing and terrifying stories from ships crewmen that arrived in Brighton. He thrived for experiences like theirs.

"Now Archie," his father said as he rested his hand on his son's shoulder, "this is an exciting opportunity. You will get to see a part of the world and bring it back to us. And tell us all your stories. Son," he said looking Archie in the eyes, "you don't want to be in Brighton the rest of your life, do you? Look around you, there's a whole world to see. Your mother and I will be fine while you are away."

Archie looked up at his father and saw the mixed emotions in his face. His father did not cry, but Archie could tell his father would miss him greatly.

"Arch," his father said with a smile, "bring me back something special from the New World."

Archie smiled at his dad, as tears slowly rolled out of the corners of his eyes, "I will. I will bring back something unique for both of you."

The three of them embraced each other. Joy had tears streaming down her face, as she knew her boy would not come back the same young man. Archie would always be her baby, but this adventure would change him.

The family had dinner that evening in relative silence, only speaking when they needed more food. After dinner, Archie was lying in bed and eyes closed and he thought about pirates and sea beasts and gold and silver and all the jewels a king could ever want. He would greatly miss home, his family, and the comforts of Brighton. More importantly, he would dearly miss his time spent with Olivia. He wondered how she would react when he told her tomorrow. As he pondered this last thought, Archie fell sound asleep.

"Oh Archie!" gasped Olivia as she flung her arms around him. She hugged him tightly. Olivia continued as they released each other, "Do you have to go?"

"I am afraid I must as the Great Merchant's apprentice. I do not want to leave you, but this is a chance that might create a better life for us," Archie said hopefully. "I will come back as soon as the Great Merchant will allow. I will be as rich as a King, and be able to adorn you in silk. My coffers will be piled high with gems and jewels, gold and silver. We will be able to run off to any part of Europe and build our castle." Archie smiled and said with a wink, "You will finally get a proper proposal too."

Olivia looked at him fondly and whispered, "I wish it wasn't for so long. I will miss you."

"I will miss you too. I will write if I can and send them on the ships headed back to Brighton."

"I'd like that. And when I read them, I shall know you are safe and thinking of me."

Archie pointed toward the moon that was just becoming visible in the twilight evening, "Each night when you look at the moon, know that I will be looking at the same one. That way it will not seem we are so far from each other. You and I will basically be side by side as we are now."

"Archie," Olivia whispered as she choked back on her tears, "that's the silliest thing I've ever heard. You will be around the world, how possibly could we be next to each other?"

Archie knew this was a rhetorical question and wrapped his arms around Olivia and squeezed her close to his body. Olivia nestled her head in Archie's chest. The two lovers stood there together oblivious to everything around them.

• 3 •

Archie and Olivia spent Archie's last month as normally as they could, but it was difficult to ignore Archie's impending departure for the West Indies and its indefinite duration. Neither his mother and father nor Olivia wanted to acknowledge the fact that Archie was leaving, and he did not desire extra attention or press anyone to give him any.

On his last evening, Olivia came over and had dinner with Archie and his family. After the meal was blessed, everyone around the table said a prayer for Archie, and wished him the best and safe travels. Everyone ate in silence because of the sorrowful realization that this might be his or her last meal with Archie for a couple years. No one at the table could fathom the worse case scenario, but it was highly possible that Archie would never return to Brighton because of the perils in the Caribbean.

At the conclusion of dinner, Archie walked Olivia back to the main road. They kissed for a long time, pretending that this action would ensure that tomorrow did not arrive. Olivia felt Archie's lips imprint the unforgettable sensation of love and longing in her memory. Then they stood in the road and embraced each other promising to see each other soon. Both knew that "soon" was just a word of comfort more than of reality.

Before Olivia departed, she gave Archie a small piece of parchment that had been folded up tightly and neatly. Archie looked at the small piece of folded paper no bigger than the palm of his hand.

Olivia said, "Only read it when you really miss me. When you really mean it. You are going on this adventure and will meet amazing people and experience a new world. I will only hear stories. I want you to take my poem to remember me when you are away. To not forget me."

"Thank you. I could never forget you," Archie said softly. "I don't have anything to give you right now, but when I return I will bring back worldly treasures that only you deserve."

Olivia shook her head in despair as she began to cry.

"I love you," Archie whispered affectionately, "and when I see you again, we will get married."

Olivia could not muster any words. Her throat was choked up and her chest was welling up inside her with emotion. Her tears trickled down her face like raindrops on a window.

She kissed him on the lips and barely audible said, "Until then Archie. I love you."

Before he could say anything more, she turned and started walking toward her home. After a few paces, she turned around and waved one last time. Archie could see more tears silently running down her cheeks. As each tear fell, Archie felt as if he was driving a dagger into her heart.

Archie began to cry himself as he watched the love of his life walk into the distance. He brushed away the tears with his sleeve and said somberly, "One day you will be my Queen."

———

An hour before daybreak, Archie was with his parents saying his final goodbyes and confirming he had everything he might need. His mother gave him an extra bar of chocolate, a special treat he usually only received on his birthday. His father gave him a knife, which according to his father had saved his life on many occasions. Archie was skeptical of this claim since his father was a handyman and a carpenter and faced almost no peril in his daily work. Nevertheless, Archie was warmed by his father's generosity. He hugged both his parents for a long time, only leaving when his father gently nudged him out the door toward the town and docks.

As Archie approached the docks, the Great Merchant appeared overenthusiastic about the voyage and the business trip that was soon commencing. Archie always knew the man to be excited, but there was a rare zeal about him this morning.

The Great Merchant glanced over his shoulder as he saw Archie approaching, "Ah good my boy, you didn't get cold feet. Cheer up; the first day is the hardest. Once this adventure begins and you won't miss Brighton in the slightest."

"Mornin', Mr. Hollis," Archie responded, trying to sound as excited as possible without the gloominess of leaving his home overshadowing his demeanor.

"From now on, call me First Mate Grant," Mr. Hollis said chuckling and looking toward the *Charlotte*. "I really like the sound of that," speaking to no one in particular. "Maybe if all goes well, I can buy my very own fleet of Merchant vessels, then I will truly be the Great Merchant of Brighton." Turning back toward Archie, "So, since you are my apprentice and have been under my teaching for some time, I figured you could be my second mate on the ship. Oh and before I forget, our captain is William Jasper."

"Thank you for the position," Archie said, as his excitement started to grow.

Archie glanced down the dock and took in the area trying to capture a lasting, mental image for himself before they left. He looked back at Mr. Hollis, who was now aboard the ship and impatiently motioning for Archie to come aboard. Archie quickly picked up his trunk and scurried up the plank and onto the deck of the *Charlotte*. Mr. Hollis showed Archie to his quarters and gave him a brief history of the ship as they toured it.

As they entered the Captain's Quarters, Mr. Hollis introduced Archie to their Captain, "And here he is Will, this is the young man that has been my apprentice for near eight years. Archie, this is Captain Jasper."

"No need for the formalities Grant," Captain Jasper said shaking his head disapprovingly. "Amongst friends we can be less formal. Any friend of the Great Merchant is a friend of mine. How do you do Archie?" The Captain extended his hand in Archie's direction.

"I'm fine, Captain. Excited to see the other side of the world and be on a new adventure," responded Archie shaking the Captain's hand in turn.

"Well then, you've certainly joined the right ship and been the apprentice to the right man. However, you might need to find a new captain," joked Captain William. "I am hoping this is less of an adventure and more of an uneventful sail to the New World."

The Great Merchant spoke up with a greedy gleam in his eye, "Nonsense. Without any risk there is no reward, and the plan is to get rich and come back with a few stories."

"You've always had a flare for the dramatics Grant," the Captain said.

Archie continued to listen to the chatter between the Captain and Mr. Hollis and knew that this adventure was going to be unlike any other story he had ever heard on the docks from other sailors. He was looking forward to whatever might be coming his way.

"So when do we set sail?" inquired The Great Merchant.

"Quarter of an hour, I'd reckon," replied the Captain.

"Archie, go to your quarters or be on deck. Just stay out of the way of the crewmembers, but enjoy yourself," The Great Merchant said.

He turned back toward the Captain and they continued their

conversation in whispered tones that Archie could not overhear.

Archie stood on the top deck as the *Charlotte* slowly left the harbor. He watched the town slowly, ever so slowly, become smaller and smaller as they inched westward. The cool morning sea air brushed against his face and speckled it with flakes of salt. He thought of Olivia and her sweet, rosy smell and her incredible kindness and joy. He could feel her head nestled into his chest and her soft lips against his. He thought of his parents and their lovingness, compassion, and encouragement.

As the sun rose higher into the sky, the vast, open sea surrounded the *Charlotte*. There was no turning back now. Archie was on his adventure, and he was going to gain new experiences that would transform him into the best man he could be. One day when, or rather, if he returned, he would marry Olivia and gallivant with her all around the world. She would be his strength on this unknown journey.

The Great Merchant found Archie on the deck and spoke as he approached, "Archie, my lad. I have a gift for you."

Archie turned and watched as Mr. Hollis sifted through his pockets on his coat and removed a leather-bound book and handed it to Archie.

"This journal will be good for you. It'll help you write down all the stories you want to tell your parents when we return. Plus, it'll give you something to do over the next five to six weeks while we make this crossing."

"Thank you so much, Mr. Hollis," Archie said taking the journal in his hands and massaging the dark, genuine leather with his thumbs. He could feel the quality and knew instantly this was an expensive journal. "How will I ever repay you?"

"My boy, you won't need to repay me. It is a gift. Just make sure that you write down everything and journal your experiences. It'll be wonderful to have one day when you are old like me. I wish I had written down more of my life," the Great Merchant said reminiscently.

"Well, thank you Sir. I will make sure to write it all down."

• 4 •

Olivia woke to the sunshine gloriously spreading itself through the window and warming up her room. She rushed to the window and could see the ocean in the distance. She thought she saw a black speck on the horizon, which she concluded must be a ship, and her thoughts immediately went to Archie. She would miss him. She recalled that dusk evening when he first approached her running down from his hill to ask for her hand in marriage. She recollected all the fun afternoons they had spent with each other by the seaside, swimming and reading her stories and poetry to him. He always loved her writings and always encouraged her to write more. She continued to stand motionlessly by the window as she reminisced.

Olivia's mother entered her bedroom and greeted her warmly, "Good morning sweetie."

But Olivia did not hear her. Olivia had blocked out the rest of the world and was deep within her thoughts. How long would it be until she saw Archie again? When he came back, would he be the same? What if he never came back? These endless questions were revolving around her head.

Her mother said louder, "Good morning Olivia."

Startled, Olivia turned around surprised and hastily answered, "Good morning mother. I'm sorry, I was thinking about Archie. Do you need help in the kitchen?"

"Yes. Wash up and dress quickly, after breakfast we are headed into town."

"What for?"

"You and I are going to buy you a new dress."

"Really?" Olivia said excitedly.

"I know this is a difficult day with Archie leaving and I think it would be fun for the two of us to do."

Olivia was beaming. Her mother and her had not gone shopping for a new dress for over a year. She rushed to the washroom and started to bathe.

In town, Olivia was giddy with excitement. She was looking in all the shops windows anticipating seeing a dress she would fall in love with. They walked down the main street until they approached the smart clothing store—Martin and Taylor: Men's Suits and Women's Dresses.

As Olivia wandered through Martin and Taylor's, Olivia's eyes lit up at each dress she passed. Then all of a sudden her eyes fell upon the dress she wanted. It was a light blue, elegant dress with white decorative lace on the collar and cuffs.

Martin, the tailor, glided over to Olivia, "That is a lovely dress, Madame. It will look exquisite on you. Would you like to try it on?"

"Yes I would," Olivia's eyes still fixated on the dress.

Martin allowed Olivia to try it on and as Olivia was standing in front of the mirror, he said, "It's made of good fabric and it's a top quality dress. It will last you several years."

"The dress fits amazing and I love the feel," Olivia said as she turned around in front of the mirror admiring herself. "I'll take it."

Olivia's mother was happy to see her daughter so pleased, and she purchased the blue dress for her daughter.

Back at home, Olivia put the new dress in her closet and could not wait for the day to wear it and show it off for Archie.

She strolled over to her window and gazed outward toward the sea in the distance. The sun's rays bounced off the water and reflected upward making the sky a beautiful, vivid, baby blue. Olivia's mind longingly flashed back to the long weekend afternoons when she and Archie would sit by the sea and listen to the waves gently crash against the shore. He would hold her tightly as she laid her back against his chest and watched the ocean roll in, wave after wave. They had had nothing but time for so many years. They spent hours just the two of them, embraced, and loving each moment whether it was in silence or fits of laughter or softly kissing.

Archie would whisper in her ear his fantasies for them. All the plans of romantic trips and fantastic voyages to see exotic cities, taste rich foods, and spend lavishly on their estate. Archie's playful dreams made Olivia's heart swirl with excitement. She wanted to live out each and every part, because it all sounded so wonderful.

As Olivia closed her eyes, she could hear Archie's voice in her ear, his scruffy beard brushing against her cheek: He would say, "The sun will rise to greet you and you will look down the magnificent countryside from our castle. You will have a servant bring you breakfast each morning and dress you in the finest East Indian silks. We will attend parties where the Dukes, the Counts, and the Royal members of the Court will all be in attendance. You will be the envy of all the women in attendance. And when we have had enough, I will whisk you away upon our noble stead, Winston, and we will ride into the night upon our next adventure."

Olivia tenderly brushed a tear from the corner of her eye. With Archie gone, maybe everything they had wished for and dreamt of together had been just that, a fairy tale, just daydreams of youthful hearts.

• 5 •

Archie pulled out the leather bound journal and opened it to the first, clean page:

18 September 1667, Day 5

The days have been very long. The ocean extends endlessly in all directions around the Charlotte. The seas have not been too rough but storms have been seen far in the distance. We might hit some terrible weather later in the journey. The crew has been friendly and they have taught me how to gamble and play cards. I am getting really good at poker and throwing dice. Since I don't have any money of my own, I can only watch and learn.

The crewmembers also have good stories to tell and have seen many places around Europe, but for many of them, this is their first journey to the New World too. There is an excitement to see what kind of people are there and what treasures are available to take home. I do not mind sailing, but it is very slow.

---

27 September 1667, Day 14

Something terrible has happened. In the last twenty-four hours the crew has been coming down with a horrible illness. The Captain has quarantined the infected crewmembers. Those crewmembers are violently ill and have been running extremely high fevers. Their eyes are bloodshot and they cannot eat anything because they will throw it up. I can hear them moaning at night and it sounds like a living hell. I hope I do not come down with their illness.

---

30 September 1667, Day 17

One of the infected crewmembers has died. We held a service for him today, and then sent his body to the bottom of the sea. Captain Jasper said a nice prayer for the man, but you can tell the crew has been shaken by the death. There are still three other crewmembers that are gravely ill. I hope they do not die and worsen the morale of the ship. The Great Merchant seems anxious all of a sudden too. He spoke to me today, and he seemed worried about his own health. He has locked himself in his cabin for days at a time to try and avoid the sickness.

---

5 October 1667, Day 22

Of the three men that were still sick, two more have passed away. The last man has slowly been recovering and looks as if he has survived the deadly, unknown illness. Captain Jasper has asked me to help with some of the duties that the three deceased crewmembers worked on.

The best news is the sickness seems to have passed. No one can pin point where it came from, but I am relieved to not have come down with any sickness. Working on the ship helps make the time pass faster. I was talking with the Captain and he was inclined to believe that we were within two weeks from reaching our destination. It's been a long journey, and the loneliness and homesickness has consumed my happiness and thoughts.

Spending two more weeks on this ship will be easier since I will be working more. This journal is helping too. It has helped me practice writing my emotions and thoughts and I am looking forward to sending a letter to Olivia.

I did not necessarily want to use this journal as a personal diary for my emotions. But I feel like I must. This journal is a reflection of what I am experiencing and going through. I miss her. I wonder what she is doing today *and every day. I constantly ponder what she is up too. After the last three weeks, I know that I will definitely write her at the first chance I get.*

Archie was standing in the Captain's Quarters with Mr. Hollis and Captain Jasper. Archie stared and observed the map spread out upon the Captain's desk.

"How much longer until we land in Port Nassau, Will?" Mr. Hollis probed.

"In the distance, there is the a mighty storm coming our way. If we can avoid it, it'll be clear sailing all the way through to Port. But it'll take a bit of skill to navigate around this storm. From the looks of it, it's huge and spreads over many leagues," responded Captain Jasper as he pivoted his compass across the map.

Archie perked up and asked, "Captain, is there any chance that I will be able to send a letter home to family when we get to Port Nassau? I would like to let them know I have reached the New World safely."

"Certainly. If you write your letter, I will direct you to the nearest Royal Post as soon as we step foot on shore," Captain Jasper said looking up from his work.

"Thank you," grinned Archie as he started drafting the letter inside his head.

Archie was sitting in his bunk and scribbling as best as possible as the boat rocked and swayed violently:

7 October 1667, Day 24

We have come across the dreadful weather that Captain Jasper wanted to avoid. As I write this, it's nearly impossible to keep writing legibly. The ship is swaying back and forth and the wind and rain are howling outside. The bombardment of rain and ocean are flooding the upper deck making it impossible leave my bunk to see the Great Merchant and Captain and ask them how long we must endure this storm.

8 October 1667, Day 25

The storm has still not abated. It doesn't look like it will end soon and the sky is as black as the night. The crew has been working tirelessly for the last day and a half to keep the ship on course to Port Nassau. I was asked to help serve food during meal times and other miscellaneous tasks. I like helping out any way I can. The work keeps my mind off how much I miss home. I can hear my father and mother's voice at night before I go to sleep; although, it is hard to sleep as the waves crash thunderously against the ship.

9 October 1667, Day 26

Still stuck in my cabin. This storm is relentless. I have not seen the Captain or Great Merchant for the last three days. I hope Captain Jasper finds a way to get us out of this dreadful storm.

———————

11 October 1667, Day 28

The storm has finally stopped. The ship has taken a beating. The sails are ripped and the crew looks exhausted. I spoke with the Captain and he indicated that we were thrown off course and it would take a day to try and figure out where exactly or approximately we are located.

The Great Merchant is on edge. He is ready to get off the boat, and start his business. He has been agitated for the last two weeks. He is not much of a sailor it seems, plus he is older and has not handled the obstacles of the journey well.

———————

15 October 1667, Day 32

The Captain says the storm knocked us off course too far North and we must be careful to not tread in foreign waters too long. As we approach the West Indies, pirates might cause us harm if we are spotted and perceived as a target for pillage and plunder. According to the Great Merchant and Captain Jasper, we should be arriving within the next ten days to Port Nassau. We will stop to get our supplies restocked and rest up for a couple days before making the final trip to Port Royal.

The Great Merchant tells me that once we have landed in Port Royal, his friend and past business partner is selling a sugar plantation. The Great Merchant's friend is tired of the West Indies as he has made good money, and he would like to return to England and see his family before he dies. The Great Merchant is going to purchase the plantation and try to make as much money as possible to live the life he has always dreamed about.

If all goes according to his master plan, he intends to expand to another island and purchase more land. At this point if I would like to return to Brighton, he would gladly purchase my passage home. I would then be his contact person and lead merchant in Brighton. I would handle shipments of sugar and other cash crops to then be distributed throughout the English mainland and empire.

I am excited for the Great Merchant's plan. I am thrilled to have such an integral role in the business and am anticipating vast mounds of gold and silver piling up in my coffers one day. I will finally be able to purchase Olivia a magnificent ring, one that sparkles and dances like fire in the setting sun. It will be the finest diamond known to man.

---

27 October 1667, Day 44

We have finally arrived in Port Nassau. We did not run into any trouble with pirates, but we did run out of food. The last two days we have been rushing to get to Port Nassau. The storm we endured half way through our trip destroyed some of our provision barrels and rats also managed to get into our food.

Thankfully, the sea over the last week has been calm, but the wind has been in our favor. I am most looking forward to stand on firm ground and finally have the taste of fresh food without the salty sea taste in my mouth.

I have started my letter to Olivia. I think she will enjoy reading about the Caribbean and how much different of a world it is compared to England.

• 6 •

Rémi Montre was in big, bold, black letters at the top of the wanted poster. In smaller print, the rest of the poser read:

> *Wanted for piracy, robbery, murder, and crimes against the Crown. Handsome reward for the capture or death of this criminal. Ship is L'île Rouge. Other alias: Le Capitaine d'Or'*

The poster also contained a sketched picture of a youthful looking, French man with a scruffy beard and long hair. The portrait appeared to be completely generic, as if no one had actually seen the man in person before. Archie studied the face hoping one day to be the hero to capture the infamous pirate.

Archie continued to walk around Port Nassau stretching his legs and enjoying the feeling of solid earth beneath his feet. He noticed how different and yet how similar Port Nassau was to Brighton's town. The fashion and the buildings architecture reminded him of home. The weather was extraordinarily better, and he wished he could be sharing this moment with his parents and Olivia.

He placed his hand inside his jacket and into his inner breast pocket. He felt the small folded piece of paper, still unread, but kept as close to his heart as possible. He thought many times on the ship to pull it out and read it, and each time something stopped him. Archie remembered how he should only read Olivia's letter when he desperately missed her. He yearned for her, but he was trying to allow himself some freedom to enjoy this new journey without becoming too homesick. It would be an emotional event to finally unfold the tiny poem and imagine Olivia reading it to him.

Despite Archie's present reminiscing, he caught some strange movement out of the corner of his eye. He quickly withdrew from his thoughts and spun his head around to the right to see a short man slip into the shadows of a nearby alley. Archie stood there deciding whether or not to peer down the dark alley and see where the man had disappeared too. He started to venture toward the dark alley when three British soldiers came bursting out of a nearby side street and saw Archie walking conspicuously across the square.

The three soldiers, guns and bayonets at the ready, sprinted up to Archie, and one of the soldiers demanded, "Have you seen a pirate run through here?"

Archie stood motionless. The vigor and authority of the soldier's question caught him off guard and his voice was paralyzed. He simply pointed down the dark alley in which the mysterious man had run down. Without a word, the three soldiers sprinted down the alleyway.

Still standing in the middle of the square, Archie could not help but visualize the crimes the man, or pirate rather, had committed. Suddenly, he heard a gun shot ring out. Archie's head spun in all directions trying to see where the shot had come from. Then another "bang" resounded and this time it clearly came from the dark alley.

He sprinted towards the dark alley and slammed his body against the barrels sitting next to the alley's opening. He peered over the barrels to catch a glimpse of the action. The alley way faded to blackness, however he could make out three red coats in the distance.

Two soldiers were standing and one was lying flat on the ground moaning in agony.

The short man must have shot one of the soldiers, concluded Archie. The two standing redcoats quickly rallied off one shot each and a shriek of pain pierced the air. Archie was still as a statue as he held his breath waiting for the next move to unfold.

The two standing redcoats slowly advanced deeper down the alley until they were no longer visible. The redcoat soldier on the ground managed to prop himself upright and rest his back against the alley walls as he held his side. A minute later, the two British soldiers emerged dragging the alleged pirate, who was moaning in agony and cursing vile obscenities. The injured British soldier motioned for the others to continue on.

As the British soldiers walked past Archie dragging the short man in tow, Archie noticed something he would never forget. On the pirate's forearm there was a tattoo of the word "d'Or". Archie made eye contact with the short man, for a split second and the short man spit in Archie's direction. He watched as they dragged the short man off through the street in the direction of the fort.

d'Or, thought Archie as he recalled the Wanted Poster. I will have to ask the Great Merchant what the translation is.

That evening at supper, Archie listened to the Captain and the Great Merchant discuss how the world was changing and how much progress mankind had made in the last couple centuries. Both of them drank heartily; glad to have made it safely to Port Nassau. Archie sat silently enjoying the joviality of his two companions and appreciating the warm, October night. Archie glanced at Mr. Hollis and thought to himself that he would be just like the Great Merchant one day: prosperous, jovial, and a traveler; although, he would do the Great Merchant one better because he would be married to the most precious girl in the world.

The following day, Archie eventually came around to asking Captain Jasper about the incident he witnessed, because the Great Merchant was in Port Nassau conducting business.

"Captain," Archie began, "what does 'd'Or' mean?"

"It means 'of gold' or 'golden'. It's French. Why do you ask?"

"Yesterday when I was walking through town, I saw a man with a tattoo that said 'd'Or' and there was a standoff between this man and three British soldiers."

"Aye," the Captain looked around to see if anyone was nearby to overhear them, "lemme explain to you what you saw. Since this is my first time here, obviously, I don't know e'erythin', but I have heard that men marked with 'd'Or' belong or were once pirates for an infamous pirate..."

"Rémi Montre," Archie interjected, remembering the wanted poster.

"Precisely. Captain Montre is said to mark all the men who join his crew 'cause it's said that he believes the mark unites his pirates. They form an unbreakable bond—a brotherhood. Being inducted into this brotherhood or Montre's crew is a lifelong commitment. The tattoo is a symbol of that eternal commitment. Montre is a vicious pirate and often ne'er leaves any survivors from the ships or towns he sacks."

Archie nodded in silence. He thought back to the short pirate with the "d'Or" tattoo: so he was a part of Captain Montre's crew. The thought of seeing an actual pirate excited Archie and scared him at the same time.

"Gotta be careful of some of the people around here Archie. Not all of 'em are lookin' out for your best interest. Some of these men are vicious criminals and will murder a young lad like yourself without a second thought. If I were you, I'd see about talking with Grant and getting yourself a pistol. You ought to know how to defend yourself in a worse case scenario."

"I'd like to learn how to shoot a gun," Archie replied with a big grin on his face. "I will see if I can't get one before we get to Port Royal. I want to take down Captain Rémi Montre."

"Aye, you'll have to learn shoot, especially since you seem so eager to find another pirate."

And with that Captain Jasper turned and walked off in the direction of his quarters. Archie decided to explore Port Nassau a bit more. He did not see the next opportunity in which he would return so this might be his only opportunity to enjoy the British port.

The sun was already high in the sky and the mild temperature was perfect for a walk outside. The sun warmed him up and yet the sea breeze was cool and refreshing. As he strolled along, he saw a couple boys fishing off the dock and some of the men loading and unloading barrels and crates off ships. It was similar to what he saw in Brighton with one major difference—the landscape.

For the first time, Archie took in the beauty of Port Nassau. Palm trees, numerous types of green plants and foliage, beautiful sand and crystal, blue water like he had never seen. The nature in the West Indies was truly magnificent. He wished he could capture all of it in a bottle and share it with Olivia. She would be able to describe and paint the gorgeous area with her elegant words. Oh, how he wished she could see this.

Archie decided to stroll down the beach and took off his shoes. As he went the sand beneath his feet molded to his every footstep and he felt the sand mush in between his toes. Much different than the stone beaches he was accustomed to in Brighton. He preferred the soft sand.

Along the beach, Archie came across a young man, a little younger than himself, drinking from a brown ball. Archie looked at him with avid curiosity.

The young man noticed Archie and looked at him saying, "Whatcha lookin' at?" He sounded irritated at the presence of unwanted company.

Archie genuinely asked, "What's that you are drinking? Or eating?"

"Coconut. But this one's mine, so ya ain't havin' any." The man was eyeing Archie, taking a defensive position as he became aware of the evident size disadvantage between the two of them.

"A coconut? How can I get one? I've never even heard of it

before."

"They come from the palm trees. Just find a rock or somethin', look up into the trees and find a brown coconut. Then try knockin' it down," the young man instructed, gripping his coconut tightly. "Once you got one, just poke a hole in it with somethin' sharp and drink. The coconut meat's good too but you gotta drink the milk first."

Archie thought for a moment. He considered his options: one, going after the coconut alone would probably take him much longer; or two, he could persuade this man to assist him and probably get a coconut much faster.

Archie went with the latter plan and proposed, "How about I let you in on a little secret plan?"

The man eyed Archie suspiciously, but was intrigued enough to nod his head affirmatively.

"Promise not to tell anyone?"

Another nod.

"Good. You and I are business partners. We'll work today a couple hours and knock down as many coconuts as we can find. Once we have our stash, we will take the coconuts into town and sell them. Then we split the shillings we earn. You know how to get the coconuts and I know how to sell them."

"Coconuts are free, anyone can come and get one," the man said playing devil's advocate. "They grow on all the trees 'round here."

"Not everyone has the time to search out ripe coconuts and knock one down though," replied Archie. "Once they realize we have done all the work for them they will pay us for the coconuts, because they don't have to take the time and now they can enjoy the coconut milk."

The young man took a sip of this coconut and thought for a moment. He took another sip then spoke, "Sounds like a good plan. I am in. What's your name anyway?"

"Archie," and he extended his hand.

The man shook Archie's hand and said, "Thomas."

The two of them started out in search of their coconuts. At

first, they had difficulty finding ripe ones, then as luck would have it, they struck a dozen or so palm trees that were full with ripe, brown coconuts. The two men picked up as many palm-sized rocks as they could find and started pitching the rocks at the coconuts to dislodge them from their resting spots.

Over two hours later, Archie was exhausted from throwing rocks. He massaged his right shoulder with his left hand and said, "I think we have enough."

Thomas, looking equally fatigued, glanced one last time at the rock in his hand, dropped it, and sat in the sand. Archie looked at the pile of coconuts they had amassed. Nearly a dozen and a half, seventeen to be exact. Archie took off his shirt and shorts and dove into the ocean to cool off. Following his lead, Thomas followed suit. The two swam in the cool water enjoying the small victory of their hard work.

Once they had savored their rest, Archie again regarded the pile of coconuts and said, "Ready for the next stage of the plan?"

"I'm ready," Thomas replied as he shook his head to remove the water from his eyes.

"We need to get all these coconuts into a barrel and push them back to the main square in town. Once we are there, we can start selling them." Archie was excited; this was going to be his first business venture.

The Great Merchant had always told him: if you can find a product or a good that is not already in the market place but you see potential, then it is something that can be sold. Archie saw the coconut drink as huge potential since it was a hot day and people would love to have a drink to sip on. More importantly, there had not been anyone else in Port Nassau selling coconuts when he was strolling around. He was not sure how good a coconut was; although, if it was good enough for Thomas, he reckoned it would hopefully be good enough for others.

After piling all the coconuts into the barrel, Archie and Thomas began the journey of pushing the barrel through the sand back toward town. It was much more difficult than Archie had anticipated. He was determined to succeed though. It took the two of them nearly an hour to push the coconut-filled barrel into the square. Both were sweating again and their lower backs were screaming in soreness from having pushed the heavy barrel through the unrelenting, sand blockade.

Archie popped open the top of the barrel, removed the sharp knife his father had given him and cut an opening in the first coconut. The shell of the coconut was hard to crack into too, but the warm milky-water on the inside was worth the effort. Archie took a long sip, when all of a sudden Thomas punched him hard in the arm causing Archie to drop the coconut and the coconut milk began to spill out.

"Don't be drinkin' 'way our money," Thomas said scowling at Archie.

"Hold on!" Archie responded angrily, as he hastily picked up the coconut to stop the spillage. "I was tasting it to make sure these are good enough to sell. We can't sell them if they aren't good."

"I wouldn't have been throwin' rocks at bad coconuts," Thomas said incredulously. "You told me to take you to ripe coconuts, so I did. Now, let's make the money you promised."

"Fine."

Archie was taken aback by the roughness of his business partner's actions; although he had to admit, he liked how focused Thomas was. Archie started working on the few people in the square. He would ask them about their day and inquire if they were missing anything. Most people said they were sure they had everything they needed, but Archie quickly corrected them saying that they were in need of a fresh coconut to drink from on the next hot day. He allowed his potential customers to have a taste of the oddly sweet, yet milky substance. A few people downright disliked the coconut's warm taste and spat out the liquid. Others however, fancied the drink after having tried it.

Thomas was a good judge of character and knew how much a person had in his or her purse. As Archie brought over the customer, Thomas would quickly survey them, their clothes, and other small details. He would ascertain and estimate how much money they would be willing to spend on a coconut. So with each customer, the price changed. For some it was a handful of coppers; while, for others it was one shilling.

The sun was beginning to set when Archie and Thomas were down to their last coconut. Archie beamed at Thomas who was counting their revenues – thirty-six shillings and fifty pence. Archie picked the last coconut out of the barrel and returned to the square to sell it. Without much difficulty, he spotted a potential customer. Across the square an older woman was shopping alongside what appeared to be her daughter and Archie assumed that it would be his easiest sell.

He approached confidently but stopped short when his eyes met with the young woman's eyes. She had green eyes, hazelnut colored hair, and her skin was bronzed. She was wearing a white sundress and was stunningly beautiful. The young woman held her gaze with Archie then turned her head and said something to her mother. Her mother looked over at Archie and they approached him. Archie hesitated, trying to find the words that were stuck in his throat.

"Hello ma'am," Archie said politely and shyly.

"What are you selling today?" the older woman said.

"My friend and I are selling coconuts. This is our last fresh coconut of the day. Would you like to purchase it?" Archie lifted the coconut up, so that the woman might inspect it.

"I will. If you would be so kind and open it so my daughter can drink it on our walk home."

"Yes ma'am, of course."

Archie withdrew his father's knife and cut a hole in the topside of the coconut. When he looked up the young, green-eyed woman was standing in front of him. Archie handed her the coconut trying not to show his innocent nervousness.

"Thank you," she said sweetly and took a tiny sip of the coconut milk.

"You're welcome," Archie said quietly.

The mother handed Archie a shilling and they walked off. Archie returned to Thomas.

He motioned in the direction of the girl and mother and asked, "Thomas, do you know who that is? The girl, the one with her mother."

"Aye course. That's the Guv'na's wife and daughter. Guv'na Raymond has been here for as long as I cared to notice. And I think his daughter is twenty or twenty-one. Her name is Isabel. She's beautiful. I'd marry her in a heartbeat. But since I'm an bastard and younger than her by a year or so and livin' on the streets, I doubt that'll e'er happen."

"You live on the street?" Archie said shocked by this news.

"Aye, I forgot to mention that. My mother is a whore and I never knew my father. He was a sailor on some ship that been through Port Nassau some twenty years ago. One thing lead to another, and here I am." Thomas was looking down at the money they had earned and said, "Most money I've e'er had in my life."

Archie feeling uncomfortable with the new information wanted to change the subject, "You should come to Port Royal with me. We can make it big together. We will split our earnings and be able to make twice as much if we are both working together."

"I'm not sure," Thomas said. "I got a pretty good way of life here. I know the area, where it's safe, and how to make it day to day."

"How about this, you come with me to Port Royal. We work hard and make some good money. We will come back to Port Nassau and you can marry the Governor's daughter, unless she fancies me more," Archie concluded jokingly.

"Sounds decent. Aye, this first plan of yers has worked out a'ight," Thomas held up the coins in his hands. "When do ya leave for Port Royal?"

"Tomorrow."

"A'ight Archie. I will come. If we keep makin' money like this, I will follow you 'round the world."

"Sounds great. Be at the dock at first light tomorrow so that you can be on the ship when we leave. The name of her is the *Charlotte*."

Archie took his share of the money from Thomas and they parted ways both satisfied with having met a new friend. Archie was looking forward to Thomas' company for the remainder of his time in the West Indies.

Archie was laying in his bunk, before dinner, mulling over the day. He thought about Thomas out on the streets and considered he should have invited Thomas aboard the ship this evening. Although he wanted to run the idea past the Great Merchant, he was confident it would not be a problem. He also wanted to talk to the Great Merchant about buying a pistol. The knife his father had given him had worked out favorably so far, and he could only see the benefits of owning a pistol for protection, especially against the infamous d'Or. He had walked past more wanted posters on his way back to the ship this evening. The scowling, young, yet rugged face stared blankly out from the poster. His eyes were never moving and yet seemingly watched Archie's every movement.

Archie's thoughts meandered to the Governor's daughter, Isabel. He closed his eyes washing her away from his mind, and his thoughts replaced Isabel with the girl he truly missed—Olivia. He wanted to be with her terribly. His heart ached, and each day seemed only to increase his pining for her.

He sat up on his bunk and grabbed his coat from the hook on the wall next to him. He lifted the small, folded piece of paper from its protective pocket and began to unfold it. His heart began to race and he could feel his palms beginning to sweat. He blinked his eyes a couple of times as the words became visible on the page.

Archie first noticed how nice Olivia's script was: *My dearest Archie....*

At that moment, there was a loud banging on the door followed by, "Archie, mate. Dinner's bein' served in da Capt'n's quarters right now. He'd like ya to attend."

"Thanks," Archie responded startled.

He folded up the piece of paper and returned it to its pocket. He jumped up and headed toward the Captain's quarters.

"Evening Captain. Evening Mr. Hollis," Archie said as he entered the quarters.

"Good evening, Archie," the Great Merchant and Captain Jasper responded in unison. They looked at each other and burst into laughter.

Mr. Hollis through gaps of laughter said, "Archie, a little bird tells me you made quite an impression on the Governor's daughter this afternoon. They have extended an invitation for you to join them for dinner tomorrow evening. If you would like to go, we will wait one more day; if however you'd prefer not to, we can always keep to schedule and leave in the morning. My boy, it's not everyday you get the chance to dine with the aristocracy, so consider the invitation an honor."

Archie sat down at the table speechless. He tried to say something but no words were forming. He was honored by such a gracious invitation, but he immediately felt like he would be betraying Olivia if he accepted the invite and went to dinner with Isabel and her family. Archie wished he could ask his father for advice.

Captain Jasper broke the silence, "Let's eat dinner while it's hot. Archie, you can decide after dinner. It'll give you some time to consider what you'd like to do."

Captain Jasper and the Great Merchant continued making jovial conversation. The spirits and morale of the table were definitely higher after the two days rest in Port Nassau. The wine was flowing freely at dinner, and tonight Archie helped himself to several full glasses to calm his nerves and anxiety over his decision.

As dessert was being placed in front of Archie, the effects of the wine had taken over. The warm, fuzziness filled Archie's head and his body was tingling. The happiness swam through his veins and he felt lighter and freer. The night was speeding by and he lost track of time.

He had stopped thinking about his decision, so when the

Captain asked, "Archie, my lad, what have you decided?"

"I'll," Archie responded louder and slower than intended, "go to the dinner."

"Splendid, lad, just splendid," the Great Merchant said boisterously, slapping Archie on the back.

"I will make the necessary plan changes in the mornin' with the crew and the Port's master," Captain Jasper said happily.

Archie then spoke again, "I've also met a friend I'd like to bring on the trip, Captain and Mr. Hollis. Will that be ok?"

The Great Merchant smiled, "As long as it's not the Governor's daughter, I don't mind. Does your friend know the plan? He understands he will be in Port Royal and Kingston for the next couple years?"

"Yes, I told him everything I knew, and he still was up for the journey."

"Have him come aboard tomorrow so he can settle in that he will be ready to leave."

"I will," assured Archie.

"Well then, good friends, I must retire," the Great Merchant said rising. "Today has been a busy day and if I get one more day in Port Nassau, then I am going to try and be equally as busy and effective tomorrow. For I bid all thee a good night."

And with that, the Great Merchant slumbered out of the dining room.

The Captain looked at Archie and said, "You'd best be getting to bed too. I know those glasses of wine are feeling splendid now, but tomorra you will have a bit of a headache. Rest up, you have quite the date tomorrow eve."

"Night Captain."

Archie rose and left obediently. He swayed a few times as he mindlessly walked to his quarters. He entered his room and took out Olivia's parchment out his jacket and clasped it in his hands. Archie finished undressing and rested his numb and weary head on his bedding. He glanced at the paper in his hands, but his eyes closed.

Before he could unwrap the parchment, he was sound asleep like a baby nestled in a mother's arms.

• 7 •

Olivia was still noticeably depressed with Archie's absence. She missed the time she used to spend with him after his workdays and during their free weekends. Each morning she looked in her closet and saw the light blue dress and looked forward to the day when she could finally wear it to Archie.

The months continued to roll by without any letter from Archie. Christmas came and went, and the new year began. Olivia began to worry about Archie, but she knew that he was probably just busy working with the Great Merchant.

On a chilly, spring morning there was a knock on the door. Both Olivia and her mother looked at each other not expecting a visitor. Olivia's mother strolled over to the window and peered out toward the front door. There she saw a man standing by the door with a satchel marked with the Royal Post emblem. Olivia's mother continued toward the door and opened it ushering the postman inside.

"Thank you," he remarked as he shivered.

He rummaged through his satchel and withdrew three letters.

"Is there a Ms. Olivia Hunt that lives here?" inquired the Postman.

Olivia's heart began to race as she heard her name, "Yes, yes. I am Olivia."

Olivia truly smiled for the first time in months. She took the three letters from the Postman's hand and sat at the table. Her nibble fingers slipped open the first letter that had scribbled on it *October 1667* in Archie's hand. The first letter was short; but for Olivia, it was a comfort to read:

Dearest Olivia,

We have arrived safely in Port Nassau. It took us much longer than expected because we ran into terrible weather during the crossing. The weather in the West Indies is incredible. Beautiful and sunny and warm. Even in October! I have met a new friend, Thomas. He is an orphan, but he and I get along really well and have become good mates. He is nineteen years old, but we are compatible despite the age gap. I will write again soon. I just wanted to let you know we have arrived safely.

Love you,
Archie

After reading the letter, Olivia turned to the Postman who was sipping on a warm cup of breakfast tea and munching on a sweet biscuit.

"How come it took so long for this letter to get here? It's been nearly five months!" she inquired.

The Postman looked at her slowly and swallowed the biscuit before speaking, "Well, word has it, that pirates have been aggressively attacking merchant ships and transport ships with any type of good. So, I'd imagine it took so long because they are only sending letters on ships that have safe passage accompanied by heavily armed convoys making the journey here together. But who knows when they were actually sent. They might have been written a while back and sent only recently. There could be a lot of reasons." The Postman took a sip of his tea. "You should be grateful any letters arrived. I have many people asking me about their letters and packages, and I can only imagine that those poor souls may never get their mail from loved ones. Once a ship is sunk, well, there's no letter to deliver."

Olivia responded retrospectively, "Oh, well I'm happy I received my three letters."

She peered down at the unopened letters and proceeded to open the second letter marked, *November 1667*. This one was much longer:

To my dearest Olivia,

The work here in Port Royal is going slowly. Mr. Hollis has completed the purchase of the sugarcane plantation in the Colony of Jamaica and we have started to work feverishly to improve the production process and the Negros work ethic. Sir Mathis is helping to teach Thomas and I the ways of slaving and sugarcane production and what to look for to determine if it's going to be a good or bad crop.

Thomas and I, most days, find ourselves wondering around the plantation, practicing our swordsmanship and shooting pistols at old cans. We have become used as work overseers and we watch the Negros labor in the hot, blistering sun. The work, like I said, is pretty monotonous though. I hate when I have to discipline the Negros for poor work performance.

I am hoping that the Great Merchant is able to make a profit so Thomas and I get paid for our work so I may return. I intend to save all that I make to ensure we can start with something. I will open my own shop and work with the Great Merchant as his distributor for the raw sugar. It'll all fall into place; we just need the operations here to start earning a profit.

Thomas says hello. He was born in the West Indies and has never been to Europe. He wants to come back with me, so hopefully you will get the chance to meet him. He's funny, but he is kind of rough around the edges. He has quite a temper when he is angry and can make some rash decisions. But he is savvy and very shrewd when it comes to dealing and judging people.

I hope you are fairing well. What's it like back home? What have you been up to this Autumn? How is your writing coming along? I bet your poems and words even make the cherubs in Heaven cry tears of joy.

Thank you so much for the poem you wrote for me. It brings me to tears each time I read it. I love it, Olivia. You are such a wonderful writer. I cannot imagine how many poems I am going to be able to write when I am alone. I am looking forward to my return, our presence, and your passion for me.

Overall, I am doing well and am enjoying Port Royal and Kingston. I think you would really like it here. The beaches are pristine, and the water is clear blue, which is marvelous for swimming and fishing.

With all my love and prayers,
Archie

The Postman quietly left and Olivia's mother was looking at her daughter thoughtfully.

"Liv, darling, I know you have been waiting for these letters ever since Archie left, but once you're done with that last letter, don't forget you are still helping me prepare dinner today for your father and the company we are having over this eve."

"I won't be too much longer mother," Olivia replied.

Olivia's eyes began to read the third letter. Moments later, she dropped the letter to the floor and placed here head in her hands as tears formed in the corners of her eyes.

• 8 •

The Governor's Mansion was massive, ornate, and awe-inspiring compared to the rest of the homes in Port Nassau. It was truly a site to behold, especially for Archie who was being treated with special attention since he was the main guest of the evening.

Earlier that day he had awoken with a throbbing headache, just as the Captain had predicted. He then informed Thomas they were delayed one day due to his engagement with the Governor's dinner. Thomas accepted the news without the slightest congratulations for Archie. Thomas was jealous of Archie's opportunity to dine with the Governor's daughter, Isabel, whom he fancied. Nonetheless, Thomas was determined to start a new life and Archie was his ticket to such a promised life. Thus, Archie's dinner did not persuade him to discontinue his journey to Port Royal.

Archie and Thomas went into Nassau and purchased pistols with their earnings from selling the coconuts. They both enjoyed admiring their new, flashy weapons. They cavorted around the port pretending to shoot robbers, pirates, and each other in mock duels.

In the evening, the horse and carriage pulled up to the Port's main dock and whisked Archie away toward the mansion. As Archie's eyes fell upon the mansion, he stared in quiet disbelief. He thought to himself, I will build a mansion one day just like this for Olivia and myself.

Archie stood in the mansion's entrance under the bright, candle-lit chandelier. He looked around at the paintings decorating the walls and the marble busts of immortalized men. Up until this moment, Archie's day had flown by and time had frozen still. Archie looked at the staircase as Isabel descended toward him. She drifted down the stairs. She was radiant, beautiful, and graceful all at once. Archie smiled at Isabel, and she smiled back at him.

"Hello, Archie. I'm glad you could make it for dinner. My parent's are already in the main room, we can go and join them."

Isabel walked past Archie and he obediently followed beside her. As they walked down the long hallway, his head was turning left and right as his eyes darted amongst all the expensive vases, busts, antiques, and pictures. He loved looking at all the ornate treasures, as he had never seen any objects quite as precious or valuable in his life before.

One object stood out to him in particular. He stared at a green dagger, appearing to be carved from stone. It was deep green, with lightening, light green veins running through it. It was recently polished and looked delicate as it sat perched upon its stand. Before he could ask Isabel what it was, his thoughts were interrupted.

"Aww Isabel darling, how wonderful you look this evening!" exclaimed Mrs. Raymond giving her daughter a kiss on the cheek.

"Archie, it's a pleasure to have you over for dinner this evening. Our daughter thought you were innovative the other day selling coconuts when coconuts are free on the island," said Governor Raymond shaking Archie's hand.

"Thank you, Sir," Archie responded modestly. "I only intended to make a bit of my own money before heading off to Port Royal."

"Money is the motivation that inspires many of us," Governor Raymond said laughing. "It also tends to get us in trouble with the women. But enough of that, let us go and enjoy the meal my chefs have prepared for us."

The party of four left the main room for the dinner table. Archie sat across from Isabel with the Governor and his wife at the head of each end of the large dining table. The dinner was delectable and each bite inspired new adjectives to describe the freshly caught fish.

The table's conversation revolved mostly around Archie's story and his background. He answered each question directed towards him. He did not want to overstep his bounds and was careful not to ask too many personal questions about the Governor or his affairs.

The dessert was brought to the table and Archie devoured it quicker than a rabbit running out of the farmer's vegetable patch. Irrevocably stuffed and overly satisfied, the party retired to the drawing room for coffee and tea.

Governor Raymond sat down in his magnificent, gold-painted chair and lit up a cigar.

He then turned his attention to his guest and spoke in a serious tone, "Archie, tell me. What are your plans in Port Royal? I think I could find you a suitable position here in Port Nassau. After speaking with you this evening, I've ascertained you to be an intelligent, driven, and ambitious young man. We could use your energy here in Port Nassau. I am certain your wage would be more than adequate for a handsome living."

Archie absorbed the Governor's words, "I do not know what my exact duties will be in Port Royal, Sir. But I do intend to go with my mentor, Mr. Hollis, and my friend, Thomas. I plan hopefully to make enough money to return to England within two years."

"Yes," the Governor paused as he took a long puff on his cigar. "Yes, I remember you saying that at the table," the Governor said as he blew a few smoke rings from his mouth.

Then the Governor looked at Archie and Archie felt his mind

being searched by the Governor's probing eyes, like a thief looking for a way into a flat.

"Consider the opportunity as an open invitation. You seem resolved to go to Port Royal and work with your mentor, Mr. Hollis. If however, during your time there it becomes unsatisfactory, come back to Port Nassau. I will see to it that you are given an integral position and satisfactory wage. The money in the sugarcane industry is definitely lucrative if you have the right luck. Some men find themselves swimming in gold, others however, run on tough times and they end up with nothing in their pockets." The Governor took another big puff of his cigar and concluded, "Before you return to England, I'd like you to come back to Port Nassau. Certainly, it'll be your decision, but like I said, it's an open offer."

"Thank you, Sir. I cannot express how tempting your offer is," Archie replied sincerely.

"Enough of this business talk," Mrs. Raymond interjected politely. "Let Isabel and Archie have some time to get to know each other better. Isabel, why don't you show Archie the grounds before it becomes too dark?"

"Cynthia, my love, you are right. I have taken all of Archie's time. Isabel, darling, I apologize. Your mother and I will let you and Archie have some time together. Goodbye Archie, it was a pleasure meeting you, and please don't forget about my offer," and with that the Governor motioned to his butler to bring over a tray to ash his cigar.

"Thank you Governor Raymond and Mrs. Raymond for your kindness and hospitality," Archie said shaking both of the Raymond's hands.

Isabel rose from her seat and the two of them took their leave. They walked out into the back garden. The temperate, fresh, evening air filled their lungs making both of them more relaxed. Both remained quiet as they slowly down the pathway toward the palm trees and jungle at the rear of the property.

As they strolled Archie turned toward Isabel, "Thank you for inviting me this splendid eve, because I had a lovely time meeting you and your family. Honest, I intend to leave tomorrow for Port Royal but your hospitality means the world to me."

Isabel did not respond, but she stopped walking and took hold of Archie's hand.

As Archie and Isabel looked deep into each other's eyes, Archie felt himself go weak, and his mind went blank. His palms began to sweat and he could feel his heart beating faster. He felt himself in the crossfires of emotions he couldn't control.

She finally spoke, still gazing into Archie's eyes, "You have dangerous, yet soft, blue eyes. I can't help but lose myself in them."

She slowly leaned in gently and kissed Archie on the lips softly, yet purposefully. Archie was paralyzed by a sweeping and intense wave of sensuality that is brought on by a first kiss.

Then all of a sudden she pulled away and whispered, "Safe travels Archie, until next time." And the powerful emotion vanished as quickly as it had come.

Stunned and glassy, Archie responded with the only words his mind could think of, "Yes."

While Archie's mind tried to comprehend his emotions, Isabel led Archie hand in hand silently back toward the mansion to the front door. The butler opened the door for Archie, and there at the bottom of the stairs was a horse and carriage awaiting him. Before crossing the entrance's threshold, Archie turned to face Isabel. Isabel smiled cheekily at him; then without saying another word, she turned and disappeared down the hallway to join her parents in the drawing room.

Archie slowly made his way down the stairs toward the carriage. The entire ride back to the *Charlotte*, he played and replayed the evening in his head and Isabel's kiss. Something deep inside him was different. Was it guilt? Or was he feeling lonelier? The kiss changed him, but how? This was a new emotion that he could not put his finger on. He did not know how to describe it. He felt like a different person than when he arrived at the mansion. He was not different in his ambition or his desire to go back to England. He still loved Olivia and missed her. He was certain of this. But Isabel's kiss had knocked him off his feet. Her soft lips and sun kissed skin and her green eyes and genuine smile. She was captivating. Archie's emotional confusion turned into a twisting river of excitement and irritation. Isabel was a beautiful, exotic vamp, but she was different and enticing for love.

Archie was disappointed and ashamed for dropping his guard and decided he would not tell Thomas of the evening's incidents. The carriage pulled up to the docks and Archie rushed aboard the *Charlotte*. He found Thomas lying in the bunk.

"Aye mate," Archie said as he entered.

"Arch, how was the dinner?"

"Good. They eat like kings in the Governor's mansion."

"I bet."

"One day, we will eat like as they do for every meal."

"We better, you prick," Thomas said under his breathe.

"What's that Tom?" Archie said undressing.

"Nuthin'," Thomas lied. "Just ready to git to Port Royal and start makin' money."

"Course, me too."

The next morning would be the beginning of a new chapter in their lives, which they both needed to be prepared to head face on.

• 9 •

The journey to Port Royal was smooth and expeditious. The waves were rough at times, but the wind was in the *Charlotte*'s sails pushing ever onward to its destination. Port Royal was bustling with people and businessmen, ships, crewmen and soldiers. The atmosphere was electric.

The Great Merchant, Archie, and Thomas loaded up the carriage with their belongings as they readied themselves to head to the sugarcane plantation. Captain Jasper indicated he would only be in Port Royal for a few days, as he would be carrying cargo and doing other business in the West Indies.

"I can't be a sitting duck in the water," the Captain laughed. "This old sailor must keep the sea breeze upon my face or I might die. When I come back to Port Royal, I will check in and see how you are doing, Grant. I know you won't be headed back to England, but I don't intend to spend the rest of my life here."

"That is fair, Will," laughed the Great Merchant. "I will see you soon then, my friend."

With that Captain Jasper pivoted and headed down the dock in search of the nearest tavern.

The carriage bounced down the road and farther into the Colony of Jamaica. They passed palm tree after palm tree. The landscape never changed. The horses slowed down and the carriage stopped outside a magnificent white house surrounded by sugarcane and palm trees.

"This is the place," the Great Merchant exclaimed not being able to conceal his excitement. Then he suddenly coughed uncontrollably into his handkerchief.

"You ok Mr. Hollis?" asked Archie.

"Yes, yes," the Great Merchant responded waving away the question.

The Great Merchant was singularly focused on, enjoying this moment of finally arriving at his future plantation, as it had taken nearly two months and a small fortune to get here. The Great Merchant had the right to be excited and nervous. Archie and Thomas grabbed the bags and clambered toward the house with the Great Merchant striding fast beside them.

"Grant," a booming voice came echoing out of the front door as it opened to reveal a short, robust, yet extremely well dressed man. It was evident this man had accumulated massive wealth over the last two decades.

"Sir Mathis," the Great Merchant whispered to Archie and Thomas before bellowing back, "Benedict, my friend, it's good to see you. How have you been? Looks like you've eaten the entire dinner already and forgotten about us!"

Sir Mathis patting his enormous frame, "It was delicious too. You really missed out on a tasty roasted, maple boar."

As the trio arrived to the front door, Sir Mathis shook hands with the two young men as the Great Merchant introduced them.

"Lads, you can leave the bags for my Nigger butler to carry up to the rooms. If you want to go bathe and get ready for dinner, you must be hungry. Clarence, Clarence, come fetch these bags," hollered

Sir Mathis.

"Comin' Sir," Clarence replied appearing out of nowhere, taking hold of the trunks from Archie and Thomas.

Archie and Thomas hurried up the stairs in search of their rooms and the bath.

"Grant," continued Sir Mathis, "I am sad to be leaving this beautiful plantation, but I know it'll be in superb hands. But we can talk business tomorrow when I show you the property and give you the financial details of this place. For now, tell me how is England and old Brighton. Come inside, would you care for some brandy, whiskey, or rum? I must say though, you have to taste the rum here."

"Then I'll try the West Indies rum," chuckled the Great Merchant before coughing again.

The two gentlemen traded stories and memories and talked throughout dinner and late into the night catching up.

Archie and Thomas feasted on the delicious roasted, maple boar, before touring the property. This would be their home for the next year or more, and both of them were excited to see what the future had in store.

The following day, the Great Merchant and Sir Mathis finalized all the paperwork and financials to complete the transfer of the property and slaves over to Mr. Grant Hollis' name.

Once it was finalized, Sir Mathis shook hands with the Great Merchant, "Congratulations Grant on the wisest business transaction of the century."

"It feels excellent. I will say...," the Great Merchant had to stop because he could not control his coughing.

"Grant, do you need me to call for a doctor? Your coughing has been getting progressively worse since you arrived here."

"I'll, be...alright," managed the Great Merchant through intermittent coughs.

"Ok, well, if you believe you will be fine then it is time to celebrate as it is the dawn of a new age for both of us," Sir Mathis said as he slapped his friend on the back. "Let's cheer to our futures over cigars and the island's best rum."

Unfortunately the celebration was short lived because over the next couple of weeks the Great Merchant's illness worsened with each day. Sir Mathis began to call every doctor in the Colony to get their medical opinion on what was ailing the Great Merchant. To Archie and Sir Mathis' dismay, none of the doctors could diagnosis the Great Merchant's illness or prescribe a remedy to relieve the Great Merchant of his high fever.

Each doctor would say the same dismal phrase, "I'm sorry, but there is nothing I can possibly do. I am not sure what the problem is."

As the weeks passed and the Great Merchant's health continued to decline into mid-December, Sir Mathis continued to oversee the plantation's operations. But assuming the worst for his friend, he began teaching Archie and Thomas everything he had learned over the last decade about sugarcane farming, the sugarcane market, and slave management.

He taught Archie and Thomas how to discern between quality of slave labor and lazy labor, and quality of a good crop and bad crop. He taught them about the weather patterns in the Colony of Jamaica, when to harvest the sugarcane, and how to produce the raw sugar. Most importantly, he taught them about networking, marketing, and selling sugar at other Ports. He taught them basic economic principles of supply and demand and the theory of scarcity.

Archie and Thomas tried to absorb as much as they could and asked hundreds of questions in order to understand the process behind running a plantation. Both of them sensed that Sir Mathis was going to eventually leave, despite the Great Merchant's poor health. Thus, they took Sir Mathis' lessons seriously knowing that they would be running the plantation until the Great Merchant had fully recovered.

One dark evening only days after Christmas, the Great Merchant summoned Archie into his bedroom.

"Archie," the Great Merchant wheezed and spoke through frequent coughs, "I am afraid, my time has come. I can feel it in my body...my body is weak. I am not going to last much...much longer.

This illness and fever have taken their toll on me. I have fought hard, but I have lost. I am deeply sorry to have to put this burden on you...."

Then the coughing stopped his speech completely, and Archie stood there helplessly. Archie could not believe his mentor; he did not want to believe it.

The Great Merchant took a sip of water and continued, "As my apprentice, since I have no kin to inherit this plantation, you are the natural heir to my estate." The Great Merchant took another sip of water. "Once I pass away, I intend for you to own the plantation and slaves."

"Mr. Hollis, I couldn't...," Archie started.

"This will be your ticket to achieving a better life than you or I could ever have dream of. Look at Benedict for example."

The Great Merchant coughed and grimaced in pain. He closed his eyes shut for several minutes as his breathing became labored and his forehead started to sweat.

"Benedict," the Great Merchant continued exhaustedly and through obvious discomfort, "made a fortune and you can too. This is my wish for you. If I give you the plantation will you promise me to run it? Give it your best shot, don't sell it off. We have worked too hard for this. I," the Great Merchant moaned in pain, "I...believe in you Archie."

The Great Merchant rolled over on his side and pointed to a piece of paper on the bedside table next to various medicine bottles, "That paper there is my will. I am leaving you as the sole owner of the Hollis Shipping Company back in Brighton and owner of the Hollis Sugar Plantation, which includes this property and its slaves. Bring it to Benedict for me, so that he may be a witness. I must rest now."

Without another word, he rolled onto his side and closed his eyes. Archie silently moved over to the bedside table, slipped the paper into his pants pocket and left without a sound.

Before Archie withdrew and closed the door, he looked back over his shoulder and stared at the Great Merchant. The Great

Merchant had become a fraction of the man Archie had gotten to know over the last eight years. The fight, the confidence, the zeal had been unmercifully stripped from the man.

"Goodbye Mr. Hollis. Thank you for everything," Archie whispered as he slipped away and shut the door. He just hoped the Great Merchant was wrong, and one day soon the Great Merchant would recover and be able to run the plantation.

Two days later, the Great Merchant passed away. They held a small service at the plantation and mournfully buried the Great Merchant. His epitaph read: *The one and only Merchant of Brighton, who inspired all to worldly achievements.*

Following the small service, Sir Mathis and his lawyer from Port Royal read the Great Merchant's Will and Testament. They had Archie sign the necessary documents that gave him full legal ownership to the Hollis Shipping Company and the Hollis Sugar Plantation.

"You are now the proud owner," the lawyer stated flatly, "of Mr. Hollis' estate and company."

"Looks like you are now the Little Merchant, Archie," Sir Mathis added. "If only it had happened under different circumstances, and many years down the road."

Archie did not know what to say. He stared blankly down at the piece of paper with his signature on it. The Little Merchant. He was not very little standing at six feet one inch, but certainly this is not how it was supposed to happen. He was supposed to be going back to England in twelve months time with the money he had saved.

He looked up at Sir Mathis, "I take it you cannot stay around too much longer."

"No, my boy, I cannot," replied Sir Mathis looking solemnly at Archie. "I wish I could help you in this difficult time, but I have taught you and Thomas all I know about this business. Plus, I must be selfish, because I want to see my family in England before I end up like poor ol' Grant."

"I understand," Archie said. "Thank you for everything you have done."

"You're welcome. I will be around for a little while longer if you have any questions and need help with the transition as the new owner, but as soon as I find a good, strong ship headed for London, I am going to leave."

"Understood," Archie said still stunned by the events of the last seventy-two hours.

———————

A week after celebrating the New Year, Sir Mathis announced at dinner that he had found a ship leaving for England in the coming week and was intending on going unless anyone had any major objections. Archie did not protest despite his desire to keep Sir Mathis as his mentor for as long as possible. Thomas and Archie both thanked Sir Mathis for the wisdom he had imparted to them. Both of them were going to miss the jovial, round man once he was gone.

The night before Sir Mathis left, Archie knocked on his bedroom door.

"Come in," Sir Mathis said.

Archie entered the room. "Sir Mathis, I have these three letters that I would like to send back to Brighton. They are for a young woman named Olivia Hunt, who lives in Brighton. Will you please bring them back to England for me?"

"Certainly, just write her name on the envelope with the address and I will make sure they get to her in Brighton when I arrive at my home in London."

Archie walked over to the desk in the corner, and quickly wrote Olivia's name and her home address on the front of the parchments.

He handed the three letters to Sir Mathis and said, "Thank you, Sir, and safe travels."

"Good luck to you, Archie. May fortune shine upon you."

• 10 •

Olivia's mother picked the letter up from the floor. Upon reading its contents, Olivia's mother realized why her daughter was so distraught and in tears. She looked with concerned eyes at her daughter and then gazed out the window into the cool mid-March morn.

The sun was struggling to poke through the thick, grey, overcast sky. Another dreary day. Olivia had finally received word from Archie, only to have the last letter incinerate all the cheerful feelings that his letters had brought. Olivia's mother glanced down at Archie's *January 1668* letter nestled in her hand and reread it:

> *Olivia, my sweetheart,*
>
> *Happy Christmas and Happy New Year. I am writing to tell you of the terrible events that have transpired over the last four weeks. Mr. Hollis got awfully ill and did not recover from his sickness. All of the doctors tried their best to heal him, but to the great dismay of all of us, Mr. Hollis passed away. He is now with the Lord and hopefully*

looks over me as I take on his business.

Before Mr. Hollis passed away he entrusted me and gave me his shipping company and his sugar plantation that he has purchased here in the Colony of Jamaica.

Now that I am the owner of the shipping company and the plantation, I am not going to be able to come home as expeditiously as I thought. I have decided to continue what Mr. Hollis has started and see it through. I haven't any idea how long it will take. I will write as much as I can and I will work day and night to get back to you sooner.

I have been given the task to run the business and am no longer a mere pawn on the board, but I am the King. I am in charge.

Although it may take me longer than I expected, I will return to you and to Brighton richer and more affluent than the Great Merchant could ever have dreamed. We will get to share in this wealth. I will place upon your finger a ring that no other man can give you. It will be as precious as your smile and shine as bright as your eyes. This I promise you. Take care my love and my heart will always be beating for you.

> *Yours truly,*
> *Archie*

Olivia's mother sat down next to her daughter and hugged her tightly. Olivia embraced her mother and cried into her shoulder.

Olivia's mother thought to herself as she comforted her daughter: Olivia is twenty-one years old and it is about time she starts looking for a good husband. With Archie deciding to run the business and remain in Jamaica indefinitely, Olivia's mother knew it might be time for her daughter to look at other suitors and prospects. She liked Archie, she really did. She would have gladly loved to have seen her daughter married to Archie and have him as part of the family. She aspired great things for her daughter and she also selfishly wished to have grandchildren too. She would not be pushy or bring it up now;

but, she would definitely begin to suggest to Olivia to venture out into the world and start seeing other fine, English gentlemen.

• 11 •

The beginning of 1668 proved to be a brutal learning curve for Archie and Thomas as they began the process of applying their knowledge to the sugarcane plantation. The slaves worked hard, but the sugarcane yield was poor. Determined to succeed, Archie hired Captain William Jasper to join the Hollis Shipping Company as the primary Captain and distributor of the Hollis Sugar. Therefore, the *Charlotte* would be utilized as the main shipment vessel for their sugarcane exportation, once they produced enough to sell. Slowly, as the weeks of winter rolled into spring, Archie became more refined in his knowledge and techniques of the sugarcane business.

Finally in the spring, the Hollis sugarcane plantation boomed with productivity. Archie and Thomas both said it was only by the grace of God that they received the boost they needed or else they would have gone broke.

As a business partner, Thomas became an invaluable asset. Thomas frequented Kingston and Port Royal as the Hollis Sugar networking liaison. On his trips into the cities and Ports, he had a proclivity to frequent the bars and brothels, but he always returned with the local rumors, news of large business transactions, and the latest on pirates and privateers. Somehow, someway, Thomas knew the pulse of the Caribbean, and it helped Archie immensely to have such critical information when making business decisions. Archie never asked Thomas about his sources or his methods, and trusted that he was good for his word. Archie's trust in Thomas seemed to be well placed as the knowledge was always correct.

At the end of the spring, after collecting enough sugarcane to meet the minimum requirement for economic feasibility, Archie promoted Thomas to be the Head of Distribution. Archie instructed Thomas to broaden his networking range and venture to Port Nassau and to the growing French colony—Saint-Domingue.

"Each month, I want you to locate potential buyers, manufacturers, and any other news or information that might be relevant," Archie ordered in a business tone. "These are important trips for us, Tom. The scouting you will be doing is intended for us to obtain new clientele not for you to meet new women," Archie continued sternly. "I know you like to frequent the taverns and brothels, but with the company money, we can't be lackadaisical. Just like this winter, we could hit hard times at any moment."

Brushing off Archie's concern and stern tone, Thomas replied, "Archie, ya worry too much. Life's good mate. The crops are doin' fine. We have almost mastered the techniques and cycles. I've been through hard times, this ain't it. I'll take care of the local merchants and find us some good buyers. You trust me mate?"

"I do Tom," Archie responded, wondering if he truly was worrying too much. "You have a point, we have become quite good at this business over the last four months. The summer and autumn will only bring better weather and higher yields."

"See," Thomas said smiling, "that's the type-a-talk I like to hear. Now, where would ya like me to travel first? North to Port Nassau and see your lovely lass, Isabel, or straight to Saint-Domingue? I could also swing South and..."

Before he could finish his sentence Archie cut him off, "Nassau, Saint-Domingue, home. That should take you around two weeks or three. Then you will be here with me for two weeks helping out, and then off you go again. Captain Jasper has accepted to take a percentage of the sale as payment, since we have nothing to pay him currently."

"A'ighty, Nassau then Saint-Domingue. I'll see you in a couple weeks," Thomas called over his shoulder as he boarded the *Charlotte*.

"See ya, Arch," Captain Jasper called from the deck. "I'll try and keep an eye on this wily cat."

Thomas laughed, "Capt'n, you're such an ol' timer. Only in your dreams could ya catch me."

Archie watched the ship pull away from the harbor and begin to sail out of the bay. He was confident with the right information and the inside scoop Thomas could acquire, he would make his sugarcane plantation the most profitable on the island. But before he sold one gram of sugar, he wanted all the market information he could get.

———————

For the next three weeks, the sugarcane business took every waking minute of Archie's time. He was always planning, strategizing, managing the slaves, and keeping records and documents of nearly everything that was measurable. He became meticulous in his work and started to really enjoy owning and managing the many moving parts of the plantation.

Archie felt like he had finally earned the Merchant title, or as Sir Mathis had put it—the Little Merchant. One day he would be the Rich Merchant. He smiled to himself as he looked outside his office window onto the expansive sugarcane field stretching into the distance. The green, tall sugarcane stalks swayed slightly in the wind, which weaved itself like a snake between the gaps.

Archie thought to himself as he studied his crop: This year is going to be booming, then I can make plans to return home, I can feel it. The singularity of his intentions to get home was for the sole purpose of marrying Olivia. He understood the longer he stayed in Jamaica the less likely she would be available when he returned.

Olivia was young, beautiful and unattached. Archie knew that she was most likely highly sought after by over half the eligible men in Brighton and probably even more from outside of the town. Would Olivia wait for him? She would definitely wait, Archie thought. The true question would be, for how long?

Breaking his train of thought, a carriage drove down the long, straight path that led to the front of the mansion. Archie left his study to greet Thomas, who was coming back from his excursion. Three weeks came and went faster than Archie could believe.

"Thomas, my friend, I can't believe how quickly the time has flown by. I hope your travels were fruitful with information."

"Unbelievably so, the ladies in Saint-Domingue couldn't get enough of me. I almost didn't come back," Thomas said laughing. "You're lucky I am a loyal mate. It was you or this lovely lass named Le Saphir. She's a gem, truly, and extraordinary in bed. She's a real charmer. Lemme tell ya, she does this one position..."

"I'm glad your personal pursuits were so rewarding," Archie said grinning and patting his friend on the back not wanting to hear Thomas' sexual exploits. "Let's chat about your trip and the prospective buyers for our sugar."

Thomas and Archie discussed Thomas' journey late into the night. Thomas rambled on about his trip to Port Nassau and Saint-Domingue.

While in Port Nassau, Thomas stopped by Governor Raymond's to pay his respects as part of the courtesy of the Hollis Shipping Company and to inform the Governor of Mr. Hollis' death and Archie as the new chief in command.

"Isabel sends a kiss along with her best wishes for you in your new position," Thomas said winking at Archie. "She really fancies you. I'd go for it if I were you. I know you got that lass from back home, but ya could really do well down here. Owner of a sugar and shipping company, married to the Guv'na's…"

"That will be enough Thomas," Archie said cutting him off. "I appreciate Isabel's thoughtfulness, but I don't intend to pursue her."

"Your loss mate. She's a catch. Where was I? Aye, I forgot to mention she is also gettin' engaged, so looks like you might be off the hook. It's some ugly, overweight bloke from Port Nassau that has made a fortune in the slave trade. I thought maybe you could save her from such an awful fate and be 'er hero."

"Thomas I know you are always looking out for me. But please continue on and enough about Isabel."

"You got it mate."

Thomas continued on with his story, this time with no interruptions or jokes. "Port Nassau definitely has buyers for their sugarcane. They'll take it and either refine it or they will buy it and resell it to England. I think Port Nassau is a location we should definitely sell too," summed up Thomas. "As for Saint-Domingue, well, I ain't sure. Saint-Domingue is beginnin' to boom and word has it that Spain wasn't gonna challenge the bloody French for the coastal territory the French has started to colonize on Spanish soil. France's influence will be there for a long while, probably as long as you and I are doin' business down 'ere."

"Interesting," pondered Archie. "What are our chances that we will be able to trade with the French as a British enterprise?"

"Lemme finish," Thomas interjected. "The infamous pirate Rémi Montre heavily influences Saint-Domingue's trade. Saint-Domingue is not you like here. Montre has been burning the British and Spanish merchant ships that do not trade directly through him and his associates. He brings all of the gold into Saint-Domingue. He cares about gold only, not a flag. The booming economy has been funded almost entirely from Rémi's treasure and gold," Thomas continued. "The man is startin' to create a small empire in the region it seems. Saint-Domingue aristocrats will be safe of course to trade with; but, there are definitely concerns as to how long cordial business relations can be conducted when a damn pirate is in charge."

Archie pondered as he absorbed Thomas' assessment. "It's important to know that Rémi has such influence over the region," Archie said recalling Captain Montre's Wanted Poster in Port Nassau. "He is definitely one man we should not cross and maybe, just maybe, an alliance or pact can be made with him. Is it reasonable to deal rationally with a pirate? I think it'll be best to have you continue to visit Saint-Domingue regularly to build a good rapport with the French before we try and sell our sugar there."

"I'm fine with that. Means I get to see my lady again—the fine Miss Le Saphir," Thomas said with a smile. "Anyways, I'm off to bed Arch, it's been a long day for me. We can talk more in the mornin' if ya have more questions to ask me."

The summer of 1668, just as Archie had hoped, brought robust sugarcane yields and he could not help but imagine all the gold flowing into his coffers. Sugar was a prized commodity in Europe and sugar was trading at a favorable price. He was at the heart of this booming market and could not believe his luck.

Throughout the summer and autumn, Archie continued his expansion plans into Port Nassau and began to introduce his presence in Saint-Domingue. Captain Jasper and Thomas spent more and more time traveling from Port to Port with refined sugar and sugarcane shipments to both Port Nassau and Saint-Domingue. The wealth and money the Hollis Sugar Plantation had produced by November, convinced Archie that they must be one of the most profitable and efficient sugar plantations in Jamaica.

On one windy afternoon in November, the day before Thomas was to make another trip to Saint-Domingue, Archie noticed Thomas standing in the doorway to his office.

"What is it mate? Did you want to talk about something?" Archie asked.

"Aye, I was wonderin' if I could have another advance on my

payments or take out a loan 'gainst this next shipment?" Thomas asked sheepishly.

"Why? Is everything ok? I thought I paid you just a week ago."

"Aye, e'erythin' is fine. I just owe some blokes a bit of gold. Not much, just need a bit-a-gold to cover it."

"You're not in any trouble are you Tom?" Archie asked worried. He knew that Thomas liked to gamble, but it had not been a problem to date.

"No. No, I'm not. And don't you be my parent," Thomas responded getting angry. "Will ya give me the gold or no? It's my share anyway."

"Yes, ok," Archie said taken aback. "I'll write you an advance for your percentage of the sale, unless you need more. You can take it out as a loan now, then you can pay it off in installments from the next few sugarcane sales."

"Whatever you write down," Thomas said flatly.

Archie took his quill and scribbled down a note for Thomas' allotment of gold from the next sugar sale.

"Thanks," Thomas said as he took the note from Archie and walked out of the office.

Archie watched as his friend leave the office. He returned the quill to the inkwell and went back to his current predicament. He could not think too much about Thomas' gambling problems currently because he had his own personal problems.

Over the last two months, he had received four letters from Isabel asking him to come visit her in Port Nassau. Her letters were overtly flirtatious, as she wanted to see her "favorite Englishman" as soon as possible. Despite Archie's unresponsiveness to her letters, she was persistent. He looked down at the blank piece of paper waiting patiently on his desk. The paper stared blankly back at Archie. Archie stared back at the paper, then picked up his quill again and dipped it several times in the inkblot and placed it against the virgin parchment.

When he finished, he pursed his lips and blew the fresh ink dry, then reread his missive:

Isabel,

Your words and flattery have truly been touching. I am so happy you think so highly of me. As you wish, I will come to Port Nassau next summer before continuing onward to England. With how well the sugarcane plantation has been performing, I am going to return home and promote Thomas to run the Jamaican plantation. Also, I understand you are getting married soon. Congratulations!

I hope you and the rest of your family are healthy and have a wonderful Christmas season. Pass on my regards to your father and mother for me too.

Warmly,
Archie

That evening at dinner he handed the letter to Thomas and said, "Tomorrow when you leave for your trip, will you and Captain Jasper stop by Port Nassau before Saint-Domingue and deliver this letter to Isabel Raymond for me?"

Thomas could not help but smile as he looked down at the letter.

"It's 'bout time mate. You might be too late; although, dependin' on what words are on this paper, ya just might've found yourself a wife."

"Thank you Thomas," Archie responded ignoring Thomas' usual, playful comments.

Thomas left the following day. As Archie watched the carriage pull down the road, he considered when he should tell Thomas of his plan. Archie's ultimate plan was to move back to England next summer and expand the business to Brighton in order to ship the Hollis sugarcane and sugar derivatives directly to England, thereby skipping the middle trader in Port Nassau and Saint-Domingue. The expansion would make their operation more profitable and he would be able to return to England, which was the primary motive.

Archie had saved nearly all of his own and the companies profits to expedite this grand plan of his. He projected that within another six months they would be able to buy one more ship and hire one more captain. With two ships, one ship would make the regular crossing to England, preferably with Captain Jasper; while, the other captain and ship would continue to trade locally within the West Indies region. Thomas would run the plantation and the local trade. Archie would run the trans-Atlantic trade and work with Captain Jasper. Archie would setup a distribution center in London or Brighton, depending on where Olivia wanted to live. He would tell Thomas of the plan sometime in the new year.

The new year began filling Archie with renewed hope in his soul that he would be back in Olivia's arms. He marked a day on his calendar—5 June 1669. This would be the day he and Captain Jasper would depart the West Indies for England with a load of sugarcane.

Despite the continuation of improved crop yields and increased profits during the winter and spring of 1669, Thomas more regularly began asking for advances on his commission and taking out loans from the Hollis Company. Even though this behavior should have been a red flag to Archie, he did not notice the increasing tendency because he was focusing all of his attention on purchasing a new ship and hiring a new, trustworthy captain to begin Hollis Shipping Company in the summer.

One beautiful, spring morning in April, Archie pulled out a quill and paper from his desk. Archie dipped the quill into the fresh inkwell and smiled as he began his letter. He was writing to Olivia to alert her of his intentions to return home by the end of the summer. He informed her of how well the company had been doing under his management over the last fifteen months and that he was going to expand to England.

Archie was proud of himself, all his hard work was paying off. He was destined to return home at last. He had had his adventure in the Caribbean and had made it more worthwhile than he could have ever anticipated. He ventured to Port Royal in the morning and slipped the letter into the Royal Post. Enjoying the lovely day, he strolled around the Port deciding to take the day off from work.

Archie noticed a familiar wanted poster and walked over to it. Sure enough, it was the same man he had met when he first arrived in the West Indies. There looking back at him was Captain Rémi Montre.

"Thank goodness my ship has never been pillaged by him," Archie whispered to himself. Archie was thankful that Captain Jasper and Thomas had been able to avoid the fate of death early in their business careers.

One day Captain Montre would be caught and be hanged by the neck, Archie thought to himself, and on that day our trading waters will be safer and I will not have to fear for my friends' lives or my business.

That evening while Archie and Thomas were sitting at the dinner table, Archie broke the news to Thomas about his plan to return to England. "Thomas, I have been meaning to talk to you about something," began Archie.

"What's that?" responded Thomas through a mouthful of food.

"I plan to return to England at the beginning of June and expand our operations to Europe. This spring, I've been working on acquiring a new ship to make this possible."

"Wow, this is big news." Thomas stopped eating and focused his attention on Archie.

"Yes, our operations have been so profitable it has given us the chance to expand. I am promoting you to be head of West Indies operations; while, I conduct all the European operations."

Thomas was beaming with pride. "Ya serious Archie? I would be the head of the plantation in the West Indies."

Thomas had never expected much out of life, but with the new position he would definitely be in the aristocracy of the West Indies.

"Indeed," Archie said happily, relieved his friend and business partner was so enthusiastic about the new plan. "As you know, I've always wished to return to England. Also, I believe in you and your ability to continue the operations here; while, I look to conduct our affairs abroad."

"Sounds like an amazin' opportunity," concluded Thomas. "When do you plan on returnin' to England?"

"Fifth of June."

"Soon."

"Yes, I know. In my heart, it feels like the right time."

"Well, I know we talked a while back about me goin' to England with you. But," Thomas paused, "this has become my home and I like it here in Port Royal. The ladies love me and what would they do if the love of their lives was to be gone forever?" chuckled Thomas. "What I'm sayin' is, I'm really glad you ain't sending me to England."

"I'm glad you like the plan the way it is. I know that you will do great in the leadership role overseeing the sugar operations and slave management. Since you have been sailing with Captain Jasper for the last year, it's only natural that you should be the one to lead our West Indies trade," Archie said taking a gigantic swig of wine.

"Aye, aye, couldn't agree more mate."

"One last thing before the transition is complete. I would like you to hire a scouting man as good as yourself. He will take your spot on the new ship that we purchase. I will find a captain that knows these waters like a mother knows her baby; but you, Thomas, must find a successor in the skill of salesmanship. While you are here on the plantation running the business, we will need someone of your caliber out in the waters, the ports, finding us new trade partners, and continuing to get the inside information you so masterfully acquired."

"That info comes at quite a cost," Thomas said reservedly and squirmed slightly in his seat. "But, I might've just the man in mind. His name's Trevor Cooks. Good fella, savvy. Sometimes even more than me, although he can be a bit of a pansy at times. I will shape 'im up into a stronger lad."

"That's good news Tom. Well, on your next tour in May, take this Mr. Cooks with you on the trip. Show him the ropes, and introduce him to all the people you know. Make him look slick and proper. Is he fit for the position?"

"Ya, he ain't no slouch. He works for a blacksmith now and does a'ight. He wants more money though, and I think our business can promise him that 'specially with me at the helm," Thomas remarked confidently.

"It's settled then," Archie said raising his glass toward Thomas. "In May you show our good man Trevor how to do your job, when you return, you will take my position and I will sail for Nassau. I will pay my respects to Isabel and the Governor, as I promised, then return to England with Captain Jasper. You will have a new ship and local captain at your disposal to continue normal operations."

"Cheers to that mate," Thomas said and then subsequently downed his glass. "Tonight we celebrate."

• 12 •

Olivia strolled amongst the crowded ballroom looking for a familiar face. It was December 1668, nine months after she had read Archie's third letter. Throughout the summer and autumn, her mother prompted her to meet new men and to begin to consider seeing someone other than Archie.

At first, Olivia was petrified at the thought and did not talk to her mother about the subject. She could not see herself courting anyone else. Archie was her man. But as the weeks rolled by and she saw all the young women going out with their men, she decided to go to a few parties to which she had been invited.

At the current Christmas ball Olivia was attending, she had decided to leave her young man because he was dreadfully boring, despite being from an aristocratic family in Manchester. Olivia managed to squeeze her way through the crowd to the far wall by the dance floor. She watched the couples dance around to the beautiful music. The women all looked so pretty and elegant. Olivia looked down at her blue dress. She wished Archie was with her so that they could too be dancing. She knew she looked incredible in her blue dress, and wished she could share this moment with her man.

She looked up and gazed amongst the crowd. She watched as multiple men clambered and competed for the attention of a stunning, young woman in a white dress with an ornate, pearl necklace draped around her neck. Loneliness filled her body and sent a chill down her spine. To rid herself of the feeling, she glanced toward the musicians playing their instruments ever so passionately. Then all of the sudden and rather abruptly, a handsome man brushed up against her. Olivia was startled and looked at the man standing beside her.

"The name's James Towns," James said. "You are captivating, and I couldn't let such a fine young lady be by herself." James extended his hand.

"Olivia," Olivia responded curtly and placed her hand in James' hand. James kissed the back of her gloved hand.

"Ms. Olivia, may I ask you to a Christmas dance?"

Olivia considered it for a moment, and then responded, "Certainly." She smiled at him. Deep down, she was so glad to be able to dance and not have to stand awkwardly against the wall and look so lonely. As they danced, she was not sure what to make of James Towns. But as the night progressed, she began to warm to him in spite of her misgivings. They danced to several songs and when they stopped to talk and have drinks, Olivia knew that she did find James to be a fascinating and mysterious man. As they talked, James gave told her about his life and explained how he happened to be in Brighton.

He was born in London and currently lived and worked there as a banker. He had been in finance for the last decade. He was nine years older than Olivia and was looking to settle down and finally raise a family. He was in Brighton on business and visiting a friend who had invited him to this ball.

Olivia found him overly confident to the point of arrogant and aggressive at times, but she couldn't help herself being drawn in by his charisma and presence. She also could not over look the opportunity and the promising life she would have being married to a London banker.

When the orchestra had played their last song, James asked, "May I walk you home?"

"Yes," Olivia said giggling, feeling the effects of the fine red wine.

During the walk back home, Olivia and James made plans to see each other the next day before James had to return to London.

That evening as Olivia lay in bed, she was happy with how well the evening had gone, since she had had such low expectations; but inside, she felt guilty. She was flirting with another man when Archie was trying his best to save up enough gold for their future together. She quickly rationalized to herself: she could not wait forever, as all the good men would be taken and what if Archie never came back then what was she to do?

The next day James and Olivia had a pleasant day together. Olivia read James some of her poetry and showed him her artwork. Olivia walked with James to his carriage and before leaving James said, "You ought to come to London and I will show you the museums and the theater and the galleries. You'd love it. Would you like to visit London some time?"

"Absolutely," Olivia said excitedly. "I've always wanted to visit."

"Splendid. You should come in April or May once the weather gets a tad better." James boarded his carriage and shut the door.

"Goodbye James," Olivia said.

"Goodbye Olivia. I will write and we can find a week that works for your trip."

James and Olivia parted ways and exchanged letters throughout the rest of the winter. They wrote to each other constantly and Olivia enjoyed having someone to write to that was close to Brighton. She laughed at James' letters and could not help but feel her attraction for him growing stronger.

On April 11, 1669, James returned to Brighton to escort Olivia up to London for her weeks stay in the city with him.

"Olivia, I am feeling positive about you coming to London. I think you will fall in love with the city. You may never want to leave," James said as he lifted Olivia into the carriage.

"I do believe you are right. For the last four months, I've not been able to take my mind off this trip and visiting you and seeing London for the first time," replied Olivia.

"You'd best get cozy. It'll be a little bit of a journey, probably take all day to travel to London, if not longer."

The two arrived in London and it exceeded all of Olivia's expectations. The week she spent with James was one of the best weeks of her life. James took Olivia to some of the nicest restaurants London had to offer. They went to two operas, the theater, and museums. The city seemed to always be teeming with activity and was lively and bustling.

Olivia preferred the hustle and bustle of the city, and reflected how she frequently became bored with the slow paced lifestyle in Brighton. In London, people where headed in all different directions at all hours of the day. The atmosphere made her feel more alive. At the end of the week, James helped Olivia load up her carriage that would take her back to Brighton.

"Olivia," James began tentatively, very unlike himself, "I don't want to rush you but I'd like you to move to London so that we might spend more time together. I know financially this might not be feasible for you. I'd like to move you to London on my expense. I have feelings for you and I see this going further. I don't see any other woman being a part of my life. On your journey home, would you consider my proposition?" James finished and looked at Olivia directly in her beautiful, sparkling eyes. He did not smile or seem tense but genuinely vulnerable.

"I will consider it," Olivia said with equal seriousness, yet her stomach was filled with butterflies. Then she added, "I had a lovely week with you James, I couldn't have asked for anything better." Olivia kissed James on the cheek and boarded the carriage. James could not stop himself from smiling.

"Have a safe trip back to Brighton, and I will be awaiting your letter, as soon as you feel comfortable and have a response."

"I will." And with that, Olivia slapped the wall of the carriage board, and waved goodbye to James as she left for her journey home.

One day after her twenty-third birthday in May, Olivia wrote her letter to James. She looked down at the finished product and smiled. Confident in her decision, she sent it with the morning post.

A little over two weeks later, Olivia was kissing her mother and father goodbye and boarded her carriage for the one-way journey to London. Olivia's mother waved goodbye long after the carriage had disappeared, but she was so happy that her daughter had found someone. She daydreamed of going to London for her daughter's wedding one day, and the thought of finally having a grandchild made her euphoric.

To her surprise, only days after Olivia had left for London, a letter arrived in Brighton addressed to Olivia. She looked at the markings and saw it was from the West Indies, most notably with the Port Royal wax insignia. Archie? Olivia's mother stared down at the letter. Should she forward this letter onto her daughter? Or should she destroy it after reading the contents? She did not want to see her daughter's heart broken, but at the same time she knew how much Archie meant to her daughter.

Olivia's mother pondered the topic for several days without opening the letter. She twirled it between her fingers every morning, and each day she started to lean more toward destroying the letter outright. Why bring her daughter additional potential heartache? There was no reason for that. She was happy in London and possibly going to be married by the year's end. Archie's letter would only ruin her happiness.

Olivia's mother decided that tomorrow she would read it, and then depending on the contents, she would make an educated plan.

The following morning, Olivia's mother gently and carefully unfolded the parchment and read the black ink inscribed on the sun-faded, yellow paper.

My beautiful Olivia,

    I have wonderful news. After the last fifteen months, I've turned the sugar plantation into one of the most profitable in Port Royal. I am heading to Port Nassau to finalize some business transactions in May, then I will be setting sail with Captain Jasper to return home. I can't wait to see you and look into your dreamy eyes; smell your sweet scent; feel your soft hand intertwined with mine; and kiss your soft lips. Also, you might not believe it, but I've even written a poem for you. I miss you, and I love you. My sweet Olivia, I am finally coming home to you.

        Yours forever,

        Archie

Olivia's mother reread the short letter three times, to ensure she was not misreading any part of it. Now she was in quite a predicament, because she knew her daughter would definitely want this letter. Olivia was most likely going to marry the banker from London and what a good, promising life that would be. Archie, on the other hand, had seemingly become a successful merchant and would also be able to take care of Olivia too. Plus, Olivia's mother ultimately conceded, Olivia loved Archie.

She refolded the parchment and melted new wax to seal the letter again. Olivia's mother dropped it in the post with a new, London address; despite her second thoughts.

———

Olivia looked at the letter that had just arrived from Brighton. Archie was coming home. She felt her heart jump and sink simultaneously. She did not know what to think. She was excited and could not wait to see him; but at the same time, she had just begun a new life in London with James. What was Archie going to think when he arrived and saw her with James?

Olivia hid the letter and decided to pretend it did not exist. For the greater part of the next month, she successfully pushed Archie's letter from her conscious thoughts.

On a beautiful late summer evening, James and Olivia were walking home from the theater strolling through the park. James stopped Olivia and turned to her.

"My dear Olivia," he said pulling a small box out of his pocket. "There's something I would like to ask you. I have become enamored with your personality, your beauty inside and out, and I would like to ask for your hand in marriage. I have sent a letter to your father asking for his blessing too." James paused before asking the final question, "Will you marry me?"

The question hung in the air as he lifted the top of the box to reveal a precision cut, beautiful, diamond ring. It must have cost him a small fortunate. All Olivia could do was stare at the ring. Her breathing became shorter and quicker. She looked up at him; he was staring purposefully into her eyes. She still did not respond. She could not; the words were trapped in her throat.

She closed her eyes. Archie's letter burned bright behind her eyelids. *My sweet Olivia, I am finally coming home to you.* Olivia could vividly see the black ink upon the paper. *I am finally coming home to you.*

"James, I must think about it. I'm sorry."

She felt ashamed and looked down at her feet. This man, who worked hard and bought her beautiful things and invited her to all these nice events and plays, and the theater, yet still she could not say yes.

James closed the box and placed it back in his pocket.

"Of course, you are right. This has happened all rather quickly. If you need time to think it over, then you will have time to think about it."

The rest of the walk, neither of them said a word. The entire time, Olivia wished she was anywhere in the world other than standing next to James. How ashamed she felt. Why could she not have just said yes? Archie. Archie was the reason. Was she really so blindly in love that she could not marry one of the most eligible bachelors in all of London?

The following day while looking at Archie's letter, she committed herself to the choice that if James proposed again, she would say yes. Unless Archie arrived home first, then she would surely marry him.

She needed security and safety for her future; and so far, James seemed to be her best option. She felt confident in her decision. Olivia thought to herself: Archie, it's time for you to really show how much you love me and to fulfill all your promises. If you can make it to me before James proposes again, then you will have won me forever. God's speed Archie, God's speed.

• 13 •

At the end of the long aisle next to the priest stood the dashing Mr. James Towns. The ritualistic, uplifting music was playing throughout the church and everyone was peering over and around each other as the gorgeous Miss Olivia Hunt took her first steps down the aisle. She was being lead by her father, and there were tears in her mother's eyes. Olivia's mother stared at her daughter in admiration, as her wedding dress glistened and shined. Olivia made her way gracefully up the stairs to the altar as she let go of her father's hand and stood across from her fiancé.

The moment on the altar lasted an eternity, as James' and Olivia's "I dos" were interlocking promises to finalize their lifetime commitment to each other. The congregation exploded in applause and jubilation when James and Olivia kissed for the first time as a newly married couple. The baroque organ blared to life and was triumphantly louder than all the applause and cheers from family and friends. The new Mr. and Mrs. James Towns proudly marched down the aisle and out of the church hand in hand, waving to family and friends as rice rained down all around them.

The wedding took place two weeks before the Christmas of 1669. The first six months of the couple's marriage were blissful and it seemed as nothing could go wrong. Olivia enjoyed staring deeply into her husband eyes, their nights out on the town, and the snuggling and whispering late into the night.

In the summer of 1670 Olivia became pregnant and was overjoyed. With each passing week, she became more and more excited on becoming a mother. James was equally thrilled too on becoming a father. However, he started working more and more throughout the autumn and winter because of financial trouble at the bank. The bank where James worked was going through a terrible slump with poor returns on investments. They were losing money on their outstanding loans faster than anyone knew how to remedy the issue. To put his mind at ease, James would regularly come home from work drunk. Unfortunately, his hot temper led him to take out his frustrations from work, by yelling and verbally abusing Olivia.

Every morning, James would apologize and tell Olivia he was under a lot of stress at work and that he needed to handle it better. Olivia knew James was a drinker and told herself it was just a stage. Once the bank recovered, all would be restored to the blissful state and she would not have to endure the James' sharp and piercing abuse. To her dismay, the bank continued to produce dismal, financial numbers.

During their first anniversary dinner in December, James became more drunk than Olivia had ever seen him.

He started swearing obscenities at their waiter and he yelled across the table at Olivia, "What do you do anyway? Just get fat and sit at home all day. I can't even have sex with you anymore you say now that you're pregnant. And now the bank is going to bring me to financial ruin. Me. Poor. I'll have none of it."

James continued to rave and rant as Olivia escorted him out of the restaurant utterly humiliated and barely able to control her tears.

Olivia endured James' drunken rows and fights, and continued to be loyal and stick by her husband through this most tumultuous time in his work. As the winter turned to spring, she was ready to give birth to their child, who was by now, draining her of her energy, nutrition, and health.

Thankfully, James noticed his wife needed support and tried his best to clean up his act; which in his opinion, was not to come home when he had been drinking. James started to regularly stay out of Olivia's way during the final month of her pregnancy and Olivia often worried about him.

He would occasionally venture home and give her a kiss and ask how she was doing; although, he frequently smelled of alcohol and looked like he had not stopped working in weeks. James told her the bank was on the brink of collapse, which meant they were also on the brink. But he reassured her that he could right the ship.

Olivia believed her husband, but she could not help and think to herself, at what cost?

Charles Oliver Towns was born on the 2nd of April 1671. Olivia held her baby boy in her arms and could not believe how adorable and precious he was. The bond between mother and son was immediate and powerful. Thankfully, James was present and shared the moment with her. Olivia thought to herself, Charles would be the light that brought James back to her.

Olivia watched Charles, as he slept peacefully in her arms, and she thought about James. He was still working day and night, so he said, and his drinking habits had become more and more pronounced despite the bank's slow recovery. Despite her sadness and loneliness without her husband, Olivia let the birth of her baby boy wash away all her troubles and trusted one day they could start over afresh as a family—James, Charles and herself.

• 14 •

"Wait…what?" stammered Thomas, coughing and spitting his ale everywhere.

"I'm afraid so, Tom. Port Royal has been sacked and pillaged by d'Or. Happened only a couple of days ago," repeated Captain Jasper.

Trevor, who was drinking next to Thomas, looked as utterly startled as Thomas.

"We should head back to Port Royal at once. How soon can we leave Capt'n?" Trevor said.

Before the Captain could answer, Thomas interjected, "Any word from Arch?"

"No word and we can leave immediately. I was thinking the same thing Trevor. If Archie is still alive, we'll need to be there and help him and the Port."

"If he's still alive…" Thomas said his voice trailing off as the shock started to set in. "He'll still be alive. Archie wouldn't have been killed by the bloody d'Or. He's too smart fur that lot. He's a good shot too with that pistol of his."

The three men left that afternoon and set their coordinates straight for Port Royal. The trip would take two or three days, but it was as quickly as they could make the voyage.

For Thomas the three-day trip to Port Royal felt like an eternity. Thomas could not help but blame himself. If d'Or had truly been the ones who sacked Port Royal, he had a hunch he knew why. He had been running with a rough crowd recently on his business trips and expeditions to Saint-Domingue. He knew he had many, many outstanding gambling debts to some shady individuals. Naturally, he had promised he was good for the gold; he just needed time to become head of the plantation. Obviously, these were not patient men.

How much did I owe the d'Or? Thomas thought hard about it. A small fortune or was it only a month's wages? He had gambled heavily and won mounds of gold; although, he had also lost more than he cared to recount.

The *Charlotte* anchored in the bay and the sight before the group was devastating. Port Royal was in absolute ruins, with the smoke still wafting up from the burnt buildings and charred remains of the palm trees, homes, shops, and other town buildings.

Thomas, Trevor, and Captain Jasper stared in disbelief at the wreckage and carnage before them. Blood stained the stone streets and there was the smell of death in the air. Flies buzzed around everywhere. Not a soul was in sight. Thomas, Trevor, and Captain Jasper frantically ran around trying to find someone, anyone. They ventured upon a stable with five horses crying and whining.

Thomas went inside the inn to find someone, but there was no caretaker or innkeeper present.

"Looks like e'eryone has either fled Port Royal or those d'Or bastards killed 'em all," Thomas shouted angrily.

Trevor pointed to the horses in the stable, "Seems like ain't no one will mind then."

"Let's take three of these horses and ride as fast as we can to the Hollis Plantation. All we can do is pray Archie is still there and alive," instructed Captain Jasper.

The three men clambered bareback upon the horses and rode straight to the Hollis plantation. To the group's horror, the sugarcane fields had been significantly burnt down and the mansion had been ripped to pieces, but thankfully not set ablaze.

Slowly and apprehensively, Thomas led the group into the mansion through the smashed and battered door. The wreckage and destruction inside was committed with impunity. Nothing was left upright. All the pictures, cabinets, and drawers were overturned and thrown about the rooms.

Thomas cautiously went upstairs and entered Archie's study alone. There on the desk amongst thousands of disheveled papers and business records lay a new note. Archie's father's dagger was stabbed through the top of the paper, keeping it pinned to the desk. Thomas shimmied the dagger free from the wood and picked up the parchment.

It was not addressed to anyone, but Thomas knew exactly for whom it was intended.

> *So no doubt, you know why we came. You owe us, and you owe us a lot. We cannot finance your losing gambling habits any longer. We have taken Archie as an incentive for you to pay us. He will die if we do not receive our gold.*
>
> *We will give you six weeks to deliver your payment to us. You know where to find us when you have it. When our paths cross again and if you are empty handed, you will receive a worse fate than your friend. You've been warned.*
>
> *RM*

RM? Le Capitaine d'Or—Rémi Montre. Thomas shook his head in dismay as he pieced together the initials. What had he done? His friend Archie had been given a death sentence, signed and delivered by the one and only Rémi Montre. Archie had done so much for him, and this is how he was repaying his friend. Thomas recollected Archie was about to leave with Captain Jasper in three weeks time and head home to England. But now Archie was a prisoner of the d'Or pirates. Thomas shuddered and ashamedly accepted this entire situation was his fault.

Putting away his pride, Thomas walked out of the office and found Trevor and Captain Jasper rummaging through the destruction in the living room.

"Capt'n…Trev…," Thomas shouted, grabbing their attention.

They turned and Thomas simply handed them the note. Both men read the note and stared in disbelief at Thomas.

Not needing a question to know the answer, Thomas nodded his head and said, "Aye, I'm the reason they kidnapped Archie. We've six weeks, which leaves us till the end of June."

The Captain leapt forward and tackled Thomas and started punching him violently. Thomas and the Captain rolled around on the floor and traded punches. Trevor tried to intervene momentarily but failed and backed away.

The skirmish last a few minutes and finished when Thomas landed a forceful blow to the Captain's nose, and blood started gushing from his face, speckling the floor with crimson droplets.

The Captain rolled onto his stomach moaning and holding his face. Thomas lay on the floor exhausted and did not move.

"I'm sorry Capt'n," Thomas said, in between deep breaths.

Through mumbled and gritted teeth the Captain responded, but it was not coherent.

Thomas slowly got to his feet and looked at Trevor who was standing fixed in the same spot before the fight had started.

"Trevor and Capt'n. I know this is my fault…"

"You're damned right, it's your responsibility and fault," the Captain yelled, audible this time.

"I know it's my responsibility to find and save Archie. But I can't do this alone. Will ya both help me?" finished Thomas.

"I will," Trevor responded, not sure whether or not he even had a choice to say no. He was technically Thomas' apprentice and successor, so it would reflect poorly on his character if he backed out.

Thomas looked at the Captain who was nursing his broken nose and wiping the tears from his eyes. "Captain? Will you help?"

"Aye, but I am callin' the shots, you bastard. We were," Captain Jasper grunted as he rose to his feet, "We were doing so well. Archie and I were 'bout to return to England. I was this close to seeing my family. Now," the Captain pointed an angry finger at Thomas, "because of you, we have death warrants from Le Capitaine d'Or himself."

Thomas did not reply immediately and allowed the Captain to vent his acrimony. Trevor handed the Captain a handkerchief. Captain Jasper mopped up his bloody face and looked into Thomas' eyes.

"I understand. You'll be in charge," Thomas replied, thankful the Captain would help.

Without the *Charlotte* and the Captain's expert experience of sailing the West Indies, Thomas would never be able find Archie. Captain Jasper, Thomas, and Trevor rode back to Port Royal and boarded the *Charlotte*. Captain Jasper set the heading for Port Nassau. Thomas needed to inform Governor Raymond of the current situation and see if they could gather additional resources from the Governor before setting out for the impossible search for Archie.

Apparently, Isabel's previous engagement to the slave trader had fallen through due to the slave trader's health. The slave trader's robustness, obesity, excessive lifestyle, and sinfulness would be the cause of his death, according to the Governor. Since the slave trader's doctors did not project him living much longer, Governor Raymond had called off his daughter's engagement in the hopes of finding a more suitable and healthy man.

Archie, not surprisingly, was still the Governor's first choice. The Governor had always wanted a son, but he was given a daughter; so, at the first chance he got, he would pick a desirable son-in-law, which would make up for all the years without a son.

Thus, Archie's d'Or imprisonment, the slave trader's health

problems, and Thomas' request for assistance aligned too perfectly for Governor Raymond. Immediately, Governor Raymond found the ideal compromise in his head. Not surprisingly, Governor Raymond was sympathetic to Thomas' cause to find and rescue Archie.

"So, do we have an accord?" asked Governor Raymond, as he studied Thomas's reaction to his proposal.

"Guv'na," Thomas said exasperated, knowing he was in no position to negotiate. "Lemme get this straight: Archie marries Isabel and you give us all the resources at ya disposal?

"That's the deal."

"If that's the price that it'll take to save Arch, then aye, you have an accord."

Thomas shook Governor Raymond's hand and instantly felt guilt and dread run through his body. Not only had he now put Archie in the hands of d'Or, but now he had just committed Archie to marry a woman that he did not love.

"Excellent. Here is the decree that will allow you full use of any ships, men, weapons, and supplies you might need in search of Archie. My best wishes in your pursuit. Also, there is a handsome reward in it too, if you can capture or kill the Captain of d'Or, Rémi Montre. Might be able to knock out two birds with one stone, Thomas," the Governor smiled as he spoke.

"I'll focus on Archie, Sir," Thomas responded flatly taking the note from the Governor. "Thank you for ya assistance in Archie's rescue."

"Of course. For a future son-in-law, it's the least I can do. Make sure you bring him back safe now." And with the last word, the Governor turned and left the room.

The butler escorted Thomas out of the Governor's mansion where Captain Jasper and Trevor were waiting.

"Well, what did he say?" Captain Jasper said sharply still incensed with Thomas.

"We'll have all the resources we need. He's given us this note signed with his authority to use any man, weapon, or ship we might need to find Archie with whatever means necessary."

"Fine. But we don't need a ship. We will use the *Charlotte*. Men and weapons are the priority here. Let's just get started, 'cause six weeks will be gone before we know it. And for all we know, those pirates could have hidden Archie in a remote cave on any island from here to the Brazilian coast," the Captain said.

It took four, full days in Port Nassau to acquire the man power, weapons, equipment, food supply, and other miscellaneous items before the *Charlotte* was ready to set sail. Finally, to Thomas' great relief, the ship left Port Nassau and the challenge to find Archie had officially begun.

The sands of time painfully slipped away as the sun rose and fell each day. There was nothing Thomas could do but hope and pray and look out at the endless horizon.

• 15 •

Archie sat in his cell beneath the deck unable to sleep. He sat alone, cold, and his impending death was slowly peeling away his strength as the days endlessly dragged on. He had lost all concept of time and hopelessness of his situation deteriorated Archie's usual happy and cheerful spirit. For the first time in his life, Archie was impotent and he was being treated like a caged animal.

As the *L'île Rouge* sleepily rocked back and forth headed toward some unknown destination, Archie thought about how he had arrived at this point in his life. This entire journey had all started when he decided to leave Brighton in the pursuit of a better life. If only he had never left, he would never have met Thomas. His business partner, his friend, had betrayed his trust. How had he been so blinded by his determination to return home to Olivia that he had overlooked Thomas' terrible gambling and whoring habits? He had been only a few weeks away from setting sail to England and seeing his adored Olivia. Archie looked at Olivia's unfolded poem lying in his lap as hot tears silently rolled down his cold cheeks.

During the sacking of the sugar plantation he had grabbed Olivia's poem, along with his pistol, and father's knife. He hid the poem within his clothes as he slipped out the back of the mansion and ran. He fired a few shots toward dark figures running along the fringes of the property. Unfortunately, the mansion was surrounded by d'Or pirates. Archie had only made it fifty meters before he was staring down the barrel of a pistol, which convinced him to return to the house and face Captain Montre. The pirates took away his father's knife and his pistol, but thankfully they had missed finding the poem.

Every night, when his captors were sleeping and their weary minds paid him no attention, he would take out the poem and read it several times. It was his treasure and it was the only thing that kept him believing there was a reason to live. Each time he read it, it gave him the mental toughness to overcome the bleakness and emptiness that depression brings. The poem inspired Archie and gave him energy to scheme of ways to escape, if there was ever the slightest chance. He needed to figure out a way to stay alive one day at a time.

As long as he was alive, he would fight to make it back to Olivia and keep his promise to her. He would take her hand in marriage. They would travel and she would write poems. They would dream together. Her dreams would become Archie's and Archie's dreams would become hers. They complimented each other. They empowered each other. Together, anything and everything seemed possible. Archie's daydreams of Olivia were in a constant battle each day he was aboard the *L'île Rouge* because the overwhelming thought of death clouded his mind.

He took the poem up in his hands and began committing the words to memory, so they could never take away his hope. Archie's eyes scanned slowly over each word:

My dearest Archie,

This is my poem for you. Travel safe and I will be here when you return.

My Feeling

I write this as a gift
To give you quite a lift,
So you know beyond a doubt
That I will always be about.

From the sun that is yellow
To the moon that is mellow,
You are the star in the night
That gives off the most light.

You are the smile during the day
That ensures flowers in May.
You are the friend who I trust
And the friend who is just.
You have eyes of blue
Where love rings true.

You have troubles and pain
That will be cleansed with the rain.
You are mighty and strong
And will conquer fear all day long.
It's you and me
Sitting by the sea.

For you, my love won't fade,
For you, I write this serenade.
For you, my King of Hearts,
So what we have never parts.

May this poem be an eternal reminder of what we have.
With all the blessings, love, and kisses I have,
    Olivia

The days and nights rolled by endlessly, and the *L'île Rouge* continued to sail. Archie had overheard from some of the pirates that Thomas needed to pay his ransom gold and gambling debts before Captain Montre would even consider releasing him. The lack of knowledge about his situation caused Archie to constantly fear for his life.

Archie had heard the stories about Captain Rémi Montre. No one, not even those with the gold or adequate money, lived after seeing the infamous and deadly pirate. He would not let Archie live even if Thomas managed to miraculously scrape together the required gold.

Surprisingly, one afternoon, Archie was escorted from his cell to the Captain's quarters. This was the first time he and the Captain had spoken since he was captured.

"Monsieur Archie," Captain Montre said maliciously. He was sitting at his desk, with his boots kicked up on top of the desk and he was leaning back in his chair reclining. "It's June 17, which gives your camarade, Thomas, another thirteen days to pay up. What do you think the odds he comes through?" Captain Montre smirked, as he looked at Archie.

Archie ignored the question and responded, "What do you want?"

"Oui, straight to business. Bien. I want to know 'ow much you are worth. Are you worth the riches I 'ave 'eard?"

Archie remained silent.

Montre nodded his head at a d'Or pirate who was standing guard next to Archie. The pirate punched Archie hard in the back of the ribs. Archie fell to the floor, grabbing his side, and yelling out in pain.

"My question again: are you quite wealthy?"

Archie rose to his feet grimacing as he massaged his ribs. "I am, but when you destroyed my sugarcane plantation that lowered the price of a valuable asset. But, the Hollis Shipping Company and Plantation have both done quite well in the last sixteen months. I have some savings but I was headed back to England."

"Archie," chuckled Captain Montre. "Tragically, I don't think you'll ever make it back to England. So, let's talk about your assets. You will give us your land and gold savings in addition to what Thomas owes us. Your gold will be a, let's say, the interest on Monsieur Thomas' gambling debts and poor credit repayment."

Archie glared back at Captain Montre. Inside his mind, he was thinking. He could not miss this opportunity to create a new plan with the Captain, one that might save his life.

"I want to propose another idea. A better idea," Archie said firmly.

Archie stood waiting for Captain Montre's response, as the Captain stood and paced toward the window looking out at the ocean.

Captain Montre turned and looked at Archie, "The Prisoner has a new proposal. As we are both savvy and successful businessmen, I'll grant you the chance to propose your idea. I'm sure no doubt it 'as something to do with not killing you or taking your assets. Nevertheless, I'll allow you your time to speak. Procéder."

"If you utilize me and my services and land correctly, I could make you much wealthier than you've ever dreamed. I know you have done very well in Saint-Domingue and pirating around the Caribbean. Imagine if you had an English man on your side, and were able to slowly take over the English sugarcane business and Port influences too. You would get a majority of my profits and start to acquire land and influence on English soil. You would expand your empire. Imagine, the English Caribbean could be all yours through sheer economic force, and of course your strategic pirating exploits along the way."

"You are talking 'bout war. We'll not go to war with England and take their land. Why risk that? Attacking one ship 'ere and t'ere, no one will fight that. But taking a Port, they'll surely send the entire brigade upon me."

"Not war. Become such an economic force through me that they cannot ignore you. Neither you nor any of your men can build or buy land in English colonies. I can. Use me and my company as a resource for your expansion."

"Interesting. I can become wealthier and protect myself from English power." Captain Montre continued to ponder the thought as he paced before addressing Archie, "And you no doubt want your freedom in some capacity?" Montre let out a laugh before allowing Archie to speak, "You will never be free. As it is, I am sure Gouverneur Raymond 'as already sent a fleet lookin' for ye. I understand he holds you in high regard, according to Thomas at least."

"What if I sweetened the deal and provided you with knowledge of The Queen's Jewels or The Jade Dagger as well, would those get me my freedom? Those are things that cannot be bought and they can only be stolen if you know where they are. You must be in a strategic position to acquire those," Archie replied.

Captain Montre did not respond but looked at Archie quizzically.

Archie had heard of the treasures from Thomas over the last year, and Thomas had asked if they could make a couple of side missions to find them. Despite Archie's desire for adventure and finding priceless treasures, he told Thomas to focus on sugar and less on the stuff of legends. Although by chance, Archie had come across one of the treasures in his recent past. He had not told Thomas because he knew his friend would undoubtedly encourage him to go and recover it, or Thomas would do something rash and steal it himself.

As Thomas had described the treasures, the Queen's Jewels were a priceless ruby and diamond ring and matching ruby and diamond necklace that was originally a part of the British Royal family gems. Somehow the jewels had ended up in the Caribbean, and many tales and myths had circulated claiming to know the whereabouts of them. Even King Charles II had promised a reward for anyone who recovered the jewels for the Queen.

While the Jade Dagger, although not priceless, was expensive, more expensive than any mortal man could afford. The Jade Dagger came from Marco Polo's adventures in the Far East. It had been stolen several times over the centuries throughout Europe. The Jade Dagger reappeared half a century earlier when word spread that a pirate had seized it and escaped to the West Indies. The legend went on to state the pirate's ship was caught in a deadly hurricane and the ship sank. Thus, the Jade Dagger was lost forever to the dark abyss of the ocean's floor and no one had seen it since.

Breaking a long silence Captain Montre said, "You talk 'bout those items like you know where they are. If you had the slightest idea where they are, you'd 'ave retrieved them yourself. You're lying. Do you think me foolish?" Raising his voice, "Do you think me as some... some imbécile?"

"No, course not. You must believe me; I do know where one of the items is. I have not retrieved it myself because it belongs to a friend of mine. It's also the one you should acquire last. That is, once you have followed my plan to acquire more power through economic means, when they cannot ignore you or hang you because you run such an empire."

"Which one do you know the location?"

"The Jade Dagger."

"How?"

"I didn't know it was the Jade Dagger at the time, but I know where it is. I only connected the dots recently when Thomas told me of its myth, what it supposedly looked like."

"I see. And the Queen's Jewels?"

"I'm not sure," Archie sadly admitted.

Captain Montre thought about Archie's economic power proposal and the ability for Archie to lead him to another precious treasure, the Jade Dagger. Captain Montre had not revealed this to Archie, but they were currently on their way to find and retrieve the Queen's Jewels.

Over the past twelve months, Captain Montre had been on the hunt for the Jewels and had been collecting all the information regarding the legendary Jewels. He had come across a Spanish missionary only weeks ago that led the Captain to the necessary break he had been hoping for. Before Captain Montre killed the missionary, the man had described the Queen's Jewels perfectly to the Captain and where he had last seen them. This information was divulged to the pirate in hopes it would save his life. Unfortunately for the poor man, once he had revealed the location of the Jewels, Rémi Montre shot him in the heart without a second thought.

Before sacking Port Royal to claim Archie, Captain Montre had already planned to sail straight for Trinidad where the Jewels had somehow ended up in Spanish hands.

Captain Montre began, "From what I have 'eard, the man who 'as the Jade Dagger also 'as the Queen's Jewels. Why wait? Why do we go after the Jade Dagger last in your plan, if they are supposedly together? Are you trying to 'ide information from me?"

Captain Montre knew this question was completely fictitious, but he was testing Archie's truthfulness. The Jade Dagger was completely unrelated to the Jewels, but if Archie lied about his knowledge of the Jade Dagger, then, Captain Montre reasoned, Archie's economic takeover plan was also deceitful.

Archie's throat tightened. He had just wanted to buy himself time by bringing up the treasures, he didn't know the entire history behind the myths or legends. Archie did not say anything, but looked at Captain Montre with a downtrodden face. Captain Montre took Archie's silence as evidence that he was not lying.

Captain Montre spoke, as he looked at Archie's pale face, "Monsieur Archie, you 'ave given me some topics to think 'bout." He turned to a pirate standing by the door, "Take 'im back to 'is cell."

Back in his cell and alone with nothing but his own thoughts, Archie replayed his entire conversation with the Captain. Had it been enough? Was he convincing? Did he say the right things that could possibly save him? Archie started to practice memorizing Olivia's poem to take his mind off how badly he had frozen up at the end of the conversation with Montre.

It would be nearly two more weeks before Archie laid eyes on the Captain of *L'île Rouge* again and it would be a moment that would change Archie's life forever.

• 16 •

"That's it! Huzzah!" shouted Captain Jasper in feverish excitement. "And the figurehead?"

"Aye, the figure'ead is dat Goldin Mermaid, you say 'airlier. She be holdin', what be she holdin' 'gain? Uh...uh...I thinks it'll be a pearl and a sword," the sailor finished unconvincingly.

The sailor had tried to describe as best he could the *L'île Rouge*, which he claimed he had seen only two days previously.

"Aye, that's the bloody ship we've been lookin' for mate," Captain Jasper said ecstatic to have caught a break after five weeks of hunting for the *L'île Rouge*. "Where did ya say it was headed? South!"

Captain Jasper went hollering through the tavern, "Thomas, Trev, mates."

Captain Jasper found Trevor and Thomas talking to other sailors at the bar. "Fellas, listen up, it's time to sail south. Apparently, the *L'île Rouge* is headed toward the Spanish territory far south or approximately around there. The ship was seen only two days ago. We need God's good graces and wind, but we should be able to catch up if we sail straight through the days and nights."

"What are we awaitin' fer?" Thomas asked. "Let's go git Archie and hope he's still on the bloody thing."

Over the last five weeks, Thomas, Trevor, and Captain Jasper had stopped in nearly every major and minor port south of Nassau and north of Port Royal seeking information about *L'île Rouge*'s current whereabouts and sightings.

As soon as Captain Jasper had set their heading to the southern Caribbean islands, the three men met in the Captain's quarters.

Trevor was the first one to speak, "I don't wanna to ask a foolish question, but what's our plan bein'?"

The Captain looked at Thomas almost daring him to say something. After Thomas remained silent and the Captain was content with Thomas' subordination, he said, "With the fire power we got armed on the *Charlotte*, courtesy of the Guv'na, we should be in a frightfully successful battle with the bastard Montre and his cursed d'Or crew. Once we have attacked and have 'em cornered, it'll be my hope that Archie is still alive when we reach 'im. Otherwise, we gotta take Le Capitaine d'Or back to Port Nassau and Guv'na Raymond to receive our reward."

Trevor looked between Thomas and the Captain to see if they were going to continue. "I seen dead men and I'd 'eard stories. Capt'n d'Or don't lose. He's ain't ne'er lost and if..." Trevor replied nervously.

"This'll be the day he don't win," Thomas interrupted. The finality and confidence with which Thomas spoke put an end to the conversation.

Thomas was looking at the horizon hoping to spot a ship. He checked as far as he could see in all directions. Six days had passed since they left in hopes of catching the *L'île Rouge*. They had been sailing for the last five days and nights continuously working in two shifts to feverishly catch up. Thomas knew if they were close, then it would be only a matter of time before they came across the pirate ship.

Captain Jasper was lying in his bunk when he heard shouts and yells on the deck above him. Thomas was yelling orders and shouting for all to hear. Hurriedly, Captain Jasper jumped up to take back command of his ship. He sped up the stairs and burst on to the deck to see the night crew pointing out a ship on the horizon and Thomas was holding the wheel of the *Charlotte* with a crazed look in his eyes.

As the Captain refocused his attention on the ship in the distance, he couldn't help but feel hope rush through his veins and into his heart that this was indeed the *L'île Rouge*. They had done it. Six fatiguing days! Tomorrow would be the moment of truth, and they would need every bit of energy and strength left in them to win.

As Thomas gripped the wheel of the *Charlotte*, he could feel his pulse racing and palms becoming sweaty. Thomas thought to himself as he stared at the black ship on the horizon, if there was ever a judgment day on earth for men, tomorrow will most certainly be that day when God judges his actions.

• 17 •

Chunks of wood splintered everywhere as the cannon balls began to rip through the wooden hulls and shatter everything in their paths. Nonstop gunfire drowned out the yells and moans of agony. The people yelling orders and commands could only be heard by those standing right beside them. Smoke began to hover around both ships and visibility past ten meters started to become more difficult.

Archie was crouched low in his cell hoping to not get hit by any shrapnel or ricocheting bullets. A splintering explosion sent Archie into a daze and his ears were ringing loudly as part of the *L'île Rouge* exploded into pieces only meters away from him. When Archie allowed himself to finally open his eyes and look toward the gaping hole, Archie looked out and see the battered and beaten hull of another ship taking serious damage too.

But as the battle continued to rage, Archie wondered who was winning. The bombardment of cannon fire that battered the *L'île Rouge* was impressive, and it seemed that the other ship was never going to run out of ammunition.

After hours of continuous fighting, the last moans of men were slowly, methodically eradicated with single shots. After each gunshot came a deafening silence that fell upon the entire sea. The waves lapping against the side of the ship were the only audible noise being made. Archie's eardrums were ringing, causing him to have a hard time hearing anything at all. He glanced up from his fetal position to see if it was safe to stand up. Two d'Or pirates entered the cell area and stood guard in front of Archie's cell. They did not indicate whether they had won or lost, but Archie's gut was telling him that d'Or had won against whomever they had been fighting.

Fifteen or so minutes passed, Archie could not tell, when three fiery explosions erupted on the other ship sending flaming pieces of wood splashing into the sea. Archie watched through the *L'île Rouge*'s hole as the flames consumed the opposing ship. As the flames tasted the salt water below, they hissed angrily like a snake recoiling from an enemy. As he watched the ship sink and burn, he now knew which side had won.

On the top deck of the *L'île Rouge*, Thomas, Trevor, Captain Jasper, and the other *Charlotte* crewmembers were kneeling submissively with their heads bowed. They had their hands tied tightly behind their backs and if anyone moved that individual received a brutal blow to the back of the head with the butt of a rifle.

Thomas stared down at the deck in front of him and analyzed a splinter of wood that was in the shape of a lightning bolt. Thomas looked at it and thought it was a message from God himself. God was sending the lightning bolt straight his way. There was not a thing that he could do to save himself. Thomas had received his judgment and death was going to be his penance. He could not think rationally because of his current situation; so, Thomas' mind went blank. He continued to stare blindly at the lightning bolt piece of wood.

Captain Jasper had his eyes closed. He was furious, absolutely livid with Thomas. All his anger about being captured, and losing the battle, losing his ship, and now facing death had aggregated into a bubbling, volcanic-like rage directed at Thomas. Thomas had been the troublemaker from the beginning, causing all this misfortune and dreadfulness to occur. All his life he had wanted something to one day tell his grandchildren. A story he could tell while he sat in his rocking chair in London. The hot, summer, Caribbean sun beat down on the back of his neck and sweat from his forehead fell upon the sea-salt, gunpowder mixed deck. He was not going to get the chance to tell that adventure story to his grandchildren. This is where his story ended. This is where his adventure would remain.

Trevor was in absolute hysteria. He would look up at his captors and plead with them. He was begging and making all types of promises. But all his efforts fell on deaf eyes. His mind was feverishly trying to escape. To his amazement, he drummed up a brilliant idea to escape, albeit a crazy one. He glanced toward the ocean. The ocean was going to be his ticket to freedom.

Trevor jumped to his feet and bolted for the railing of the ship. Suddenly all eyes, captors and captives, were watching as Trevor made a dash for it across the deck. He weaved in and out of the debris that littered the deck. He hopped over barrels and danced around dead bodies. He was within feet of the ship's edge. One more step then a jump and he would be a free man. Trevor could see the blue water; his mind was singularly focused on the jump.

Bang! Trevor slammed into the railing at full speed and crumbled onto the deck. A d'Or pirate lowered his rifle as smoke wafted from the barrel. He walked over to Trevor, who was slumped on the deck and a pool of crimson blood was starting to form around him. The d'Or pirate methodically set down his weapon and rolled up his sleeves. He then picked up Trevor and tossed him overboard. The d'Or pirate watched as Trevor's body hit the water with a splash. Satisfied, he picked up his rifle and rejoined the other d'Or pirates who patted him on the back.

Captain Rémi Montre stepped out of his quarters and onto the battle-ridden deck.

"Donzelles!" Montre began, addressing the captives, "whose wise idea was it to blow holes in my precise ship?"

No one responded. No one had to the courage to breathe a word.

Captain Montre continued, "I like to play this game called Answer or Death. This'll be how we play." Captain Montre paced back and forth in front of the captives as he spoke, "I ask a question and if no one responds, one of you worthless Brits dies. It'll be quite simple, but I'll forgive you for not knowing the rules. Lemme ask again, whose idea was it to fire upon and put holes in my beautiful *L'île Rouge*?"

The following silence crushed the captives' spirits as no one looked up and no one spoke.

"Mon Dieu! You British really are as thick as rocks on the sea floor. Shoot one. Maintenant!"

Upon command, the same d'Or pirate who killed Trevor lifted his rifle and from point blank range sent a bullet through the head of a captive. The captive fell with a thud and blood splattered across the faces and clothes of the other captives.

"How you liking this game? It's quite fun. I usually win, but let's see how long we must keep playing. Anyone willing to answer me?" Captain Montre scanned the crowd and was about to signal another killing when a voice spoke up.

"Me. I did." Thomas' voice was hoarse, as he had lost his voice from all the yelling during the battle. Thomas repeated himself trying hard to be loud through his croaking voice, "I did."

"Stand up, stand up, show yourself," chirped Captain Montre.

Thomas slowly and reluctantly stood up. It was time to pay for his sins and accept his fate. As Captain Montre analyzed the man standing in the middle of the captives, he could not help but allow a malicious grin to shine across his face.

Captain Montre spoke with near jubilation, "Monsieur Thomas. I should 'ave expected you to do something this rash. And yet, I still find myself surprised. Just shows how you came to be in so much debt to us in the first place—your impulsive be'aviors. No matter, no matter. I have an accord with Monsieur Archie to pay it all back, so your debt is forgiven. 'owever, now that you are with us, I can 'ave my deal with Archie commence officially."

Captain Montre swept his glance from Thomas to one of his crew standing close by. He whispered something to the pirate, and the pirate disappeared down the stairs and underneath the deck.

Captain Montre focused his attention back to Thomas, "Here's another question for you Thomas, was that by chance Archie's ship, le…" Captain Montre repeated himself as he tried to remember the name, "le…le…."

"The *Charlotte*," croaked Thomas.

"*Le Charlotte*, merci. Where is le capitaine of that sad, burnt ship?"

Thomas did not even get a chance to respond. Captain Jasper's rage exploded. He stood up and unleashed a fury of expletives and nonsensical phrases. As he spoke, his face became beet red and his eyes became bloodshot.

Captain Montre looked at the monstrous, British Captain and spoke loudly, "Ta gueule!"

But Captain Jasper did not care, he bellowed ahead. After another minute of expletives and angry gibberish, he was soon out of breathe and exhausted.

"Glad we got that out of us," laughed Captain Montre. "That was comical."

The d'Or crew mimicked their Captain's laugh to join in.

Captain Montre continued, "Will someone bring Thomas to the front and someone take the Captain to the plank. We are 'bout to 'ave some serious entertainment. I want to personally send Le Capitaine to Davy Jones' Locker."

Captain Montre strode behind two d'Or pirates who dragged the uncooperative Captain Jasper to the gangplank. The two pirates heaved Captain Jasper's wriggling body onto the plank and shoved him out toward the end of the wooden slab.

Captain Jasper's face became pale as he realized this was the end. He glanced out toward the horizon, looked down at the dark water below, and then turned his head back toward Captain Montre, who was now standing on the beginning of gangplank with a pistol pointed at him.

Captain Jasper pleaded, "I'll do anythin'. Anythin'. Just lemme live. Gimme a chance!"

"Capitaine, 'ave more decency and self-respect than to plead and beg like a common pute," Captain Montre said with disgust. "It's bad enough to 'ave a whole crew of whining British sailors. I expect you to show them 'ow to die with honor. Plus, out of respect for a fellow Capitaine, I'll kill you myself."

Captain Jasper gritted his teeth and felt panic radiate throughout his body. Without a word, he charged headlong at Captain Montre. No sooner had Captain Jasper taken two steps toward the ship, a plume of smoke billowed from the end of Captain Montre's pistol. Captain Jasper's body fell silently downward and splashed into the hungry waves below.

Captain Montre leaned over the ship's railing and watched the body sink below the dark water before turning around and calling out, "Bring Archie out. The time 'as come."

Archie walked out between two burly pirates and was shocked to see Thomas standing on the deck. Archie's face went pale. Captain Montre was going to kill both of them. Archie's heartbeat quicken with each step. Archie had failed; he was going to die. His mind shot to Olivia, he was never going to see her again. The image of her waving goodbye to him burned brightly in Archie's mind. He could see her standing there, only meters away from him, crying. Why had he let go of her? Why had he left? He thought to himself, forgive me for not holding you in my arms.

Archie's focus was brought back to the present situation when Captain Montre handed Archie a pistol. Archie looked down at the pistol. He recognized the pistol immediately. It was the one he had purchased in Port Nassau, after seeing Captain Montre's Wanted Poster. His first thought was to shoot Captain Montre dead cold.

But a cold pistol barrel pressed up against the back of his neck as soon as Captain Montre released his hand from Archie's pistol. Captain Montre looked Archie in the eyes and Archie helplessly looked back into the soul of the devil himself.

Captain Montre spoke softly and with the greatest intent on drama, "You'll kill Thomas with your own pistol. I consider Thomas' death as proof of your loyalty to me, to d'Or, to your own self-preservation, and to our plan that you have devised. If you do not kill Thomas, then you will be killed along with 'im."

Captain Montre stepped aside to reveal Archie's target. Thomas stood defenseless in front of Archie. Both men looked at each other petrified and were ghostly white.

Archie looked down at the pistol. He had bought it with the intention to save himself. He never thought that to save himself he would be required to use his pistol to kill the only person he considered to be his friend in the Caribbean. Archie's mind was buzzing. He felt like the weight of the world was upon his shoulders. The hot sun was baking his mind and he was having trouble thinking. He must come up with some creative solution; he could not kill his friend. But more importantly, he cannot die either.

Captain Montre broke the silence, "Either of you two 'ave any last words?"

"I'm so sorry, mate," Thomas said quietly, looking at his friend for the last time. "This'll be all my fault. I deserve that bullet. Thanks for believin' in me. We made a good runna it."

Archie could not take it anymore. The shock and anxiety were too overwhelming. He could feel his courage slipping. The gun still rested by Archie's side. It felt heavy in his hand, too heavy to lift.

"Maintenant Archie," pressed Captain Montre. "I'll give you to the count of trois. Un...deux...."

Archie hesitantly raised the gun, which momentarily stopped Captain Montre's count. The icy pistol barrel tingled the back of Archie's neck as it was pressed harder against him.

Archie managed forlornly, "I'll see you soon my friend." And with that his finger squeezed firmly on the trigger.

Thomas hit the deck with a thud and Archie dropped the pistol to the deck. He closed his eyes as he could not look at his friend's motionless body.

Captain Montre was smiling and slowly clapping, "Bien, bien. As I'm a man of my word, welcome to the crew of d'Or, Monsieur Archie. I did not think you were going to 'ave it in you, but you really must want to live to kill your only camarade. I thought I was the only one that cold blooded."

Archie was not listening. His eyes were looking at Captain Montre, but his mind was far away. He had gone into shock. His ears were ringing and his thoughts were of England and home. He saw his parents and Olivia, and as he had rehearsed and trained, he could hear Olivia, singing her poem to him. Archie's daze continued as the two burly d'Or pirates escorted him to the Captain's quarters and sat him down at a table. Captain Montre entered with rudimentary tattooing tools.

Captain Montre worked away at setting up the ink and needle. Archie stared blankly at the Captain and the pirates accompanying him not registering what was currently happening on the other side of the table. One of the pirates rolled up Archie's left sleeve and turned over his arm to expose his forearm for Captain Montre to inspect. As Captain Montre began tattooing "d'Or" in distinct black ink onto Archie's arm, the second burly pirate joined to hold down Archie if he were to resist.

However, Archie did not fight back and he did not resist. He endured the pain and watched as the black ink sank into his skin and permanently stained it. Once the tattoo was completed, Captain Montre put down the needle and looked at his work. He blotted away Archie's blood and looked upon the fresh "d'Or" glistening on Archie's arm.

"You're one of us—a d'Or pirate for the rest of your miserable life. You'll be 'eld accountable as such, and report to me directly once you 'ave set up operations in the English colonies. These two next to you will be your new brothers. They will be my eyes and ears and will watch over you to ensure you never double cross me or try to escape to your precious Gouverneur Raymond. If you can refrain yourself from doin' anything foolish, then we'll make a good team. With your sugar business enterprise as the newest addition, I look forward to becoming richer and more powerful." Captain Montre chuckled to himself and extended his hand in Archie's direction.

Archie was staring at the tattoo on his arm and then proceeded to look up at Captain Montre and shook the pirate's outreached hand.

"Captain, I will do everything in my power to get you what you want."

"That's the spirit," Captain Montre said. "Our little delay and charade with your camarades is over and it's time for treasure. Time to retrieve the Queen's Jewels."

"You know where they are?" Archie asked shocked.

"Je fais. We are close to them. I expect us to retrieve the Jewels within the week."

"I...I don't know what to say."

"You didn't know it, but you were always a part of the plan. From what I understand," Captain Montre said as he sat at his desk, "the Jewels are in the 'ands of a Spanish aristocrat in Trinidad. Your role is important. You're gonna confirm that the Jewels are with this aristocrat without raising any suspicion. As soon as you report on the exact location of the Jewels, then my men and I will do the rest. You are going to be our scout. If you deceive us in any way or disrupt the plan, you're signing your own death warrant and I won't lose any sleep in killing you myself. You will serve the d'Or faithfully, and I'll allow you to live. The second you cross me or d'Or or jeopardize my missions, you're as good as dead. Do I make myself clear?"

"Inescapably," replied Archie absorbing the plan as he looked back down at his forearm. d'Or forever. At least he was alive and breathing; every day above ground was a good day he thought to himself.

"Excellent. Leave me and get yourself acquainted with your new family, they should be down in the lower quarters. Lacazette, the chef, should be able to find you a bunk. Just talk to 'im after the meal."

Archie nodded obediently, stood up, and left Captain Montre. He joined the rest of the pirates beneath the deck realizing as he did so that a new journey had just begun. He was now a free man, in the sense as he was not in a cell; but he was not truly free.

He thought about Olivia's poem: *You have troubles and pain, That will be cleansed with the rain.* Hopefully a powerful storm would come sweeping through and pick him up and land him across the Atlantic far away from Captain Montre.

Archie, after eating alone and being studied by the d'Or crew, asked one of them where the man named Lacazette was. The pirate pointed at a man standing at the end of the food table without making any eye contact with Archie. Archie treaded carefully over to Lacazette, who was a tall, fit, and muscular specimen. Lacazette's skin was leathery and tan as if he had been standing in the sun all his life. His chest, arms, biceps, shoulders, and back had black tattoos up and down. Underneath the black ink there were terrifying scars, which made it appear as if the man had been able to escape death itself many times. He looked fiercely in Archie's direction as Archie came within five meters of him. Archie swallowed and looked up at the fearsome man.

"Mr. Lacazette," Archie ventured.

"Oui," Lacazette responded, but it sounded more like a grunt than any actual word.

"I was instructed by Captain Montre to find you in order to receive a place to sleep."

Lacazette burst out laughing. He buckled over and hugged his stomach as he laughed. He said something in French to a nearby table of pirates, who all instantly joined in with roaring laughter. Archie stood there mystified and embarrassed at what was so comical.

His face became flushed as he stood in the center of the laughter and mortified when Lacazette spoke in a thick French accent, "A bed, a bunk, Monsieur, is fer Français blood," he said pounding his chest with pride. "Ye mit be d'Or, but yer an English bastard." Lacazette spat on the wooden floor. "Ye be sleepin' wit les rats on le floor."

Archie knew there was not any point in negotiating or protesting with this hulk of a man. Lacazette would not change his mind, and it was no use to complain or go to the Captain. These were the men he would have to live with and he was not going to anger them in any way.

Archie's first priority was to see tomorrow's sunrise. Survive every day. He could bide his time and wait. Archie could be patient. He must be patient. In his current situation, being reckless or arrogant would most certainly get him killed.

Later that night, Archie had difficultly trying to fall asleep as he lay on the cold wooden floor. For each time he shut his eyes, he would hear the scuffles of mice and rats nearby. The sound sent chills down his back as he imagined the filthy creatures crawling only inches away from his body.

Finally, exhaustion overcame Archie and he fell asleep. Throughout the night Archie had tortuous nightmares. The image of Thomas' body haunted his dreams. He could hear Thomas' apology, then saw the bullet murder his friend. Archie would look down at his hands and they would be dripping with Thomas' blood. Then Archie would envision himself tossing the cold, lifeless body overboard and watching it sink into the dark abyss below. Thomas was only a kid; Thomas was Archie's only friend.

Archie awoke with a start. His tattered clothing was wet from sweat. He wearily rose to his feet and stretched his aching body. He walked up the creaking stairs to the main deck and watched as the morning dawn light started to paint itself across the dark night sky. The stars above leisurely disappeared and the morning breeze brushed across Archie's face. He looked down at the black ink on his arm and gently felt the injured and inflamed skin. This was his new reality—the first day of his new life.

He watched the horizon as the sun continued to rise and at the land the *L'île Rouge* was fast approaching. The poor, Spanish settlement had no idea the fury and devastation it was about to endure. Archie could not feel sorry for the Spanish families or assume the pain they would suffer. He needed to be selfish, because whether or not he helped Captain Montre, the Captain would retrieve those Jewels. Archie's task was to stay alive; it was his time to be selfish.

• 18 •

Archie followed Señor Esperanza, the Spanish aristocrat who supposedly had the Queen's Jewels, around his grounds and listened patiently to the man's life story. Archie's cover story was quite simple, yet ingenious. Archie was pretending to have been sent by Governor Raymond as a scout in search of a foreign aristocracy for the promising invitation to marry his gorgeous daughter—Isabel.

Somehow, Captain Montre had procured a small painting of Isabel, but Archie did not know how the painting had come to be. Archie's best guess was it came from Thomas. The painting exposed all of Isabel's most appealing features. Her brilliant green eyes, her genuine smile, smooth caramel colored skin, and her youthful composition. The painting was the hook to intrigue Señor Esperanza into giving Archie a full explanation of why he deserved a chance at marrying the fair Isabel. This would then give Archie the chance to ask pertinent questions regarding the Jewels and possibly locate them.

As Archie showed Señor Esperanza Isabel's painting, Señor Esperanza was instantly enamored with her. He wasted no time in listing all his qualifications and why he would be the best suitor for the lovely young woman.

Archie thought to himself, how easy men become blinded and distracted by women. Men will do anything for a woman they lusted for or wanted. It was an incredibly powerful motivator and one that was working brilliantly on the Spanish aristocrat.

At the end of the house tour, the two men rounded a corner and entered into the drawing room. Señor Esperanza removed tobacco and a pipe from a drawer in the middle of the room. He loaded his pipe and lit it, puffing copious amounts of smoke from his nostrils. He then handed Archie a cigar and lit it for him.

"Ahora, let us discuss more about the lovely Señorita Isabel?"

"Course," responded Archie, still trying to find the right moment to ask about the Jewels.

The two men chatted a bit more about Isabel and her likes and dislikes. Of course, Archie needed to make up lies and told completely fabricated stories about Isabel, but it was all in the interest of trying to guide the conversation to the Jewels.

"Isabel," Archie explained, "is mystified by the legend of the Queen's Jewels. She loves the story and would love to one day find them. Been a childhood dream of hers ever since her daddy, the good Governor, told her. Have you heard of this legend Señor?"

"Claro que sí," Señor Esperanza responded immediately before translating. "Of course. Why does la Señorita ask about Las Joyas de la Reina?"

"She has a tendency to be marveled by things no one else can have. She is a woman of finer tastes and if she has a chance to have the Queen's Jewels, how do you say it?"

"Las Joyas de la Reina."

"Yes, las Joyas de la Reina, well, you'll have won her heart. It's the only thing in this world she has truly wanted," Archie concluded, satisfied with his elegant, conversational storytelling.

Señor Esperanza stood up and walked over to a cabinet and unlocked it. He returned with the Queen's Jewels in hand and set them down before Archie. The jewels sparkled and shined in the light. Archie was in awe and wonder as he admired each stone and the beauty that was before him.

Señor Esperanza spoke, "I do not call them Las Joyas de la Reina. If you had not explained to me what they looked like, I would not have known that these were the Jewels from the legend. I will not tell you how I came to own these, for I am not proud of the story behind it. But I will tell you the Spanish name for them—'Las Hermosas Rosas'. We named them this because the big rubies that are the centerpieces in the jewelry, decorated gorgeously by the spectacular diamonds."

"They are truly a sight to behold. Isabel will be pleased to know she has found her man," Archie said as he continued to stare in wonder at the diamonds, which glistened in the light, and the ruby, which exuded pure passion.

Archie finally looked up and spoke with a more serious tone and business-like attitude, "Señor Esperanza, if I may, I would like to leave at once to report directly to Isabel and the Governor." Archie placed his cigar down and stood to leave. "Thank you for the hospitality and I will report with news from Port Nassau on Isabel's arrival date to Trinidad."

"Excelente. Give Isabel my best wishes. I look forward to hearing from you soon," Señor Esperanza said jubilantly.

Archie left the Spanish aristocrat waving in the distance.

Poor man, Archie thought to himself as he walked down the steps to the carriage, he feels on top of the world at this moment, and little does he know he holds the item that will lead him to an early death.

Archie turned around one last time and waved, knowing it would only be a matter of hours before nightfall when Captain Montre and his men killed the man and took away his Las Hermosas Rosas, or the Queen's Jewels.

Back aboard the *L'île Rouge*, Captain Montre quizzed Archie on everything from the layout of the house to the precise description of the Jewels.

After thoroughly being briefed, Captain Montre sat back in his chair and looked at Archie saying, "Good work today. I'm glad you took this seriously. It means we can be in and out quicker than I anticipated, which will help us not get caught in Spanish waters. The Spanish Armada is ruthless down here." He chuckled, "But not any more ruthless than I."

Archie did not reply and instead looked at his hands. He started to hallucinate and could see his hands becoming red with blood. How many lives would he be a part of killing? He felt himself get nauseous and lightheaded. Thomas and Señor Esperanza.

He looked at Captain Montre, "I'm going to go Captain."

"Oui. Your part is done. I will take care of the rest," Captain Montre said distracted, as if his mind had wandered off to other more important issues.

Archie left and sat on the deck and simply enjoyed the cool dusk air. He watched from a safe spot, as the crew became battle ready and rowdy. All the d'Or crew was excited for this raid and plunder. They laughed and hit each other. They yelled and bellowed. Captain Montre and the crew left in small boats from the *L'île Rouge* and made their way toward shore.

An hour or so passed before the guns in the distance could be heard. Screams raced across the water and into Archie's ears. His imagination started to run wild with images of what the small city looked like. Archie focused his gaze in the direction of the city. Red, orange, and yellow spots became visible amongst the black landscape. Fires were being lit and chaos was consuming the city. Fear and hysteria rained over the city. Archie could not take the sight anymore and to help stem his imagination of the horrors being committed, he walked down the steps below the deck.

Archie awoke the following morning and all was tranquil and quiet around him. Not one pirate had returned from the shore. He stepped out onto the deck where the bright sun was rising above the small Trinidad city and the smoke was billowing upwards and fires were burning visibly. There were no screams or noise in the early morning light and the ocean was calm, glass-like—Narcissus would have been able to see his reflection clearly.

Finally, around midmorning, the small boats filled with pirates started making their way back to the *L'île Rouge*. The d'Or pirates looked triumphant in their return as they climbed aboard the ship; although, many looked exhausted from a long night of fighting and sexual escapades. Archie watched as the motley crew clambered around the deck situating the sails and doing their daily tasks getting the ship ready to embark.

Last but not least, Captain Rémi Montre climbed aboard and in his hand was a small brown satchel tied tightly around his wrist. Archie guessed this satchel's contents were none other than the Queen's Jewels. As if Archie had needed confirmation, Captain Montre walked over to Archie upon seeing the him standing away from the rest of the d'Or crew.

"Success," Captain Montre proudly proclaimed, shaking the small satchel in his hand.

"I'm glad, you got what you desired," Archie said quietly.

"We sail back to Saint-Domingue and set up your sugar operations. I intend to use you immediately for the economic expansion into the British West Indies, as you proposed. Gouverneur Raymond must not detect you. We will give you a new identity and name."

"Whatever it takes," Archie responded trying to start and devise his own plans on how he would escape his new d'Or prison.

The *L'île Rouge* lazily made its way back to Saint-Domingue. Once they had arrived, Captain Montre and the d'Or took the plunder from Port Royal and Trinidad and collected it all in chests. The chests were filled with gems, gold, silver and other precious valuables from the two cities. Captain Montre decided to keep the chests underneath St. Peter's Church in Saint-Domingue. He paid the priest handsomely for God's protection of his growing treasure and wealth. And most importantly, the crowning jewel of the plunder—the Queen's Jewels— was placed in a tiny purple and gold chest and locked away by itself. Captain Montre held the key on his person because he trusted himself only with such a responsibility.

Over the next month, Captain Montre and Archie completed the necessary tasks to begin Archie's sugar expansion. Captain Montre instructed Archie to go by the name of Calvin Smith moving forward in all business transactions. Archie, using Captain Montre's gold, purchased the Hollis Sugar Plantation from the Port Royal Bank. As instructed, he then renamed the plantation Smith Sugar and Company and began the process of rebuilding and restarting the sugar plantation he once owned and ran himself.

Captain Montre also directed him to immediately send a letter to Governor Raymond informing him of the deaths of Thomas, Captain William Jasper, and Archie. He signed the letter Calvin Smith, new owner and businessman of the Sugar Plantation in Port Royal. The purpose of this letter, according to Captain Montre, was to slowly build a rapport with Governor Raymond. Slowly, as Captain Montre's plan grew, he would have Archie buy more and more land slowly migrating the business from the Colony of Jamaica to Port Nassau and the Bahamas. At this critical junction, they would then own major portions of both economies in Port Royal and Port Nassau. Then Archie would run for Governor. If a coup d'état was necessary, then Captain Montre would proceed according.

For Captain Montre, the benefit of having Governor Calvin Smith as a pawn in his grand scheme, would be to allow Captain Montre to pirate with impunity and become a legal privateer under the King's authority as signed by Calvin Smith.

Essentially, Archie was going to be used as a puppet in Captain

Montre master plan to take control of the British waters and Ports. Archie would have superior status in Captain Montre's plan. He would belong to one of the most notoriously feared crews to ever sail in the West Indies. However, the advantages and positives to Captain Montre's plan still barred him from ever leaving the West Indies and returning home to his dear Olivia. She never left his mind.

• 19 •

It was October 1669, four months after the deaths of Captain Jasper and Thomas, when Archie had finally restored and managed to get the new sugarcane fields planted and the operations at Smith Sugar back up to a profitable standard. Throughout the end of the autumn and winter, using the endless gold from the d'Or coffers, Archie, acting as Mr. Smith, continued to buy more and more plantations and land around Port Royal.

By the spring of 1670, Smith Sugar had amassed nearly sixty-five percent of all sugarcane and sugar exports from Port Royal. The business was booming and the wealth Archie was generating was incredible. For him, it was like clockwork. He knew the business, and now he had the financial resources to acquire the physical and human capital he needed to build a sugar empire. Archie was enjoying himself; but in the back of his mind, the omnipotent Rémi Montre reigned supreme.

Archie reported quarterly to Captain Montre. However, Archie saw this as a mere formality. The two d'Or pirates that had become

Archie's new shadows reported regularly to Captain Montre, Archie was sure of it. Archie believed Captain Montre was never in the dark when it came to the Smith Sugar enterprise.

During the beginning of the autumn of 1670 at their quarterly meeting in Saint-Domingue, Captain Montre asked Archie, "Do you believe we 'ave enough influence in Port Royal to start and expand to Port Nassau?"

"I do," Archie responded confidently. "We own and sell nearly seventy-two percent of all sugar and cotton exports in Port Royal. Smith Sugar is basically running the economy in Port Royal. Sure, shipping is another massive industry, but the sugar and cotton crop industries keep the Port open. If Smith Sugar goes down, so does Port Royal."

"That is excellent news. Then," started Captain Montre as he stroked his beard, "I say it is time for you to make a trip to Port Nassau and inquire 'bout open land and businesses there."

"I will do so immediately."

Thinking the conversation was over, Archie knew his place and stood up to leave. But Captain Montre caught him off guard when he spoke.

"Where do you think you are going? We aren't finished 'ere."

Archie retook his seat, stung by the chastising.

Captain Montre proceeded, "I am aware you and Gouverneur Raymond have a strong connection and he might be your friend. Might I remind you that 'Archie' is dead. Archie is no longer friends with the Gouverneur. Calvin Smith is your identity. You'll not reveal your intentions to run for Gouverneur or tell anyone of your plans."

"I know," Archie replied annoyed that he was being treated like a child. "I know the plan, you don't have to tell me twice."

"I like the fire. But watch your tongue when you speak to me. You're replaceable. You may go."

This time Archie left the room angrily and made his way to his ship for the few days journey back to Port Royal.

Archie needed to start scheming and formulating a plan now

that he had the mission to expand to Port Nassau. He would require a secondary plan to Captain Montre's plan, before he had to run for Governor or worse, kill Governor Raymond in a coup d'état. He already knew the pivotal person in his plan was going to have to be the beautiful Isabel Raymond.

Archie sailed into Port Nassau in the winter of 1670 with an army of Smith Sugar employees and slaves ready to buy any sugarcane plantation available. It did not take him long to find a decent sized lot with promising potential. He overpaid for the plantation, much to the glee of the seller. Archie was not too concerned with the price, because he knew he would make it back within six months time.

For Archie, it was strange to be back in Port Nassau. He walked about the Port and city, and could not help but feel lonely knowing that his friend, Thomas, was dead because of him. If Archie had let Thomas drink his coconut in peace and not asked for his assistance three years ago, Thomas would still be alive today. He ambled aimlessly between the buildings and amongst the stalls and shops. Archie stumbled across the dark alleyway, where he relived the chance encounter with his first d'Or pirate. Reflecting, Archie realized that over the years Port Nassau had not changed. However, Archie could not say the same for himself. In Archie's ultimate plan, Port Nassau would either be the place he buried himself, or it would be his chance at escaping.

As the new year of 1671 continued in Port Nassau, Smith Sugar was drawing attention to Archie, rather Mr. Smith, as Smith Sugar's power grew in size. The company started becoming a dominant player in the sugar business and overall affairs at the Port. As such, Governor Raymond started to take notice when his business associates and sugarcane plantation owners began to complain about a "Mr. Calvin Smith" who was punching his way to the top of the industry. Governor Raymond quelled the uproar over Mr. Smith and said that the man was doing fine business, and Mr. Smith's company was bringing more gold into Port Nassau, which was beneficial to all of them.

However, throughout 1671, Mr. Smith's name began to torment the Governor. The Smith Sugar Company began to make demands of the Governor and the Port authorities. Mr. Smith started to demand tax breaks and subsidies because of the vast amount of market share his company held. By the end of the year in December of 1671, Smith Sugar owned forty-three percent of sugar and sugarcane exports in Port Nassau and seventy-five percent in Port Royal. Governor Raymond was receiving requests from both Ports about the unfair requests Smith Sugar was demanding of them.

Governor Raymond was suspicious of the Smith Sugar Company; but when an audit was conducted on its affairs, everything seemed to be in order. Mr. Calvin Smith had appeared from nowhere with a fortune in his pocket, and all his business transactions had been represented legally. Governor Raymond wondered what person or entity had funded the Smith Sugar Company because no company in the history of the West Indies had grown as fast in a year's time.

At the beginning of 1672, the Smith Sugar monopoly began to lower its price of sugar to the point where no other sugar company could compete with its pricing. The other rich plantations owners were furious with Mr. Calvin Smith as month after month they saw their market share and their profits decrease substantially. They continuously bombarded Governor Raymond with requests to hang the Mr. Smith, or at the very least, freeze his company's accounts until the man could explain how he was financing the business and charging such low sugar prices.

Governor Raymond had no idea how to settle the issue, because Mr. Smith had not broken any laws or rules to his knowledge. Governor Raymond sat in his study as he thought of all the ways to try and deal with this new business authority, Smith Sugar. After a few cups of coffee, Governor Raymond called for his daughter, who might bring fresh ideas to him.

"Darling, love of my life, what am I to do with a man who has not broken any laws and yet the people want his business shut down?" asked the Governor looking at his daughter.

Isabel looked at her father not knowing what to say. It was a rare occasion when she was ever asked for advice.

She thought hard for a moment before responding, "Well, if they haven't broken the law, then you must offer them something they want before they will consider stopping. If I wanted a new dress, and you didn't allow me to buy one; usually you have me do something for you. Then in return I receive my dress, but there is always an exchange of favors."

The Governor jumped out of his chair and kissed his daughter on the forehead.

"You are my girl," he beamed. "I need to offer Mr. Smith something he wants and in return he might stop this wretched business of undercutting all the other sugar plantations. Why didn't I think of that before?"

The Governor quickly took out a piece of parchment and scribbled away:

Dear Mr. Smith,

As Governor of Port Nassau, I would like to invite you to attend a dinner with my family and I. I understand you are relatively new to Port Nassau and have been successfully building a sugar business here, but it is to my great displeasure that we have never become acquainted. Please know it will be my pleasure to host you for an evening at my mansion so that we get to know each other better and discuss important topics. I look forwarding to hearing from you soon.

Your friend,
Governor Raymond
Port Nassau

P.S. If you have a wife you would like to bring, she is more than welcome too.

Pleased with his letter, he fetched his butler and had it sent to Mr. Smith immediately. Secretly, he hoped Mr. Smith did not have a wife, so he might entice Mr. Smith to marry his lovely daughter. She would be the best bargaining chip he could bring to the table. Otherwise, he might have to sell the mansion and all of Port Nassau to stop Mr. Smith and keep the public approval of him high.

As soon as Archie received the Governor's letter, he knew it was time to put his plan into action. His moment had come. He had drawn ample attention to himself through the outstanding growth of Smith Sugar. It was time to implement the critical move of his plan. He was to have his quarterly meeting with Captain Montre next week, and it was imperative that he set his plan in motion first, before Captain Montre could get his plan started.

Captain Montre and Archie had acquired vast amounts of wealth from Port Royal and Port Nassau over the last fourteen months. They had invested wisely and Archie had made Captain Montre one of the richest pirates in history. Captain Montre was nearly untouchable in his pirating enterprises, as he was able to afford the most powerful weapons gold could buy and bribe all the necessary officials in every port.

Archie hoped one week would be enough time to allow his plan to blossom and take action, before Captain Montre reacted to it and squashed it like a bug.

———

Four days after sending away his letter to Mr. Smith, Governor Raymond's butler knocked on his master's study's door.

"Sir," the butler said standing at the closed door.

"Yes," Governor Raymond responded from within, "enter".

The butler opened the door and proceeded into the study where Governor Raymond was hunched over multiple parchments and a wet quill was hovering above a fresh sheet of paper.

"I have a letter from a Mr. Smith for you."

The name, "Mr. Smith", caught the Governor's attention. "Yes, yes, bring it over."

The Governor quickly took the letter from his butler and opened it. As the Governor began to read his letter, the butler proceeded to Ms. Isabel's room to deliver a letter addressed to her from a mysterious man named "*A*".

The Governor read aloud:

Governor Raymond,

It would be my honor to attend a dinner at your mansion with your family. Please understand that my business is of the utmost importance to me, so I will be unable to attend a dinner until 2nd of April 1672. I know three weeks is a long way off, but my businesses in Port Royal and Port Nassau are consuming every minute of my life. I hope you understand and can wait for this date.

Also, I assume you are writing me, because you have been receiving complaints about my business ethics and practices. I have not made many friends in Port Nassau, so it was a welcome to receive your invitation, even though I expected it sooner. I will be away on business next week and will be back in Port Nassau on 30th of March. Then we can have our dinner on 2nd of April. I hope this timeframe is acceptable.

Warm regards,
C.S.

The Governor read the letter several times, trying to read between the lines and analyze it from all angles. Finally satisfied with the message and acknowledging that Mr. Smith was probably truly busy, he accepted he would have to anxiously await the three weeks before resolving the business problems with Mr. Smith. He wrote back:

Mr. Smith,

I look forward to seeing you then. This is the formal invitation to our mansion. Please bring this piece of paper with you on the 2nd of April as it will be the way to confirm your entrance to the grounds.

Safe travels,
Governor Raymond
Port Nassau

At the same time Governor Raymond was proofreading his response letter, Isabel was opening a very confusing and puzzling letter from an unknown sender, "*A*". Isabel did not usually receive mail directly from strangers, unless it was a potential suitor she had met at a party. This letter was quite different in tone and the contents startled her.

Isabel, my dear,

I am alive, but the infamous pirate Captain Rémi Montre is holding me captive. I was only just able to get this letter out to you. You must send an army to come and rescue me before these rancorous pirates kill me. I have been able to clutch on to life for all these years through the strength of my love for you. All I want in the world is to be with you, and I need you now more than ever. I do hope you receive this letter and believe me. I love you Isabel, only you and your father can save me now. I cannot wait to hold you in my arms.

Love,
Archie

As she read the letter, Isabel put her hand over her mouth in astonishment. If it was true, and Archie was alive, then she needed to save him. It was up to her. She quickly rushed to her father's study.

"Father, father," she called out as she burst into the study without knocking.

"What is it darling," he said as he handed his response letter to his butler.

The butler swiftly left the room holding Governor Raymond's response letter and to send it off to Mr. Smith directly, per the Governor's instructions.

"I have just received a letter from Archie. He is alive, but he needs our assistance. The vile Captain Montre is still holding him captive and he has only just now been able to write to me."

"What!?" the Governor was flustered at this surprising news. How could Archie be alive? The Governor's head was spinning trying to wrap his mind around the new information. Had it not been two years since Captain Jasper, Thomas, and Archie were proclaimed dead in the letter from, who was it again... then it clicked. *Mr. Smith.* The Governor's mouth dropped open. Mr. Smith had written the letter to him informing the Governor of the tragic news and death of the three men. Mr. Smith was the man who bought Archie's Hollis Sugar Plantation. The dots all started to connect. The Governor, without explaining, rushed passed his daughter and flew down the stairs as quickly as his legs would allow him.

"Gregory, Gregory," the Governor called out in between deep breathes.

The butler appeared apprehensively, "Yes, Sir?"

"Where is that letter I have sent, I need to change it."

"I have sent it by your carriage directly to Mr. Smith's plantation, Sir. Just as you instructed."

"Get it back, immediately. I must change it. Send a horse after the carriage. I have another message I would like to send Mr. Smith."

"Right away Sir," and Gregory vanished.

Returning to his study, the Governor saw his daughter slumped in a chair with the letter clutched in her hands. He would speak with his daughter in a second. First he need to clear his mind and write a new letter to Mr. Smith asking for an explanation and demanding Mr. Smith come to the Governor's mansion at once. He would also freeze Mr. Smith's accounts on suspicion of fraud and conspiracy to murder.

First, Governor Raymond drafted the letter to the bank to freeze Mr. Smith's assets in both Port Royal and Port Nassau. He also drafted the new letter to Mr. Smith, which the Governor's tone was much more authoritative and demanding. He sent off both letters with another butler, then proceeded to read Archie's letter that was still clutched in his daughter's hands.

As he inspected the letter, it appeared to be written by Archie's hand and the letter seemed genuine. Archie could definitely be alive, but why would Captain Rémi Montre keep him prisoner such a long time without any demands for a ransom?

Shedding light on this mysterious situation was necessary. Governor Raymond concluded that Mr. Smith was the key person linking Archie, Smith Sugar Company, and Captain Rémi Montre altogether.

"Please father," Isabel said breaking Governor Raymond's concentration. "Find him for me. I love Archie."

"Anything for you my dear. You will marry him, once we find him. How does that sound?" the Governor said.

"I dream about it all the time. I can't believe he is still alive."

"Isabel, we will get him. I will start preparing a brigade and ship for them to go on a hunt for Archie."

"Thank you father. What a horrible life Archie must have had the last two years under that cruel pirate. "

"Yes, yes. We will get him this time," the Governor repeated trying to assure himself, more so than Isabel, that this was a worthy mission to risk his soldier's lives.

• 20 •

"All of it," Archie said as he signed the documents. "That's right, all of it. Yes, and I am agreeing to this price. I know it's a bargain. That's why you deserve to be ecstatic."

"Sounds good to me, Mr. Smith," Sir Lester responded as he penned his name next to Mr. Smith's signature.

"Fantastic. The deal is settled," Archie said relieved. "Please transfer the gold into my account as soon as possible."

"What account would that be?"

"Archibald Rose is the name of the account."

"I will do so right away," responded Sir Lester, "any other requests?"

"Yes actually. Will you please also make sure the bank holds all of the gold when you deliver it? I do intend to close the account and head back to England soon, so I will be transporting all the money across with me to my English bank in London."

"Certainly," Sir Lester said without a second thought.

Sir Lester was astounded at Mr. Smith's apparent novice

knowledge in business sales. Mr. Smith had just sold all of the Port Royal assets, held by the Smith Sugar Company, to Sir Lester at an astonishing low price compared to its actual value. Of course, Mr. Smith made out handsomely in the deal, but he could have profited much, much more if he was not in such a hurry to sell. The Smith Sugar Company was recording major profits and basically had a monopoly on the sugar industry. Mr. Smith seemed to be in a great rush to sell the busy and quickly get back to England, so Sir Lester was not going to pass up such promising deal.

Archie's plan had officially been set in motion. Archie had needed to act quickly when he had received Governor Raymond's invitation letter. So, the following day he went to the bank with the urgent agenda to find a buyer for all the assets in Port Royal. It took two days, but finally Sir Lester bought the assets after thoroughly inspecting Mr. Smith's company's books.

After finalizing the sale of the assets, Archie had responded to Governor Raymond's letter, left Port Nassau, and set sail to Saint-Domingue to report to Captain Montre.

———

Archie arrived in Saint-Domingue and went directly to Captain Montre' hideout to consult with the Captain.

"Calvin," Captain Montre said as he waved Archie through the door, "please sit down. What have you to report to me?"

Ignoring Captain Montre's continually use of the name Calvin instead of Archie, Archie proceeded, "Mr. Smith is receiving increased attention and has received an invitation to discuss business with the Governor. It shows that we are in a position of power. We are threatening the current economic status quo in Port Nassau and Port Royal. I believe this is the opportune time to overtake the Governor and set in motion your next stage. There will be a rebellion in Port Nassau from the people if nothing is done about Mr. Smith. If we make my demands clear—that I want to be Governor—I think the people will turn on Governor Raymond in a heartbeat. They will gladly put me in as Governor, as long as I promise to stop undercutting all of them in the sugar business and sell the monopoly I have. Either way, as soon as I become Governor, then you will be able to pirate the Caribbean oceans with impunity. I have set up a meeting with the Governor on 2nd of April."

Smiling, Captain Montre just nodded his head as he listened to Archie. "I like it. If you think it's a good time, then we'll set sail in two days time for Port Nassau. You'll 'ave your meeting with the Governor where you will make your demands and request he steps down as Gouverneur."

"Precisely, and I will also make sure that you receive your Jade Dagger just as I promised."

"Bien. Make sure that is part of the deal, I love rare treasures more than a ship on fire sinking to the bottom of the ocean" Captain Montre said chuckling. "I'll get my men prepared and situated for the trip. We will raid Port Nassau. I mean, why not? With you as Gouverneur, you will give us pardons. This'll be magnificent."

"You're going to raid Port Nassau?"

"Why not? Don't worry we won't kill you, plus my men love raids and razing cities."

"Whatever you desire. Nevertheless, we make quite a team, Captain."

"Power and fear. We'll soon be unstoppable."

Archie left Captain Montre and headed to the nearest tavern to quell his nervousness. He flashed his d'Or tattoo and was given a pint of ale free of charge. There were certainly nice perks by being in the most notorious pirate crew in the West Indies. As he sat at a table alone and watched people enter and exit, Archie sang Olivia's poem to himself:

> *From the sun that is yellow*
> *To the moon that is mellow,*
> *You are the star in the night*

That gives off the most light.

You are the smile during the day
That ensures flowers in May...

You have troubles and pain
That will be cleansed with the rain...

For you, my King of Hearts,
So what we have never parts.

He sipped on his cold ale and thought about Olivia. What was she doing today? His imagination ran wild. He had a million questions. Was she married? Had she waited? Was she still living in Brighton? Did she have a family? Did she still love him? It had been three years, since he wrote his last letter to Olivia. He felt awful and was filled with guilt. He had been so close to being with her, and holding her in his arms. Then his entire world had been turned upside down. Finally though, Archie had crafted a plan that had sparked a little light, a small fire at the end of the dark tunnel, which would light his way back to her.

Archie let his thoughts slip away as the drinks tingled his mind. He ordered another ale and let the alcohol continue to seep into his body. He smiled to himself, his plan must work. Olivia did still love him. Another drink. Certainly she did, she absolutely waited. They loved each other. She had written such a lovely poem for him. He had written one for her too. Archie could not wait to whisper it in her ear. Hold her hand, kiss her lips. Smell her aromatic scent. The woman of his dreams. Archie had another drink and tried to wash away all his fears. And another. He leaned back in his chair and sipped his drink. Olivia, I am coming home.

An old man with a wispy white beard, long white hair, and bright blue eyes that shone with wisdom sat down at the table with Archie, "Bonjour Monsieur."

"Hi ya. Name's Archie," Archie slurred, glad to have some company.

"Louis Laurent," the stranger extended his hand.

Archie shook the old man's hand and asked, "So ol' timer, why do I have the pleasure of your company?"

Louis glanced around the tavern before speaking, "You seem troubled. What is bothering you?"

Archie stared back at the man. He was troubled. Olivia was on his mind. There was a heavy anxiety weighing down upon his shoulders about his life and his future. Archie fired back shortly, "That's a forward question. I don't suppose you think I am going to tell you my life story."

"Patience. I mean you no ill will. I am here to give you guidance."

"I don't need your guidance."

"Hear me out. What is the number one thing that is troubling you?"

"A woman across the world."

"I see," Louis contemplated as he stroked his beard and bobbed his head. "What about this love is troubling you?"

Archie let out a deep sigh. He did not want to spill his life out on the table. He could handle his troubles himself. He looked at the man's wise blue eyes and prefaced, "I can handle my problems myself, ya know. I don't need you. But out of respect, I will answer. I am fearful that I might die in the Caribbean and never make it back to England. To Brighton. To her."

"The love of your life?"

"Aye, the love of my life."

"And you've left her."

Archie did not answer, but sadly nodded his head and downed his ale.

"Will you do anything to hold her in your arms again?"

"Yes," Archie said exacerbated.

"I want you to consider my next questions because it is a

momentous decision to risk anything and everything for a woman. Does this woman challenge you to greatness? Does she inspire you to be a better man? Does she reflect the values you see in yourself?"

Archie absorbed the man's words and the questions bounced around in his numbed head. Archie opened his mouth to reply, but Louis raised a finger and stopped him.

"Think before your reply. The answers are vital to your decision before you risk your own life for her or ruin someone else's. Love is a unique emotion because it has the ability to cripple the mind to do evil, sinful actions and yet, it has the power to lift up the worst individuals to acts of stewardship, mercy, and grace. Love, unconditional love, rather, is the greatest gift a man can give a woman. Loving her not only for her virtues, but loving her for her vices. Loving her at her worst. Loving her when she is least deserving. It is difficult but that is true love. Anyone can love a woman at her best, when times are grand. But Archie, you must acknowledge the sacrifice this kind of love takes: the pain and patience, and the understanding and compassion. For you to acquire this love, you must realize the path of sin you might need to endure and live with. For you to make it back to Olivia, the love you are currently fighting for, you already know what must be done."

"I...," Archie started. His eyes welled up with tears as the alcohol softened him and allowed his emotions to sweep through his body. He could see Olivia standing along the water's edge in Brighton. He was fighting to give her the love she deserved.

"I miss her," Archie whispered.

Louis spoke as he stood up to leave, "If you see her again, the longing you are feeling now will be washed away, but the blood and sins on your hands will not be."

Archie closed his eyes and rubbed the few tears from his eyes. He leaned forward and rested his head on the table and his weary brain fell asleep. Louis looked upon his drunken companion, said a small blessing, and left without another word.

Archie awoke being hoisted up by two big, strong men. He was dazed and disoriented. His head was fuzzy and the first thing he remembered was an old man. Currently, he could not comprehend what was happening and why two men were dragging him from the tavern. The two men carried him outside and dropped him on the stone street. In front of his eyes was a sparkling pair of blue high heels, which surprised him. He peered up from his position on the ground and saw an attractive woman dawning an elegant blue dress looking down at him.

He stood up and dusted himself off, then inquired, "You need something from me? Misssss...."

"Le Saphir," snapped the woman sharply in a French accent.

"Aw," Archie said smiling as he acknowledged how appropriate the name was given all the blue clothing the woman was wearing. "Uh, what can I do for you?"

"I demand payment. Pay me for my services," Le Saphir said testily.

"I never slept with you."

"Thomas did, he owes me. Therefore, you owe me."

"Thomas is dead. Plus, I don't have any money, so it appears we are in a bit of predicament."

The two big men took a step closer to Archie.

Archie's voice shook a bit and started, "Of course, we can always work something out. What would you like? And how much does Thomas owe you?"

"He owes me a small fortune. He always said, 'Next time.' There have been rumors that you know where Les Joyaux de la Couronne Britannique are hidden. Montre's men are keeping it very hush, hush; but you," Le Saphir put a finger into Archie's chest, "you are Montre's la pouffiasse. Get me Les Joyaux and the debt will be paid."

Archie scoffed, "Not a chance."

One of the two men pulled out a pistol and pointed it straight at Archie's forehead.

"In that case," Archie said as he knew he was in no position to negotiate, "I will see what I can do. Give me a week?"

Life, Archie thought, I need to survive each day.

"A week and if I do not have it, I will have my men kill you."

Le Saphir turned briskly in her high heels and with her blue dress swishing walked away. The two men followed suit and all three disappeared behind a corner.

God, Archie thought to himself, am I ever going to catch a break? He could not help but laugh as he thought, Thomas, you dirty dog, you found the most attractive and deadly whore in all of Saint-Domingue. You were the best and worst business partner at the same time.

As he walked toward the *L'île Rouge*, he thought about how he was possibly going to acquire the Queen's Jewels. Although at this precise moment, the Queen's Jewels and Thomas' prostitute debt were the lowest of his priorities. Captain Rémi Montre was of the utmost concern. If he found out Archie had sold the Port Royal assets, Archie was most certainly a dead man.

———

The *L'île Rouge* had begun its journey North to Port Nassau. The seas were tumultuous and the journey was slow. The hurricane force winds and enormous waves continued to batter the ship and delay any progress toward their final destination. Archie worried that the storm might cause him to miss his appointed dinner with the Governor.

Archie rubbed his head as the ship continued to sway to and fro. Archie sat across from Captain Montre in the Captain's quarters and was listening to him rant on and on about how magnificent their plan was and had been playing out. The Captain had become extraordinarily wealthy off the sugarcane profits and Archie's hard work. Captain Montre seemed to be untouchable and omnipotent on the oceans too. No ship in any battle had a chance to outrun or out shoot the *L'île Rouge*. The d'Or crew was also the most loyal and ruthless pirates imaginable.

Exhausted and tired of listening to the boastful Captain, Archie excused himself and went to his corner underneath the deck. He contemplated and recalculated his own plan of action. His plan and Captain Montre's plan were going to overlap at one crucial point. This apex moment relied on how the Governor reacted to his letter to Isabel. The Governor would do anything for his daughter. So all Archie could do now was pray Isabel believed his letter, for his life depended on it.

Currently, Captain Montre believed Archie was headed to Port Nassau, where a transition of power was imminent whether through forceful diplomacy or murder. However, if as Archie hoped, Isabel was able to convince her father to amass a fleet to search for him, then Captain Montre, the *L'île Rouge*, and Archie were headed to a huge battle as soon as they neared or arrived in Port Nassau.

Archie forecasted this surprise battle could have three outcomes: firstly, the d'Or pirates win and Archie dies at the hands of Captain Montre, because Archie double crossed him; secondly, Governor Raymond and the British win and they liberate Archie from his captors; or thirdly, the British win and they believe Archie is a d'Or pirate because of his d'Or tattoo and he hangs from the noose with the all the other d'Or pirates. Either way, Archie was going to need luck and God on his side to survive.

• 21 •

Olivia retreated to a corner as James advanced on her angrily. Charles was crying and wailing uncontrollably. Olivia looked at her son, who was howling like there was no tomorrow. She started to speak but there was a hot knot in her throat that stopped any words from coming out. The back of James' hand smacked her across the face and sent Olivia sprawling to the floor.

"Bitch," James bellowed.

"Stop it James, you just need rest," screamed Olivia as she crawled away from James.

It was January of 1672 and the respectable James Towns had lost his senior banking position at summer's end in 1671, only a few months after Charles' birth. The bank had failed to recover to investors' expectations, and they blamed James' myopic vision and stubbornness for the poor investment performance. The last six months had become a living nightmare for Olivia and Charles. Olivia and Charles lived with a man who had once had everything: the status, the money, the respect, and the power. He had been stripped bare and was left with nothing. James' pride and ego could not take such a brutal blow. His banking reputation was destroyed and no one would hire him. His future had come crashing down around him. His resolution was to turn to heavy drinking to escape from his anger, frustration, sadness, and disappointment.

Unfortunately, Olivia and Charles had to endure the violence and chaos of this man. Olivia was tired of James' behavior and started to fight back and lock him out of the house. She could stand on her own two feet. She would not tolerate such disrespect. However, James became infuriated with her dissent and would strike her accordingly when he got the chance.

Olivia had more than once grabbed Charles and run away from the house in the middle of the night with nowhere to go. Once she had gone to a friend's house, although, her friend's husband said that James needed a loyal and supportive wife at his side and would not let Olivia stay for any extended period of time.

In this current domestic battle, Olivia jumped to her feet, finally having the strength and determination to end this fight. She grabbed a tall, candlestick holder and held it out in front of her like a sword.

James looked at her and laughed, "Olivia now, don't be daft. I swear if you don't put that down, I will hit you so hard you won't ever raise a hand at me again."

"James, you need to leave. If you don't, I will find a way to leave you forever," Olivia growled through her gritted teeth. Furious tears ran down the sides of her face, "I will defend myself and my baby against you, you, monster. You are a wretched and violent man when you drink. I won't stand for it anymore."

James grabbed a glass dinner plate on the table and hurled it at Olivia. It whizzed to her left and smashed against the wall behind Olivia. Olivia screeched as the pieces sprayed everywhere and ricocheted against her body. She sprinted around the table and threw the candlestick wildly in James' direction. She did not take a second to look and see if it hit the mark.

She swept Charles off the ground in a single bound and fled the room heading straight for the front door. She flung the door open and sprinted out into the gentle rain falling upon the empty, London streets. She did not pause to grab a coat or an umbrella. Her mind focused on getting away as far as possible from the monster she was living with and married to. Charles continued to sniff and sob as the rain chilled his small body.

Olivia ducked under a shop awning and shivered as the cold night penetrated her wet clothes and chilled her bones. She kissed Charles forehead and stood looking out watching the rain fall gently into puddles. Tears quietly trickled down Olivia's soft, perfect features. Her husband was an abhorrent beast when he drank and threatened her safety and her baby's safety.

Her mind was jumbled with thoughts. Could she run away forever? A cold snowfall was inevitable any day and she would freeze to death with Charles. The last seven months had been tortuous. James' routine and behavior was not going to change. Olivia needed a way out of her situation, but she was helplessly stuck. She had no money of her own and her husband was so controlling she feared what would happened to her or Charles if she ever brought up the idea of them separating. She would be an outcast if they divorced. Although, it was better than the nightmare she was presently enduring.

Olivia sniffed and wiped her nose. She looked down at Charles who had stopped crying. His blue eyes looked back at Olivia warmly. Her heart melted, despite how freezing she had become standing outside. Those round, baby blue eyes were the only thing that kept Olivia going and living each day. As Olivia continued to look at his blue eyes, she saw Archie looking back. Archie's blue eyes…her mind drifted off to him.

Archie always treated her so preciously. He cared about her opinions, her fears, her likes and dislikes. She would never have been in this situation if he had come back to England like his letter had promised. Olivia had resolved herself to the fact that Archie had found a woman in the Caribbean and had forgotten all about her. She could not blame him. England was a world away, and thus she was a world away from him. A handsome and caring man, like Archie, he probably was able to marry any woman he wanted. Why would he come back for her?

His letter had given her such hope that he still wanted her and desired to return to England. When he never showed up at the end of the summer in 1669, what choice did she have? She could not live by herself for the rest of her life. She wanted to have a family and a little son or daughter to dote over, kiss, love and cherish.

She looked back through the darkness and rain in the direction of her home. How much longer could she live with James? The rain pitter, pattered in the silent street and raindrops playfully splashed in the puddles. Olivia committed herself to a plan: she would return to the house in the middle of the night once she was confident James was fast asleep. She would take one day at a time and hope and pray for better days ahead.

With a little luck and secret promotion by Olivia, James finally was offered a new job with a boutique, retail company in the heart of London. The retail company, Marsh's Essentials for Men, hired James as a financial consultant. James' position was to review Marsh's financial books and help them navigate the expansion of a second store to either Ipswich or Oxford.

Olivia happened to be walking along the London streets, her private time away from her husband's hangover, when she stumbled across a flyer in Marsh's store window. The flyer was searching for a financial manager or consultant who would be able to assist in expansion. Seeing the opportunity, Olivia naturally went into the store and inquired about the position. She talked about her husband's financial brilliance and promoted his availability to their cause. Within the week, James was summoned for an interview. To Olivia's great relief, he was sober and passed the interview with flying colors. Mr.

Marsh hired James on the spot, and James began taking regular weekend and week-long trips to Ipswich and Oxford to scout out locations and speak with bank managers about financing the expansion.

James' new position granted him a second wind at life and his family. As winter rolled into spring of 1672, James stopped drinking and began to have new energy and found purpose in his work. The domestic violence and verbal abuse ceased altogether, and most weekends, James was away from the house on business and scouting trips.

According to Mr. Marsh, the utmost priority was to ensure the expansion was a success. Thus, there was not a rush if the right property or finances were not currently available. James took the new task as a personal challenge, and for the next half year, he set his mind to nothing else other than helping Mr. Marsh's business succeed.

Olivia enjoyed the peace and quiet around the house and was happy to see James finally, once again, become the man she had married. There were emotional scars from James' words and actions that could never be healed or taken back. The pain James had caused Olivia would be a lasting feeling she never forgot. She was unsure if she could ever truly forgive him, because his actions had been so deliberate and done with such impunity and fury.

One Friday morning in July of 1672, James kissed Olivia goodbye as he boarded the carriage that would take him Northwest to Oxford. Olivia slowly strolled back to the house and settled in for a nice long weekend of tea and biscuits and playing with Charles. Just past mid-morning, there was a knock on the door.

Odd, Olivia thought to herself. When James left on a business trip, no one visited the house unless it was her friends, Elizabeth or Louise. However, neither Elizabeth nor Louise was expected until tomorrow.

Olivia walked over to the window and peered out toward the front door. Standing there was a Royal Postman. She proceeded to the front door and opened it.

"Morning ma'am. May I presume you are Ms. Olivia Hunt?"

the postman said warmly as he procured a letter from his bag.

"Good morning and yes I am her, or used to be. I am now Olivia Towns," replied Olivia. "How are you doing on this fine Friday?"

"Dandy, just dandy. Busy day ahead though. There has been an influx of letters from the West Indies over the last few weeks. Apparently, there was quite the battle at Port Nassau. Hundreds dead, not sure what's happening exactly; but lots of letters coming from all over the colonies. People trying to contact family and friends, I suppose."

"Sounds dreadful. What awful news spoiling such a good start to the day. You don't know what's happened?" Olivia asked trying to get the inside scoop.

"No ma'am. Rumor has France might have been involved in the attack. Other reports say it was just an entire fleet of pirates. I also heard the attack was orchestrated by slaves, who were riding on the backs of griffins. Just rumors." The postman paused momentarily as he handed over the letter: "Lookie here. Your letter is originally from Port Nassau before it was sent here from Brighton. Do you know someone in the Caribbean?"

Olivia froze.

"Ma'am?" the postman hesitated.

Olivia took the letter from the postman. Looking down at the letter, the handwriting on the front was unmistakable. Olivia's hand quivered as the weight of the letter increased significantly upon seeing Archie's script.

"Yes," Olivia said quietly. "I do."

Olivia did not take her eyes off the letter in her hands.

Recognizing a potentially awkward situation, something he did not want to be a part of, the postman politely excused himself: "Well, I hope everything is ok. I'd best be on my way Miss Towns."

The postman retreated back to the bustling street and whisked himself and his letters to the next house to resume his deliveries.

Olivia closed the door and set the letter down on the dining room table. She glanced at it once more and then she walked to the kitchen to start her day's planned routine. She made a cup of tea, and started to work on baking the lemon, poppy seed muffins for tomorrow when her friends would visit. She would open it when her chores were done.

• 22 •

Archie awoke early in the morning, many hours before the d'Or crew would start their day's preparation for the arrival to Port Nassau. He quietly made his way across the room and up the stairs to the deck. The cool, morning, sea air and light blue, dawn horizon greeted him.

Archie was surprised to see Captain Montre standing at the wheel already fully dressed, and steering the ship toward the Port. Captain Montre did not seem to notice Archie as he continued steering the *L'île Rouge*, absent minded of the fact another person was on the deck with him. Archie did not call out, not wanting to disrupt the Captain's meditation. Archie continued across the deck to the bow of the boat and looked out toward the approaching landmass in the distance. They were too far away for him to determine what type of preparations, if any at all, Governor Raymond had started. Today was 1st of April, and Archie was scheduled for a business meeting with the Governor tomorrow. Of course, as soon as the Governor laid eyes on "Mr. Smith", the Governor would know it was Archie. Thus, Captain

Montre wanted the Governor to be taken by surprise a day early, before he could react to this shocking turn of events.

Needless to say, Captain Montre was unaware of Archie's letter to Isabel as an indirect way to hopefully utilize the Governor's power to mobilize the British Royal Navy. Archie could only pray that his plan had worked. Archie was nervous, extremely nervous. His mind could not wander anywhere but on the approaching Port and what might happen in the next few hours.

Archie felt helpless and impotence as the waves continued to splash against the side of the ship. He felt like a man who had been thrown into an enormous maze because he could not turn around and start over. And as he looked forward, he did not know which way to proceed, because all the pathways were as dark and abyss-like as the next. He no longer felt like the captain of his fate.

All around him, the ship began to come to life. The d'Or pirates readied the cannons and set the sails accordingly. They prepped the ammunition strategically and sharpened their swords. Pistols were loaded and holstered. Archie took his pistol and readied it.

One kill, Archie thought to himself, and he was my friend. As he rammed the bullet into the gun, the horrifying images Thomas' dead body flashed before him. Archie swore to himself the next body he killed would either be Captain Montre' or his own. He most certainly could not keep living this cursed life as a pirate under the control of Captain Montre. He wanted his freedom whether it was in this life or the next.

Archie had not forgotten about his beloved Olivia. He had resolved himself to writing one last letter before he died: telling her how sorry he was, telling her how much he missed her, how much he longed to kiss her soft lips, feel her soft skin brush against his, how he missed their hands interlaced together, how he missed looking in her eyes as they lay by the beach and watched the clouds roll by overhead as the waves lapped against the shore, and how he missed spending time with and having her head nestled in his chest. In the end, it would be his farewell to her. He would give her that closure and let her know he tried his best to make it home.

Captain Montre called out over the deck, "Aye, men. Ready yourselves, we're gittin' close. Roquette, what's it look like?"

"Capitaine, it looks like the Brits have armed ships docked in the 'arbor," yelled back Roquette, the d'Or pirate who was perched up in the crow's nest. "Trois British naval ships. Deux look to been fully armed, un looks to been a scoutin' vessel."

Captain Montre remained silent as he stared at the ships in the distance.

"Monsieur Smith," Captain Montre barked with an edge in his voice.

"Captain," Archie replied anxiously.

"Will you explain to me why there are two fully armed naval ships in the Port we so 'appen to be 'eaded toward?"

Archie looked at the distant ships and tried to think quickly. He felt his insides turn and his skin become hot as all eyes were upon him.

He ventured forth, "When I left, word on the street was that Governor Raymond was celebrating the pending marriage of his daughter and had invited several high ranking officials in the Royal Navy. I did not know what day of course, since I, Mr. Smith, had not been invited."

Captain Montre contemplated Archie's answer and Archie stood exposed, hoping he would not have to answer any more questions. The lie was plausible; however, Archie was motionless as he watched as Captain Montre took out his pistol. Archie's heart stopped.

"Ready the weapons," Captain Montre yelled. "If a wedding is taking place and we weren't invited, then I say we invite ourselves. I've always loved a good wedding with fine wine. I ought to 'ave been the best man of course, so I 'ave a right to be there. We attack as soon as we are within range and we take it all. Forget the plan of diplomacy, we are d'Or. Nous somme d'Or!"

The d'Or crew bellowed in unison, "Nous somme d'Or! Nous somme d'Or!"

Over the uproar of voices, Captain Montre roared, "We are d'Or, we take what we want!"

The d'Or pirates cheered with riotous enthusiasm.

Captain Montre walked down from the ship's wheel and across the deck to Archie.

"Mr. Smith, after this massacre is all over, you'll take the Gouverneur's place at the 'elm of Port Nassau. It should not be too much of a problem considering the poor Gouverneur will be dead."

Archie simply nodded, not knowing how to respond.

Captain Montre turned and laughed as he fired his pistol skyward. "Get ready to slaughter 'em all."

Archie ran downstairs below deck and grabbed a parchment and quill. He began writing his letter to Olivia. As he wrote, he paused momentarily as he heard a round of rifles volley off the deck above.

He glanced up and quietly said, "This might be my last chance to get my poem to you."

He looked back down at the paper and added at the end of his letter the poem he had always intended to tell Olivia in person. After looking over the letter to make sure he had said everything he wanted, he folded the paper and tucked it away in his clothes.

Archie checked his pistol and said a prayer. The first volley of cannon fire started to erupt from the *L'île Rouge*. Explosions began to sound all around the once peaceful, morning ocean. Yells and commands could be heard above as the pirates' frantically reloaded pistols and cannons and positioned themselves for the next volley. Archie rushed up the stairs to join the fray, and if he got lucky, eventually find a way to escape. First though, he must fight as a d'Or pirate. He was a lifelong member of the crew, and he would need to act like he was on their side.

Despite his fear of dying in the emerging firefight, he was pleased that phase one of his plan had worked perfectly. Isabel had played her partly beautifully. He wished he could have witnessed her performance, which had persuaded her father to prepare the fleet for his rescue. In addition, he could not have asked Governor Raymond to organize a more qualified naval battle-ready fleet. The pieces so far had all fallen into place. Slow and steady, thought Archie, I need to survive the ongoing raging battle of death.

Archie scanned from his left to his right looking for safety and a good vantage point to determine his next move. The *L'île Rouge* continued its course deeper into the heart of Port Nassau. The British ships had mobilized after the first round of cannon fire rained down upon them. They acted quickly, but it was still slower than they would have liked. The *L'île Rouge* was able to fire off two more rounds of heavy cannon fire before either of the British ships could respond.

The offensive Captain Montre knew how to take a battle straight to the enemy. He was always the aggressor in battles, never taking his eyes off what he wanted. Cannon balls started to whiz around the *L'île Rouge* as they were within fifty meters of the first British ship. Some of the cannonballs hit their mark, causing splitters of wood to fly in all directions creating a dangerous situation, as anyone standing in the shrapnel's way was impaled.

Archie bounded across the deck in strides only deer could replicate. He slid across the final part of the deck, ducking behind three barrels just in the nick of time. A cannonball whipped through the air where he had been running and ripped a d'Or pirate in two. The pirate fell to the floor and was dead before he hit the deck. Archie vomited immediately at the site of the severed man.

Archie heard British commands being shouted over the gunfire. He peered over the barrels and saw that they were within ten meters of the first British ship. Volleys of pistols and rifle fire thunderously exploded in unison. The British ship disappeared behind a thick, black cloud of smoke, and as it reappeared, the British soldiers where rapidly firing their weapons upon the pirates.

British soldiers began to swing across the open water and board the pirate ship. Hand to hand combat ensued between British soldiers and the pirates. The pirates, however, with plenty of ammunition and superior aim began to pick off the British soldiers one by one as they tried swinging across to board the ship. The British soldiers screams were heard mid-flight as they fell and into their watery graves between the two ships.

Archie turned his head to see three d'Or pirates who were preparing a catapult with a barrel of gunpowder as its ammunition. They are going to hurl over a massive explosion, thought Archie. The weapon could blow a hole in the British ship, but also could cause massive damage to L'île Rouge.

As Archie watched in fascination and horror, Captain Montre appeared next to the three men. He nodded the affirmative and the three pirates positioned the mortar and explosive within striking distance. One of the d'Or pirates lit the fuse sticking out from the top of the barrel. It was a fast burning fuse, and Archie panicked thinking it would explode in the middle of the L'île Rouge deck. Before he could run to the edge of L'île Rouge and jump overboard, the second pirate fired the catapult and Archie watched in utter amazement and horror as the enormous barrel of gunpowder flew through the air toward the British ship.

The British commanders and soldiers on board were unaware of the incoming explosive. The barrel silently tumbled through the air in slow motion. As it was about to hit the British deck, it erupted into an enormous, white, hot flash of heat and debris. The explosion knocked Archie off his feet and he landed hard on his back. As he stood to see the catastrophic damage the explosion had caused, he was aghast at how successful it had been.

The main mast of the ship was on fire, as were several other parts of the deck. All the British soldiers on the deck were either dead or mortally wounded. Screams and cries of agony pierced the air as the three pirates readied another barrel of gunpowder to finish the job.

Captain Rémi Montre was standing confidently in the middle of the deck eyeing the burning remains of the British ship. He looked over at the three pirates and gave them the affirmative nod. Within a minute the second barrel of gunpowder flew across the gap between the ships and again, exploded with the same fury and impunity as the first. Everything and everyone around it was destroyed or killed. The

British ship burned significantly faster as more of the ship became aflame.

"Swing 'er 'round," yelled Captain Montre to the pirate standing at the wheel. "The other British ship is beginning to flank us and we can't get caught in the middle."

"Oui Capitaine," came the response.

As the L'île Rouge began to maneuver away from the burning ship, British cannonballs again began to puncture the L'île Rouge's hull and rain down upon the deck. The d'Or pirates faced their new oncoming adversary.

As Archie looked in the direction of the new ship, he realized something was different about this one. He could not tell, but it appeared to be armed differently. The same cannonballs were being used, but the strategy of the attack was different. The ship was staying farther away using longer-range cannons as their offensive strategy.

Obviously, they did not want to end up engulfed in the same fiery explosion like their counterparts. The cannonball fire continued to batter the L'île Rouge as it made its way toward the British ship. Pirates fell dead and cried in pain as pieces of shrapnel thrashed through their bodies and became lodged inside vital organs.

An explosion on the L'île Rouge sent shrapnel in all directions and large wooden, splintered planks sprayed against Archie's body. Luckily, he survived the explosion. When Archie opened his eyes, he felt his left shoulder was on fire. There, embedded in his body was a small piece of wood sticking out.

Archie sprinted across the deck trying to find a new hiding spot. He crouched down behind a cannon that was not being used and examined his shoulder. He could feel the warm blood oozing down his bicep and onto his arm. The crimson blood stained his tattered and worn shirt. He decided it was best to leave the wooden shard where it was, and have a doctor look at it if he survived long enough for that to happen. Archie determined his injury was not life threatening, but his left arm was now immobile.

Archie scanned the deck with his pistol ready and cocked in his right hand. All the d'Or pirates still fighting were crouched low avoiding the onslaught of the British cannon fire. The *L'île Rouge* drew closer and closer. They were within thirty meters.

A group of pirates began to ready another barrel of gunpowder to assault the British ship. The d'Or pirates unleashed their own volley of cannon fire toward the second British ship. The two ships traded blows back and forth. The visibility dimmed as the smoke from rifles, pistols, and cannons clouded the air and hovered between the decks.

All of a sudden, a white, hot explosion erupted on the *L'île Rouge*'s deck. Archie was flung backwards. He hit his head forcefully on the wooden railing; and instantaneously, stars formed in front of his eyes and he became extremely light headed and dizzy. Archie looked up trying to orient himself, but the world seemed to be upside down. Archie touched the back of his head and felt thick blood and a crack in his head. He was barely holding onto consciousness; he glanced around dazed. His mind was having a hard time processing what he was seeing. He looked like a newborn baby bobbing his head around trying to follow a toy. Half of the deck was ablaze.

The area where the catapult and barrel of gunpowder had been was annihilated. Something must have caused it to explode before it was catapulted across to the British ship. All that remained in the catapult's space was a gaping hole in the deck, charred bodies, and fires consuming sails, rope, and wood. The d'Or pirates were now the ones screaming as they clung to their bodies where fresh injuries bled.

British soldiers began hollering and cheering. Archie looked up as the British ship drew nearer. British soldiers began swinging across the deck and landing on the *L'île Rouge*. There was a cacophony of gunfire and yells, but Archie was slowly slipping away. He could not focus or tell who was yelling or in which direction the gunfire was coming from.

Archie blinked his eyes rapidly trying to fight against the black abyss of unconsciousness. He swung his head lazily to his right. There in the distance, Captain Montre was standing, one of a few pirates left standing, pointing two pistols at advancing British soldiers. Captain

Montre fired two guns and two British soldiers fell. He picked up another pistol from a dead d'Or pirate lying next to him, and fired it with similar accuracy sending another British soldier to an early death.

Archie had to admit, Captain Montre was a fighter; he was quite a leader. Archie glanced down at his aching body, which was limp and unable to move. His head screamed in pain and he winced with any sudden movement. Archie felt his eyes slipping. He could not fight any longer. Against his will, the world went black, silence engulfed the ship, and his body slump to the deck's floor.

• 23 •

Archie gradually opened his eyes, but hastily shut them to shield his pupils from the bright, morning sunlight streaming into the room. He moaned as the pain in his head started to bang against his skull. He continued to rest his head and body on the stone he was currently laying on. He did not get a chance to take in his surroundings for it was too taxing at the moment. He would try again later. Archie decided to keep his eyes shut as it numbed the pain in his head, and he drifted into a dreamless sleep.

Two British guards standing in the prison hallway monitoring the prisoners heard Archie's moan. One guard walked over and stared at the weak man lying with his eyes closed shut.

The soldier walked back to his partner saying, "Notify the Commander that the Englishman is alive and he is fit to stand trial with the lot of them."

"Right away, Sir." The second British guard scurried away to inform his superior.

The d'Or pirates sat silently in their cells as they looked out through the bars hopelessly awaiting mortal judgment to be passed over them and their actions.

———————

Archie finally awoke with the ability to sit upright. He head still ached and was sensitive to movement, but the pain was tolerable. Archie took in his surroundings. He was in a cell all by himself, adjacent to the other d'Or pirates. It was dark and the only light source were two torches lighting the hallway and cells to his right and left. He saw all the surviving d'Or pirates were fast asleep and wondered how many days had gone by and what had happened after he blacked out on the *L'île Rouge.*

Archie came to the realization that Captain Rémi Montre had suffered his first loss as his entire crew had been captured. As Archie slowly scanned the sleeping bodies, he did not see Captain Montre and wondered if he had died fighting or if they were keeping him in solitary confinement.

Regardless, Archie thought, I need to be concerned with my next move. He moved his hands around body and head feeling for any and all injuries to conclude what kind of physical shape he was in. As Archie performed the self-examination, he was pleased to find that other than his head injury, he had only suffered the shoulder wound. He had survived. For all intents and purposes, he was ok. The wood had been removed from his shoulder and the wound had clotted. His arm was still stained dark red with dried blood and he could not move nor lift his arm upward. The muscles in his shoulder were inflamed and agitated. The back of his head had a contusion too and the wound was extremely tender to the touch.

As Archie looked down at his tattered and useless clothing, he noticed something odd. A piece of paper was sticking out of his waistband. That's odd, Archie thought? He carefully removed the paper and unfolded it. There before him was his letter and poem to Olivia. Archie smiled, he had not lost it. He reread his letter and it brought tears to his eyes. He missed her dearly. He pined for her each day more and more.

Was he expecting too much from her to have waited for him nearly five years? He had left her. Why in the world would she wait for his return, especially when it was not or had not been guaranteed? He had even sent a letter two years ago saying he was on his way home. He was farther away from home now than he had been when he sent that letter. Archie had gone in the wrong direction.

One tear rolled down his right cheek as he imagined Olivia kissing another man and holding his hand, making love to him, and raising a beautiful family. He let himself slip into the depressing images that were unfolding in his mind. His imagination ran wild as he watched her live life with someone else. The unknown man would undress Olivia every night and she would let her dress drop to the floor. She stood bare and vulnerable in front this man. This man touched his angel. Kissing her lips, ruining a white canvas. Archie closed his eyes and more silent tears trickled down his cheeks. That was supposed to have been him. He was supposed to be with Olivia.

Archie thought back to the first evening, he met her in the grassy field. She was beautiful, the most beautiful girl in the whole world. She was to be his forever. And now, she was probably another man's forever. She was another man's wife. She was no longer Archie's. Archie was no longer in her life. The depression swept through Archie's entire body and shivers began to run up and down his spine. Archie could not stand it anymore; all he wanted to do was die. He could care less what happened to him.

Let the British hang me as a pirate, let them, Archie thought in despair. It would put him out of his misery and allow Olivia to live her life in peace without his presence.

Archie wiped away the salty tears from his cheeks as he curled up as best he could on the ground feeling extremely alone and tired. Archie fell into a deep sleep as the sadness consumed his weary mind.

• 24 •

Archie was marched along with the other d'Or pirates out of the cells and out into the main square where a hangman's noose had been set and prepared. As Archie slowly step toward his death, he noticed the large crowd that had already gathered. They were jeering and cursing at Archie and the other pirates. Some people hurled miscellaneous objects and stones at the pirates. The people did not throw to kill, however, because they were blood-thirsty to see the hangings. A pirate's death by hanging was the most entertaining event a man or woman might ever personally witness.

On a platform directly across from the noose, stood Governor Raymond, Isabel, Mrs. Raymond, the executioner, and British Commodore Benedict Chapman. In Commodore Chapman's hand were several sheets of paper waiting to be read—the death sentences for each pirate.

The executioner made his way down the platform and across to the hangman's platform. He stood diligently at the noose checking the knot and making the final preparations. Archie was last in the long line of pirates, as he stared at the noose, he felt a sense of fear. The human instinct of survival began to accelerate his heart rate and sweat formed upon his brow. He could not die. How could he allow his life to end like this? He was furious with himself for permitting his confidence and self-value to plummet so far to the point of apathy.

The fear had kicked his mind into hyper drive. Archie's mind raced to find solutions to save his life. He looked up toward the Governor and Isabel standing solemnly on the platform. He could plead his case to them of course; but, he needed a backup plan on the off chance the Governor had little tolerance or did not believe his story.

Archie looked around quickly looking for escape routes if he got the chance to make a dash for it. However, there was no escape. The square was full of people and curious faces encircled the main square and all the pirates. The chains around Archie's hands and feet were locked tight and his mobility was limited. The only chance he had was to play on Isabel's heart strings and hope she swooned to the tune he played.

The first pirate was led up the hangman's platform and the crowd erupted in cheers and jeers. His name was read aloud by the Commodore.

"Franz Goul, as known as Le Tigre, you have been sentenced to death by the Royal British Crown. As it is my obligatory duty to judge men of their crimes, I find you guilty on the charges of murder, piracy, kidnapping, arson, rape, and robbery. For these crimes, you shall be hanged by the neck until you are dead. As is customary, do you have any last words?"

Franz gave a cold, icy look toward the Commodore. He spat on the ground and yelled in English for all present to understand, "d'Or until death."

The crowd angrily booed and screamed obscenities at Franz.

Over all the yelling, the Commodore projected his voice as loud as possible, "Before God and before man, you are condemned to death."

The Commodore made eye contact with the executioner and nodded. The executioner nodded back and pulled the lever. Franz fell sharply as the platform opened up underneath him. His neck snapped as the rope tightened and jerked him upward. Franz hung motionless. The crowd applauded and cheered. The noise was overwhelming and the mob-like mentality of the crowd was infectious. It spread to everyone: man, woman, and child. Everyone wanted to see more death; they wanted to see another hanging. The noise and jeers only became louder with each pirate that was led to the hangman's noose.

Every pirate before they were hanged said the same last words, "d'Or until death." As the line of men in front of Archie became shorter and shorter, he began to wonder where Captain Montre was. Would he not have been one of the first pirates to be hanged?

Archie was next in line for the noose. Twenty-six pirates had fallen to their death. He was the last "pirate" standing, number twenty-seven. The executioner prepared the noose and a soldier forcefully grabbed Archie and led him up the platform to the awaiting Grim Reaper. Archie began to panic.

The sun had risen quickly over the last two hours and it was beating down on the square. The square was brimming with people, but many people had retreated to find shade and protection from the burning sun.

Archie shuffled his feet back and forth as the soldier placed him in front of the noose. The executioner slipped the noose around Archie's neck and tightened it. Archie swallowed hard as the prickly hemp rope scratched his skin and constricted his throat. Archie felt an icy chill sweep across his body as the Grim Reaper placed his bony, emotionless hands upon Archie's shoulders, ready to usher Archie to the afterlife. His heart was beating as fast as it ever had. His palms were clammy and sweaty. His throat was dry and his forehead was drenched in a cold sweat.

As the executioner went through his routine and the Commodore pondered over the last piece of paper in his hand, Archie was looking directly at Isabel trying to make eye contact with her. He needed Isabel to notice him before it was too late.

The Commodore looked up from his paper and grimaced at Archie in disgust.

Archie must have looked like a man who had been to hell and back. His clothes were in tatters and bloodied. His hair was unkempt and straggly, his beard was fully-grown and he smelled like a pigpen. The crowd and people gathered did not seem to mind because the last, repulsive pirate was going to be a dead man soon enough, so it didn't matter what he looked or smelled like. As Commodore Chapman began to speak, the riotous crowd quieted down, as no one wanted to miss the last portion of the day's entertainment.

"Now," began the Commodore looking at the disheveled, wounded, unshaven man standing before him, "Explain to me who you are and how a British man became a pirate for the infamous d'Or crew? It was my understanding the d'Or only allowed French blood to join their ranks; but obviously, I stand corrected."

Before Archie could respond, Isabel gasped loudly. Then stammered, "Oh…oh my heavens. Ar…Archie? Is that you?"

All eyes fell upon Isabel as her outburst resounded across the square.

Finally, thought Archie.

He and Isabel had been staring eye to eye for the last minute or so and he was becoming frantic that she would never identify him. It took her longer than he expected to recognize his blue eyes, the same ones she had fallen for three years earlier.

Archie twisted his neck around trying to get the noose off his throat so that he could talk, "Yes," he croaked, "it's me Isabel, Archie."

"Archie," Isabel said relieved, "I thought you were dead."

Whispers and murmurs began to sweep through the crowd as they realized Isabel knew this pirate personally.

"Isabel," the Governor commanded, "please remember your place. Archie is on trial and obviously has some serious explaining to do. He has the mark of the d'Or upon his arm. He is a pirate, and will judged as guilty until proven innocent. No prisoner is inked with the d'Or tattoo."

"Father, you must not think that. You know Archie was a captive, you read his letter."

"I'll only tell you once more. Remember your place in this affair."

Isabel closed her mouth obediently and sat silently.

"Archie," continued the Governor addressing him directly, "Commodore Chapman asked some poignant questions that I would also like to know the answers to."

"Sir," Archie maneuvered his neck around again to loosen the noose a tad, "do you mind removing the noose so I plead my case?"

"Commodore," the Governor turned toward the military man.

The Commodore motioned his right hand upwards absentmindedly as he stared at Archie trying to assess the new situation. The executioner removed the noose from around Archie's neck.

"Proceed Archie," indicated the Governor.

"Short story or long story?" Archie jested anxiously, but the joke missed the mark.

Governor Raymond said sternly, "Remember you are guilty of piracy. I hardly think this is the time for quips."

Archie stood center-stage in the most dramatic hanging Port Nassau had ever witnessed. The crowd had never seen a man receive a chance to save his own life. Most of the convicted pirates accepted their fate and were hanged without so much drama. The crowd was as silent as a coconut falling into the sand, and only the seagulls in the distance could be heard. The crowd was intent on catching every word that seeped out of the convicted man's mouth.

"I was captured about two years ago," started Archie. "Then Thomas and Captain Jasper were captured by Captain Rémi Montre and his crew while they were trying to rescue me. Captain Montre killed Captain Jasper and then he forced me shoot and kill Thomas to save my life. If I had not, he would have killed Thomas and I regardless. Afterwards, Captain Montre initiated me into the d'Or crew and held me under his command as his British sugar merchant and plantation owner. The sugar profits went to him and his pirates as he continued his expansion in the British colonies using me as his puppet. He was intending to expand his influence over the British territories so that he could rule and pirate the Caribbean waters with impunity. Captain Montre is the one who financed the sugar plantations in Port Royal and Port Nassau. He gave me a new identity to use as to not attract any attention while I ran his sugar plantations. I was a captive in his master plan."

Archie paused not knowing whether or not he should reveal his identity as Mr. Smith. The mob surrounding him might lash out and kill him themselves if he revealed the alias; so Archie concluded that it would be wise to bite his tongue. He paused momentarily and allowed his story to sink in. He watched as the Governor and Commodore looked at each other and exchanged words he could not hear.

Before either of the superior figures could speak, Archie continued, "During the last two years, I was watched at all times by two d'Or pirates to make sure I didn't flee or double cross Captain Montre. My only goal was to survive and I did whatever I had to in order to see the next sunrise."

The Commodore did not seem to buy Archie's story as he stared back at Archie with his icy, stone, cold eyes.

The Governor spoke first, "Remarkably, Captain Montre vanished during the fight. We could not find him or his dead body. Somehow, someway, he escaped. We initiated a vicious manhunt, but our soldiers believe him to be dead and multiple accounts state that his body was last seen sinking to the bottom of the sea. Thus, he cannot confirm or deny your story."

The Commodore immediately followed, "If I might add, you must have been pretty content working with a villain such as Mr. Montre for two years. You had status, money, women, and probably a better life than most men will ever attain. Why should we believe you? Plus," added the Commodore, "You are going to tell us you never have a chance to kill the Captain yourself and flee. Certainly, over two years time, there was a moment when you could have escaped?"

"Commodore," implored Archie, "you must recognize we are talking about Captain Montre—the smartest, most savvy pirate in the West Indies. I was not going to try to out maneuver the man."

Of course this was a lie, as Archie had out maneuvered Captain Montre when it counted, but he needed any and all sympathy to save his life.

Archie proceeded, "Captain Montre knew three moves ahead what was going to happen. I am simply a merchant's apprentice from the small town of Brighton. I ended up in this situation after a string of unfortunate events fell upon me. I wanted to make it home. I wanted to survive. I was a prisoner who Captain Montre used as leverage to increase his coffers and his power."

"Commodore, may I have a word with you?" the Governor said as he glanced over toward the bloodthirsty officer.

Turning away from Archie without saying a word, the two gentlemen retreated to an alcove away from the crowd and far away from earshot.

The crowd was stunned and they began to murmur restlessly. Had the pirate done it? Was he truly innocent? Were they about to let this pirate go free?

One man in the crowd hollered out, "Hang 'im. All pirates ought to be hanged by the neck. Hang 'im!"

Similar sentiments rumbled throughout the crowd, as they slowly began building into the mob-like, volatile group they were before.

"Hang 'im! Hang 'im!" the crowd chanted.

The yelling behind Archie grew. He fleetingly peeked over his shoulder at the tumultuous horde. If the noose did not kill him, then the mob would surely bury him if he was released. They seemingly did not want a pirate alive in their city. Archie closed his eyes as sweat dripped down his brow. He began to say Olivia's poem in his head, as he awaited his sentence:

You have troubles and pain
That will be cleansed with the rain.
You are mighty and strong
And will conquer fear all day long.
It's you and me
Sitting by the sea.

The conversation between the Commodore and the Governor seemed to be taking an eternity.

For you, my King of Hearts,
So what we have never parts.

"Archie," Governor Raymond said now that he was back on the platform in front of the noose.

Archie's eyes remained closed as he tried to savor his last moment before this final sentence, which would determine his fate.

"Archie," repeated the Governor louder.

Archie took a deep breath in, opened his eyes, and looked directly at the Governor. Archie noticed that the Commodore had not returned with the Governor to the raised platform.

"By the power vested in me by the Royal British Crown, I pardon you of the charges against you: murder, piracy, collusion, and treason. You'll have a clean slate from this day forth; however, this pardon carries with it one condition."

The Governor paused for dramatic effect and took his daughter's hand. Isabel stood up and looked at her father inquiringly.

"You must marry my daughter, Isabel, as she is in need of a fine husband, and the Raymond family is in need of an heir."

Archie let out a sigh of relief. He had done it. He had survived. How many times would his life hang in the balance? He had survived Captain Montre and now he had survived the noose and Grim Reaper.

The crowd all around the hangman's noose erupted in

confusion. Some jeered and called the Governor a traitor; others clapped trying to stay loyal to the Governor's curious proclamation.

"Do you accept the terms of the pardon?" asked the Governor in a softer more personable tone than before.

What choice did Archie have? Did he want to marry Isabel? When the choice is between the noose and Isabel, Isabel wins every time.

"I do," Archie said exhausted.

He looked into Isabel's eyes as she beamed at him.

"Thank you," he mouthed to Isabel as two soldiers grabbed his arms and led him down from the hangman's noose.

Archie and the two soldiers slowly navigated their way through the confused and rowdy crowd. Archie was taken to a private room within the fort, where the chains around his ankles and wrists were removed. Archie massaged his wrists as the two soldiers left the room and shut the door behind them. Archie walked over to the window and looked out over the bustling Port of Nassau below. The adventure, Archie thought, I will be able to tell my father and mother if I ever make it home. They will never believe me.

For the first time in a long time, Archie was able to breathe as a free man. He enjoyed and savored the moment. The sun seemed to shine brighter and the ocean seemed to be a limitless expanse of opportunity once again. The palm trees swayed peacefully in the sea breeze and hope filled Archie's spirit.

Archie began to recount all the events that had happened in the last few days. He was to marry Isabel Raymond, Captain Montre was supposedly dead after the failed assault on Port Nassau, the entire d'Or crew was dead and most importantly as he removed the parchment from the pocket of his trousers, and he could send his final letter to Olivia.

The next phase of his plan would commence. He had not fully developed this next section of his plan because of the many unknown directions the battle of Port Nassau could have taken. Fortunately, since Archie had survived, it was an appropriate time to scheme a way to make it home—his escape from the Caribbean and back to Olivia.

However, as he continued to stare out the window, one thought kept lingering in his head: Captain Montre and his crew are gone. The Queen's Jewels are up for the taking. No one in Saint-Domingue would know about the collapse of d'Or yet.

The Queen's Jewels naturally reminded him of Thomas' debt with Le Saphir. Archie mentally brushed her aside. She was a minor problem, nothing the Great Archie could not handle and overcome. If he could acquire the Queen's Jewels and Captain Montre's treasure and add it to the small fortune he had made selling the Port Royal assets....

Archie's thoughts were interrupted when Governor Raymond entered the room. Behind him entered a bald, shorter man with measuring tape, chalk, and clothes over his shoulders.

"Archie, this is my personal tailor, Bennett, and he will fit you with some new clothes that will replace those," the Governor paused as he searched for the right description, "hideous rags you are currently wearing. I am returning to the mansion, and please join us for dinner this evening once you have finished with my tailor, showered, and have had a chance to clean up."

"Yes Sir. And about today, how can I ever thank you for my life?"

"Provide me with a grandson." Governor Raymond winked at Archie and left.

Bennett went to work, took Archie's measurements, and chalked and pinned the clothing accordingly.

"I will be back this afternoon with your suit, Mr. Rose," Bennett said as he left the room.

Archie thanked him, showered, and took a much needed nap. Bennett returned later that afternoon with Archie's fitted suit, which was the latest fashion and style from London. Archie smiled as he looked at himself in the mirror. He looked smart, very smart indeed. Archie's confidence had returned; he felt invincible, like he could take on any challenge and succeed. Nothing was impossible. He had championed Death itself.

Archie walked to the carriage that would take him to the Governor's mansion and told the driver, "Take me to the nearest Royal Post, then we shall head to the mansion."

"Right away Sir," responded the driver respectfully and he whipped the horses into a trot.

Archie looked at the letter to Olivia one last time and decided to add a postscript. He reread the final love letter and poem. Archie kissed the letter, sealed it, and handed it to the Postman. He would have to escape the Caribbean soon, because he would not allow himself to break another promise to Olivia again.

"On to the mansion, good driver," Archie stated as he clambered back into the carriage.

"Rightchu are, Mr. Rose."

The carriage bounced up the stone road to Archie's new home, his new life, and soon-to-be wife. Archie looked out the carriage window as the red, orange, pink, and yellow sunset sky created a majestic end to the day. He sat silently and enjoyed God's evening painting. As he rode along the palm tree decorated path, coconuts hung high in the trees and Archie smiled fondly at them.

Port Nassau's sunset and evening breeze gently swept over Archie as he closed his eyes and thought to himself: From an apprentice to a merchant, to a pirate then to a prisoner condemned to hang by the neck, and now to a liberated man about to marry the Governor's daughter. The last four and a half years had felt like a lifetime of adventure squeezed altogether.

The carriage pulled up to the front doors of the mansion and Archie slowly stepped out. Archie strode up the steps and as he entered the mansion, he experienced déjà vu. He looked up as Isabel came flowing down in an elegant, green-blue dress with white lace decorating the cuffs and edges. He inspected the entryway, glancing to the left and right, and looked upon the same pictures, busts, and vases he had done three years previously. Nothing here had changed, and yet, so much had changed.

Archie turned his attention to Isabel, as she floated across the marble floor to him. Without a second's hesitation, Isabel pressed her body against his, stood on her tiptoes, and softly kissed Archie on the lips.

"Hi Archie," she said warmly.

She looked stunning and smelled of lavender. The intoxicating warmth of Isabel's lips made Archie feel fuzzy inside. Archie looked deeply into Isabel's eyes and thought to himself: I must stay focused.

• 25 •

Olivia placed the lemon, poppy seed muffins on a decorative plate, took off her apron, and made her way over to the table where she had placed Archie's letter. Her hand quivered as she pulled and unfolded the wax sealed parchment. Olivia's eyes glided across the lines:

My love, my Olivia,

This might be the last time I get to write you. I have survived many trying and dangerous events, too many to recount on this piece of parchment. I will tell you all my stories if I survive and make it back to you. I am writing this because today I may die at the hands of pirates and wanted to let you know how I feel about you. I love you. Always have. I have missed you ever so dearly. I am sorry I never made it back to you sooner, but pirates captured me.

I have not gone a day without trying to devise a plan to get back to you. I understand if you have a family and could not wait for me. I just wanted you to know, you always had my heart. Here is my poem that I have written for you, since I might not get to tell you in person.

Sails of Your Heart

For you, who falls asleep first,
Let your dreams burst.
Let your imagination flow.
And let the winds blow
The sails of your heart in whichever
Direction they may go.

They may take you far and wide,
Or near and dear.
Wherever your dreams may take you by night,
Just remember me,
The brightest star, second on the right.

For you, my Queen of Hearts,
So what we have never parts.

With all the love I have,
Archie

P.S. I survived the Battle of Port Nassau, where the insurmountable odds had been stacked against me. Before the year's end, I plan to return to Brighton. I know I promised this years ago, but I intend to sail in autumn on the first ship to England. I intend to see you soon, my love. I will write again as soon as it is feasible. I have so much to tell you, if I tried to write it all down it would require an epic to document.

By the end of the letter, she had tears forming in the corners of her eyes. Archie loved her just as much as the day he left. She wiped away her tears and she stood up and took the letter to her jewelry box. She placed the letter away, so that James would not find it. It would be her little secret she shared with Archie.

She did not really believe Archie was going to return home after all this time, plus she could not permit her hopes to rise only to come crashing down, like the last time Archie had made such a claim and heart-felt promise. For Olivia, she found it more comforting to know that the man she loved still loved her back. She picked up baby Charles and kissed his forehead.

Olivia could stand on her own two feet and live the life she had chosen. She could handle James and the obstacles that lay ahead. Olivia was content believing that Archie and her would share a love than no one else could take away from them and Archie's letter solidified that eternal bond.

James Towns was her husband, but he did not bring her nearly as much joy and happiness as Archie had in those young, summer days and winter eves back in Brighton. Olivia thought to herself, Archie was her first and only true love; and if there was ever a day when they could spend their lives together, she would let it happen.

———

James came home from work late on Monday evening from his scouting trip to Oxford and did not inquire about Olivia's weekend. He had stopped drinking, but his relationship with Olivia had become secondary to his work. His work had become an obsession and his new love. Olivia was not obsolete, but she certainly was not a priority in his life. Olivia was saddened by the lack of affection and love from her husband; yet, she had to admit it was much better than the drunken rants and beatings.

As the summer of 1672 marched on, the days came and went without much consequence. The relationship between James and Olivia mundanely flowed without emotion or passion. Charles took up the majority of Olivia's time; while, Mr. Marsh and the expansion took all of James' time and attention. Olivia and James started to become independent of each other both physically and emotionally. Olivia still relied on James financially, and James of course, relied on Olivia to raise their son. When James did have the chance to be at home, he loved to spend time with his son—his blood.

He wanted Charles to grow up to be handsome and strong; he wanted the best and the world for his son. He allowed Olivia all the freedom she wanted to raise him, because he knew she would do an amazing job. She was a natural caretaker, a natural mother.

James recognized his flaws as a husband and father. He would never ask for forgiveness or acknowledge his flaws openly, because his ego was too great. Admitting to any problem outwardly would be devastating to his self-confidence and manhood. His pride would never allow himself to be humbled by asking for someone's forgiveness.

James' stubbornness and vanity lodged a wedge between him and Olivia that he willingly ignored; but, Olivia was overcome by loneliness and craved emotional attachment. To fill the widening void, she frequently reread Archie's letter on evenings when James was out of town on business.

She found comfort in Archie's tender and loving poem. The letter warmed her heart. She longingly wished to nestle her head in Archie's chest, as he wrapped his arms around her and held her tightly, gently squeezing her, bringing her ever closer to him. Archie would never let go. She looked out of the window onto the street full of the August sunshine and whispered, "Come back my King of Hearts."

• 26 •

Port Royal's bells rang loudly and clearly slicing through the midmorning silence alerting everyone in the Port of the celebration about to take place. However, the bells were merely a formality because no soul had forgotten about the event. How could a person in their right mind forget the wedding day of a pirate and the Governor's only daughter? The union of such a couple would be legendary. The story would live on and be retold long after Archie and Isabel were dead. With each retelling, the tale would gain new twists and turns. It would only be a matter of time before the wedding became a permanent fable in the West Indies' history.

The May, morning sun shone warmly against Isabel's beautiful face. The woman was truly a sight to behold. Her tanned skin and green eyes stood out against the stark white, elegant, wedding dress. Isabel held onto her father's arm as he slowly and joyously guided her down the numerous rows of chairs lining the path to the aisle. As the music played on, people stood to look upon the bride and the Governor. The congregation smiled as they stared, for they all knew,

Isabel was the happiness woman in the New World.

Archie stood next to the pastor at the altar. His gaze fell upon Isabel and the Governor as they proceeded toward him. His heart skipped a beat as Isabel and Archie made eye contact. He knew that one day he would break her heart, and he despised himself for it. But what choice did he have? His heart already belonged to someone else.

Governor Raymond released his daughter's hand, and she took her place beside Archie. A hush swept through the crowd and the music rolled into silence.

The pastor bellowed to the congregation, "I have the privilege, on this glorious May morn, to wed an extraordinary woman, to a…" the pastor paused looking for the right word, "a unique man."

Archie smiled inwardly, "unique" was much kinder than he was expecting. The city of Port Nassau had respected the Governor's wishes to allow Archie to be reinstated as a full, British citizen. All charges against him were dropped, but of course, more than half of the Port's individuals, families, and shop owners disagreed with the Governor's pardon and frequently let Archie know they would never forget his crimes. Archie became accustomed to not being permitted to enter certain shops, taverns, and other establishments. Some vendors and storekeepers would also not allow him to buy their items and wares. Archie was an outcast; albeit, he did not mind because he was a free and alive outcast.

The pastor continued with the ceremony, "Sweetest Isabel, do you take this man, Archie Rose, to be your husband as evidenced by man and by God?"

"I do," replied Isabel as she shot Archie a sweet, fleeting glance.

Turning to Archie the pastor said, "And do you, Sir, accept the responsibility, courage, and sacrifice it will take to be a loyal and faithful husband, spouse, and father for this woman?"

"I do," Archie responded and as the lie slithered out of Archie's mouth. Guilt immediately flooded his veins and he could feel the poison grip at his heart.

"I am happy to have the honor to pronounce you husband and wife," the pastor proclaimed to the silent congregation.

Archie pivoted toward Isabel and lifted her veil from her face. Tears of joy were rolling down her cheeks, yet she was smiling brightly. He bent down and kissed her, and as he did so, the congregation erupted in applause and whoops and hollers. The cheering was exuberant and the musicians, who were also applauding, stopped clapping suddenly, realizing they had missed their queue to start the music. The musicians immediately took up their instruments and added their glorious tunes to the jubilant atmosphere.

Archie and Isabel walked down the aisle hand in hand and waved to family and friends. Isabel was the envy of all the young women in the congregation, and Archie was most certainly on the death list of every bachelor in attendance.

The newlyweds strode to the carriage that whisked them away to the banquet hall at the Governor's mansion where their wedding party would take place for the remainder of the day and last late into the evening. The party would be the biggest the Port had seen since Governor Raymond took office many years ago.

The party was full of life, laughter and the wine was freely flowing. Archie casually sipped glass after glass as he watched the entertainment and enjoyed the festivities, quietly sitting in his chair at the center of the table. Isabel was being fawned over by every single girl and young woman at the party, and she could not resist being in the center of the spotlight.

Isabel, late in the evening after they had eaten, grabbed Archie's hand.

Archie, who now was drunk and slow to react, turned his head and said as coherently as possible, "What's it you desire my lovely wife?"

"You're drunk," Isabel giggled and she kissed him on the cheek. "Won't you sober up, so that we may dance?"

"Certainly," Archie replied and leaned over and pecked his wife on the cheek too.

She smiled warmly at him, tipsy herself, as she placed a glass of water in front of Archie.

Archie observed the party and guests dancing on the floor in front of him as he sipped the water. He felt stuck and out of control. How was he ever to get back to England and Olivia now? The thoughts running through his head swung wildly from one extreme to the other. He would remain in the Caribbean for the rest of his life married to Isabel, raise a family, and die. This seemed to be a reasonable and plausible outcome of his life. Another option was to run away, which would cause him to be a wanted man in both the British colonies and the French-d'Or influenced colonies. Running away seemed to lead only to a long life of always looking over his shoulder. In addition, as a marked pirate and the husband of Isabel, it was unlikely Archie would ever go anywhere in Port Royal or the Caribbean without being recognized or noticed. He had created quite a name for himself. Archie continued to scheme as his dazed mind and tingling body fought against him.

Before he knew it, he was sidestepping and dancing with Isabel, then another woman, then back with Isabel. Archie's mind went in and out, time seemed to be speeding past at light speed.

Finally when his mind checked back in, he saw he was dancing with Isabel again. She smiled kindly back up at him in a goofy, cute way. Archie did not really think about what he was doing, but the moment seemed right. He leaned close to his wife's ear and sucked gently on her earlobe. Isabel shuddered as the sexual sensation ran down her neck and into her spine.

Archie whispered into her ear, "We should go somewhere. Just you and I."

He was craving Isabel's beautiful body and his mind was singularly focused. The alcohol had worked its effect and he was unable to process anything but primal instincts. Archie looked deeply into Isabel's eyes as his mind began undressing her on the dance floor.

Isabel excitedly whispered back, "Where should we go?"

"Wherever you'd like," Archie responded dumbly not taking

command of the situation.

"How about Europe? I've never been. Will you take me to Europe?"

Archie blinked twice. Her response did not immediately sink in. He quietly retorted confused, "Europe, but that's so far. How could we make it there tonight?"

"Not tonight silly," Isabel smiled. "I meant will you take me to Europe one day?"

Absent-mindedly Archie responded, "Sure Isabel, I'll take you there."

Isabel nestled her head into Archie's chest as she wrapped her arms around his waist. Archie looked around the dance floor, as couples spun around them. Trying to get his bearings, he searched for an escape route from the dance floor. Archie spotted an opening and did not waste another second. He took Isabel's hand and led her swiftly through the crowd and out of the banquet hall.

Once in the hallway, he pushed Isabel up against a wall and kissed her passionately. Isabel reciprocated and returned his kiss and the two of them were locked together in a hungry embrace. The newlyweds found their way to the stairs and took two steps at a time as they made their way to Isabel's bedroom. Once they had both entered, Archie quietly shut the door and turned his full attention to his stunning wife.

Isabel deliberately unlaced her white dress. She moved with a purposeful sensuality. Archie's eyes were fixed on her every movement. The white dress fell to the floor exposing the matching white chemise, corset, stockings, and underwear. Archie assisted her to undo the corset that was tied tightly against her body. The corset fell to the ground. The sensuous body that stood before Archie made him swoon. He could not get his clothes off fast enough. Isabel placed her index finger against his lips and Archie stopped completely. The couple remained silent for a moment looking deep into each other's eyes. Archie's blue eyes and Isabel's remarkable emerald eyes locked together building the sexual tension.

Isabel slid off Archie's shirt and Archie removed his trousers. The two began kissing and made their way blindly to the soft, warm bed. The sheets caressed both of their naked bodies as they made love for the first time. Archie nibbled tenderly on Isabel's neck, and Isabel's finger nails scratched Archie's back. Their tongues danced around each other and the ecstasy was exceptionally satisfying. Sensations, passion, and lust consumed both of them in the darkness.

When they had finished making love, Isabel shimmied and snuggled up against Archie. He rolled over and kissed the top of Isabel's head, and closing his eyes fell into a deep slumber.

Archie awoke the following morning with a splitting headache. He peered out of one eye as he observed the room. His clothes were in a pile on the floor as were Isabel's. He rotated his body, but Isabel was not lying in bed next to him. He gently rested his head back on the soft, caressing pillow and massaged his temples. What exactly happened last night? He remembered only bits and pieces. As he continued to lay motionless, Isabel entered the room and sat on the bed next to him.

"Good morning," she said cheerily, obviously not suffering the same negative effects of drinking excessive wine.

"Morning," croaked Archie, his mouth feeling like it was stuffed with cotton wool. "Breakfast is ready downstairs when you are."

"I'd love some food. Beans and toast?"

"Yes."

"Sausage and eggs?"

"Yes, that too."

"Orange juice?" prayed Archie.

Isabel smiled and kissed Archie on the lips. She crawled on top of him and rested her head on his chest.

Christ, thought Archie, I am going to break Isabel's heart.

As the couple lay on the bed enjoying the warmth the sun was casting through the window, Archie could not help but feel pangs of guilt and remorse. His black heart felt like it was being ripped into two pieces. He had consummated the marriage with Isabel, but loved Olivia. Lied to Isabel about his love for her; nevertheless, pretending to love her anyway so that he could one day leave her to marry Olivia. He had broken promises to Olivia but still promised he would return to her. He head was pounding against his skull. Archie's feverish desire to return to Olivia had cost Archie his clean conscience. It was stained, spoiled, and marked with sin, sorrow, and shame.

Isabel whispered something.

"What was that my darling?" Archie asked.

"I said I cannot wait for our trip. I've been dreaming about it all morning."

"What trip?" inquired Archie. "I love trips."

"You don't remember?" Isabel's voice rose abruptly, slightly taken aback.

Archie's mind went immediately into his short-term memory banks trying desperately not to say the wrong thing. He began rummaging through all the fragments of memory he had from the previous evening and all the conversations he could recall.

He weakly responded, "Yes...yes, I mean, no. No, I haven't forgot about our trip. I was only jesting."

His answer seemed to suffice for the time being, because Isabel slowly rose from the bed and joked, "Alright mister, I'm not going to let you lie around all day. Let's go get breakfast."

Archie forced a smile, "Ok, I will be right there. You go. I'm going to bathe quickly."

He would have gladly remained in bed all day and slept.

Isabel left and Archie reluctantly started his day. He bathed and joined Governor Raymond, Mrs. Raymond, and Isabel at the breakfast table.

"Good day, Arch," Governor Raymond peppered at Archie, louder than necessary.

"Morning, Governor."

"You have a good time last night? I'd say it was splendid. People did not leave until the wee hours of the morning."

"Yes Sir. It was quite the wedding celebration. Thank you."

"No need to thank me. I would not have wanted to send my daughter off in any other fashion," responded the Governor as he returned to his breakfast and the morning missives lying around his plate.

"Good morning, madam," Archie said bowing to Mrs. Raymond.

"There is no need to bow Archie. You're family now. I'm certainly glad you had a pleasant time yesterday. Isabel was telling us about the trip you both plan to take. It sounds utterly exciting. I haven't been back in ages; well that is since we moved out to Port Royal so he," she nodded in the Governor's direction, "could take over as Governor."

"Yes," Archie replied, "I'm quite speechless about the trip myself."

Isabel chirped in, "I was just telling mother there are two parts I am looking forward to most: one, I cannot wait to see the shops in London, and two, the chance to visit your home in Brighton."

The words hit Archie in the chest like a cannonball and nearly knocked him out of his chair. He stared at Isabel in disbelief. Was she talking about a trip to England? Surely, it was too good to be true.

Mrs. Raymond looked at her daughter fondly, "You will bring me back something, maybe a dress or some jewelry. It takes forever to receive anything if you send for it from here. By the time the dress arrives, it will already be out of style in London."

"I'll buy something that will make you look glamorous, mother."

"Thank you darling."

Archie's mind was processing the new information. He was headed to England, or at least that seemed to be in the cards. He was actually going back. He was not going to question the trip or ask how it came about. Obviously, he must have brought it up or suggested it last night, or maybe Isabel initiated the trip. Archie shook his head, it did not really matter. He took a sip of orange juice as he sat passively next to Isabel and Mrs. Raymond as they continued to chat away. In the end all that mattered was the destination, which thank the good Lord was England.

A month after the wedding, Isabel and Archie had finalized their honeymoon plans to Europe. The couple would embark on a two-month trip to Europe and then return to Port Nassau. They would leave on the 1st of September 1672 and tentatively return in December, preferably before Christmas.

Archie looked at the map of Europe and traced their journey with his finger. They were to land in England and immediately spend the first week in Brighton, before returning to London for three weeks. Archie's mother and father would have the privilege of meeting Isabel and hear about Archie's adventure and his survival against all odds in the d'Or crew. After the four weeks in England, the honeymoon would continue to Paris for three weeks, before returning to London for the last couple of weeks. The couple would then find a ship returning to Port Nassau and they would make the journey to Archie's new home—the Caribbean.

Archie studied the map looking for a clear answer and plan to try and never returned to the Caribbean. Those first four weeks in Brighton and London were going to be crucial. He was going to have to find and make contact with Olivia, if he was ever going to have a chance to be with her.

If Olivia loved him, as much as he loved her; then, in Archie's mind, there was no chance he would ever return to the Caribbean with Isabel. He would rather be hanged by the neck for treason. Archie would rather die than falsely pretend to love Isabel any longer. It was exhausting and he knew he was a horrible sinner for falsely pretending to love Isabel. God would certainly send Archie to Hell for what he had done with Isabel's heart and her love. She loved him, and he was abusing her kindness, love, and loyalty. God would not have mercy on

Archie's soul come judgment day.

He did like Isabel however; there was no question about it. She was loyal, affectionate, beautiful, compassionate, and thoughtful. Any man would be lucky to have her as their caring wife. Nonetheless, Archie had already found the woman he wanted to spend the rest of his days with, and she had captured his heart many years ago on that day when she was strolling across the green, grassy field.

Archie sighed and closed his eyes as he leaned over the map lying on the table thinking: Thomas, mate, you really put me through some gauntlet just to get this opportunity to return home to my woman.

That evening as Archie and Isabel snuggled in bed, he could not fall asleep because the warm, humid night air was keeping him awake. He glanced through the window and saw the bright, full moon rising timidly above the sea below. Archie felt this unquenchable desire to retrieve Captain Montre's treasure and the Queen's Jewels from Saint-Domingue.

After receiving his freedom, the Governor would not let Archie out of the mansion without an attendant or some valet always accompanying him. Archie had originally assumed that this is how the rich lived, always being doted on hand and foot. Unfortunately, he realized too late that the omnipresent valet was to ensure he did not try and escape. The Governor was keeping eyes on Archie at all times. Archie had to hand it to the Governor; he was a witty and sly man. Archie supposed any government official had tricks and cards up their sleeves and Governor Raymond was no different. Knowledge was power.

Archie patiently played the Governor's game and did not make any moves to try and recover the treasure secretly. This game of patience had cost Archie precise time. A month and a half had gone by until he had gained the Governor's trust and the attendant finally allowed Archie to take excursions to the docks and into town alone.

The moon rose and disappeared from the window's frame and out of Archie's sight. He lay motionless in the darkness and resolved himself to making a trip to capture Captain Montres' treasure and the jewels within the fortnight. He must do it before Isabel and he left for England, because he might never be back. He wanted desperately to be able to award Olivia the prized Queen's Jewels for her patience. It would be a symbol of his deep feelings for Olivia, his gift to her that no other man could ever give. Archie dreamed himself away into sleep: *For you, my Queen of Hearts, I will present thee with the Queen's Jewels.*

• 27 •

Archie smiled and waved from the deck of the small vessel as it disembarked on its voyage. Standing on the dock waving back stood Isabel and Governor Raymond unaware of Archie's true intentions and destination. Archie was on his way to Saint-Domingue to recover what was left of Captain Montre's loot and hopefully the Queen's Jewels. Naturally, he did not tell the Governor of his plan when he asked for the funds to charter a ship and hire crewmen. He fabricated a conceivable story that he would like to return to Port Royal to the Hollis Sugar mansion and retrieve any personal belongings that might still be there after he was taken hostage by Captain Montre and his crew of thugs. The Governor believed the story and allowed Archie to charter a ship.

Archie, after his years with the d'Or crew, knew exactly where to set the heading and sailed directly for Saint-Domingue. After only a few days, Archie slowly maneuvered the small vessel into an alcove tucked away from the main port and city. Archie planned to be in an out of the city within one night, but if it took him two nights, then so be it. It would be tricky as he was unsure of the stability of the city without the d'Or's omnipotent presence. A power struggle would have certainly formed and Archie was unaware of what the current situation was within the Port. His "d'Or" tattoo would no longer be a source of protection in the French territory.

"Give me forty-eight hours," commanded Archie. "Under no other circumstances should you leave or move the ship."

The last thing Archie would need is to be stranded in Saint-Domingue after coming so far to survive and be so close to returning to England.

"A'ighty, Sir," acknowledged Captain David nodding.

"Good. So here is the plan: I am going to enter the city at nightfall in that small rowboat. I will return within the forty-eight hours as I specified at which time, we will embark and head back to Port Nassau."

"And if forty-eight hours pass and you ain't back?" inquired Captain David.

"Come get me of course," chuckled Archie.

"Really?"

"No. You should definitely leave at first light after the second night. You can assume I've either been captured or killed and won't be able to make it back."

"Aye, and what should we tell da Guv'na? I mean, we ain't gone to Port Royal, and ye'd be missin'?"

Archie pondered for a moment trying to come up with an appropriate response. "Tell him I've died from a slave rebellion at the plantation in Port Royal. You can be as imaginative as you'd like."

The Captain nodded and shrugged his shoulders.

Archie did not waste any more time as the sun was beginning its descent below the black water. He climbed into the small rowboat and the crew lowered him into the water. Archie positioned the oars and began the silent journey to the edge of the port. He spotted a watchtower and waited patiently in the distance as the calm, ocean water lapped against the side of the rowboat. He waited until complete darkness had dispersed itself throughout the port and across the water. Only the dim, crescent moon lit Archie's way.

When the rowboat's bottom scrapped against the sandy shore, Archie hopped out into the knee-deep shallows and tied off the boat to a nearby palm tree. He heaved the small rowboat further onto the beach and assessed his surroundings. Not a soul to be seen. In the distance there were faint candles and lanterns burning in people's homes. Archie hastily strode down the beach ducking and dodging in between the palm trees until he found himself running along the cobblestone streets.

Archie gradually and cautiously made his way through the dark streets and alleyways trying to remember to the best of his ability where St. Peter's Church was located within the city. As he ran across a lantern-lit street to get to an adjacent alleyway, he spotted a woman in blue high heels and revealing blue dress. The prostitute did not notice him as she entered a tavern just a twenty paces away. Le Saphir! Archie recognized her immediately. He stopped and rechecked his surroundings to see if her two henchmen were close by. Holding his breath trying to remain as silent as possible, Archie strained his ears to catch the faintest of movements. Those two men were the last two people he wanted to run into on this island. He placed his hand on the pistol tucked into his holster, ready to be drawn and shot in a second. The moment passed. There were no movements or sounds around him. Archie turned away from the lit street and darted down the dark alleyway.

After an hour of strategically maneuvering in and out of the shadows, Archie finally heard it—a church bell ringing. He paused and listened intently trying to determine which direction the bells were coming from. He was close. He could tell by the loudness of the church bells. Awfully late for the priest to be ringing the church bells, pondered Archie. Was it a trap? Was someone trying to help him find the church? How could it possibly be a trap, no one knew he was in Saint-Domingue. The bells stopped and silence filled the void. Chills ran down Archie's neck as an eeriness and fear settled around him.

Archie confirmed his path to the once ringing church bells and slowly proceeded, hugging the walls of the shops. As he turned one last corner, he spotted the church. Behind it laid a graveyard, then a palm tree forest. St. Peter's Church stood alone at the end of the street. The vacant, French street leading up to it was as quiet as a monastery in prayer.

Archie remained in his hidden location and surveyed the church from a safe distance. He was not in any rush. Keeping a low profile was of the utmost priority. He had plenty of time until he had to be back at the ship. He continued to check up and down the street to make sure that no one was approaching or patrolling the streets.

As the crescent moon rose higher in the sky it spread a dim, white light across the church and Port below. Finally, Archie saw them. Two figures emerged from the church carrying a handful of bags over their shoulders. The figures were talking in low hushed tones. One of the black silhouettes pointed, then they both scurried across the courtyard and disappeared into the city's shadows. Archie cursed, what if those two goons had taken everything?

He could not wait any longer or there might be nothing left for him to bring back to England, and then this whole treasure hunt will have been futile. Archie initiated his approach toward the front gates of the churches courtyard. He bounded across the empty street and hopped over the waist high gate. He dashed across the church's courtyard and slid to a stop before the front door. Archie placed his hand on the door's handle and gently pushed. He winced as the door creaked loudly. Despite the door's continual groaning, he continued to push it ajar to the point where he could slip inside. Once inside the church, Archie shut the door behind him as quietly as possible.

Archie navigated his way blindly through the dark church, bumping into pews and more than once other objects. He stopped occasionally and listened to make sure there were no other footsteps or sounds from unwanted company. He finally found the side door, which would lead to the basement underneath the altar where the treasure and Queen's Jewels would still be hidden, if they had not been stolen by the previous intruders. He pushed on the wooden door, but it did not open. He tried again with a little more force, but again, the door rattled and remained closed. Archie vigorously pushed and shoved the door, but it did not budge. Archie ran his hands around the door in the blackness and felt a lock and the latch. Sure enough, it was locked. He removed his knife and started the nimble process of picking the lock.

An hour passed and Archie had not prevailed. The lock seemed determined to stop Archie in his mission. Archie, more than once, thought about taking his pistol and shooting the bolt off, but decided against it considering how much noise that would make. Also, he needed to save his bullets in case one of the thieves did return. Archie gallantly remained perseverant and continued his attempt to pick the lock. Finally, he heard a click and the lock popped opened.

At last, he thought to himself as he let out a sigh of relief. He removed the lock and the door swung freely open. He slowly descended the stairs. As Archie reached the bottom he could not see anything. The basement had no light source, which forced Archie to return to the church, where the moon's dim light provided some visual stimulation. He scanned the church for a candle or lantern. Archie's eyes fell on the altar. He walked over to the altar and picked up the candle and box of matches beside it. With the lit candle, he descended back down the stairs and into the basement.

As he stared into the basement's cavernous space, Archie's mouth dropped. Everything was gone, the lot of it. All of Captain Montre's chests were smashed and pieces of wood were littered across the floor. Archie tenderly stepped on the wooden shards and surveyed the mess. The candle shed light on the destruction and Archie bent down and rummaged through the rubble.

Archie spent the entire night in the basement clearing wood and searching for the special purple and gold chest that held the precious Queen's Jewels. He was certainly disappointed that the d'Or treasure and fortune was gone; but after considering it, he should not have been the least bit surprised. Any ambitious man would have been chomping at the bit to claim the d'Or treasure once they knew it was up for the taking.

As Archie knew, Captain Rémi Montre did not keep the Queen's Jewels in the same standard chests as the rest of his treasure, which encouraged Archie to spend the evening searching the massive basement. Archie slowly made progress across the room, getting weary of the tedious job and poor light the candle was providing him. In the silence, Archie heard a rooster making its morning call. Gradually, the first rays of sunlight began to drift down the stairwell and permeate the darkness.

As the sunlight spread across the room, Archie blew out the candle, which was nearly at the end of its life. He stood up and re-examined the room with the new light. He noticed something he had not seen in the darkness when he had first arrived—at the far end of the basement laid a body. Archie instinctively placed his hand on his gun and drew it. He cocked and pointed it at the body as he cautiously crept over to it. Archie looked down at the motionless body and holstered his pistol. Archie shook his head as he identified the dead man.

At Archie's feet lay the priest who had allowed Captain Montre to hide his treasure beneath his altar. Archie crouched down and checked the man's pulse. The body was cold, but there was no sign of decay. Those intruders must have killed him, Archie contemplated. Archie thought back to the church bells: had that been a signal that the priest was dead?

Archie was saddened that the priest had to die, but nevertheless, he could not be found in the presence of a dead French priest. The French authorities would certainly hang his British soul without a trial. As he stood, he saw something in the priest's robes that stopped him short. One of the robe's outer pockets had a crinkled missive sticking out of it. Archie removed the note, unfolded the tightly folded paper and read:

Francis, Secrecy is imperative. Here is the key to the Queen's box. Don't let either the box or the key out of your sight. Die defending it if you must.

Archie carefully removed the priest's outer robes, patting every inner pocket praying that he would find the key. Finally, Fortune smiled on him as his hand touched something small. He placed his hand inside the pocket and slowly withdrew a small brass key.

Archie reread the note. The Queen's Jewels must still be here. It must be. The priest had died defending the key and the Queen's Jewels. He began to run around the basement searching every nook and cranny. Archie checked in every spot imaginable. He looked through the shelves and bookcases; he looked behind the pictures and recklessly kicked wood out of the way to reveal what might lie underneath them.

Exhausted and with heavy eyes, Archie paused momentarily breathing heavily. Think, Archie, think, where is that purple and gold box? Then it came to him. Archie knew in a flash where the priest had hidden the Queen's Jewels. The box would not be in the basement that would be too simple. *Don't let the key or box out of your sight.* The hiding spot was so ingenious and clever. A place no one would look and Father Francis would always have his eyes upon it. Archie rushed up the stairs and straight to the altar. He cursorily made the sign of the cross and opened up the tabernacle.

Nestled beside the ciborium, sat the purple and gold jewelry box. Archie gingerly reached in and picked it up. He slipped the box into his jacket pocket along with the key. He closed the tabernacle and turned around to leave the church. To his horror, there at the entrance of the church stood two burly men.

Archie froze, startled to see the men's presence. Both men raised their guns and took aim. Archie ducked in the nick of time behind the altar. The bullets ricocheted off the altar. Archie peeked around the altar. He saw both men reloading their weapons as they started to approach the altar in stride. Archie cocked his gun and fired.

The bullet missed wide, but it momentarily stopped the men's approach. They took cover behind separate pillars. Archie fumbled to reload his gun. He needed to think quickly. A firefight was not his strength as he was low on ammunition, but he could hold his own if he was able to kill one of the two men with his next shot.

Archie repositioned himself and glanced down the church's nave. Two opposing gunshots rang out, both missed. Archie sprang up and took aim. He fired and watched as the bullet flew true and landed itself in the chest of one of his assailants. His body fell to the floor with a thud. Archie did not miss another moment as he sprinted down from the altar and slid behind a pew as another shot rang out from the remaining enemy.

Archie reloaded his pistol and glanced above the pew to spot his adversary's new location. The man however seemed to have vanished. Archie looked again and still could not find him. Cautiously, he took a longer look surveying the entire church. Then he spotted the man. The man had climbed the stairs in the back and was situated on the church's balcony next to the organ. Archie ducked as the man fired in Archie's direction. Archie took aim, however, before he could pull the trigger a woman's voice sent a chill down his spine.

"Archie, Archie. It's been longer than a week," Le Saphir said coldly. "We've waited patiently, but it's time for you to pay your debt."

From his hiding place Archie called out, "How'd you find me?"

"I have eyes everywhere you sweet thing. Finding you was not hard. Waiting all night to kill you was the hard part. Did you find it?"

"Find what?" Archie said angrily.

"The Jewels, of course."

"No."

"That is a shame. I've been here so many times looking for them myself. The priest would not tell a soul. Last night, we were finally able to move the last of the treasure, but the Jewels evaded us. I gave that priest a choice; sadly, he chose death. I guess the legend of those Jewels will live on. But if you had found them, I think we could have worked out some type of deal. You give me the Jewels, and well,

I could please you in any way you desire."

"I don't pay for pleasure, you murderous whore."

Le Saphir revealed herself from behind a curtain and called out, "I am a woman that has power. Does that scare you? That I have power over men. Men are weak. Men are simple minded, lustful idiots, who will forfeit love, money, and all they hold dear for sexual pleasure. I hold all the power over them and can make them bend and break at my will. Sex, Archie. Sex separates a weak woman, who gives pathetic men, like yourself, everything you desire for nothing in return. An independent woman, like me, who uses sex to increase her status, wealth, and position in life."

Archie remained silent strategizing his next move.

"Enough of playing this frivolous game of cat and mouse. Reveal yourself. I know you found the Jewels."

Archie peered above the pew. He saw Le Saphir gliding close to the church's entrance looking directly at him. She was dressed the same as she had been last night—the royal blue revealing dress and the blue high heels. He glanced up. Her remaining henchman had his finger on the trigger of his rifle pointing it at Archie. He was waiting for Le Saphir's command.

Archie crouched behind the pew and checked his pistol. He had one shot left. His chances at escaping alive were slim, but it was now or never. He took several deep breaths and slowed down his heart rate as he prepared himself for this finale. He closed his eyes. *Olivia, I am coming home.*

Archie opened his eyes with an electrified, confident energy. He jumped up suddenly, turned, and shot directly at the man on the balcony. He did not watch to see if the bullet made contact and instantly dashed across the church's floor toward the front door. The man on the balcony was caught off guard and Archie's bullet lodged itself in his shoulder. He hollered in pain and dropped his rifle.

Archie continued sprinting toward the front door. Le Saphir raised her pistol and fired it at Archie. The bullet barely missed as it whizzed past Archie shattering the stained glass window to Archie's left. Archie did not pause and kept his entire attention on slipping through the church's slightly open door. He barreled into the main door and busted it wide open as the sunlight stung his pupils. Through squinted eyes, he sprinted as fast as he could across the courtyard as he heard another shot ring out behind him. He jumped the church's fence in one leap.

The morning sun had woken up the city and people had filled the streets going about their daily activities. The sudden commotion and gunshots from the church caused people to stop what they were doing and watch as Archie hurtled away from a woman who was shooting at him. Le Saphir began to scream at the bystanders in French, while simultaneously pointing at Archie. The bystanders took action immediately and began to chase Archie yelling angrily at him. The chase was on.

As Archie sprinted down the street, he peered over his shoulder at the group hunting him. He was going to have to lose them before he could return to his rowboat. Archie took a sharp turn down an alleyway and headed toward the palm tree jungle. The group was gaining slightly on him. One young man had incredible pace and would certainly catch Archie if he did not evade him soon.

Archie plunged into the palm tree forest and began hopping over bushes and arbitrarily veering left and right through the foliage. He continued to sprint without any direction or heading in particular. He just ran to escape. He glanced over his shoulder again and then slid to a halt. He paused as he held his breath. Angry French voices could be heard, but he had lost them momentarily. He hid behind a tree as he watched the vicious group separate to continue their search in pairs. The pairs slowly dispersed themselves in different directions amongst the palm trees and disappeared from Archie's view.

Archie collapsed and sat in the sand resting his back against a tree. He exhaled deeply letting out a long breath and closed his eyes. He was so fatigued and weary. Archie could have easily fallen asleep, but he would not allow himself to do so.

He rested and waited until he felt enough time had elapsed to start to navigate his way back safely to the beach. Archie stood up and looked around. The jungle looked ubiquitous in all directions. He was completely lost. He knew vaguely the direction of the city, or at least he thought he did. Archie picked a direction and began walking as the sun heated the air and the humidity swarmed around his body. He was hot, dehydrated, and drenched in sweat as he mindlessly trudged along dragging his feet in the sand.

Archie was on the verge of calling it quits and giving up until the evening when it cooled off, when he heard the faint sound of crashing waves. The welcoming sound sent joy throughout his body and he quickened his pace in its direction. He sprang through the last part of the forest and found himself standing on a beach staring at the ocean. The virgin, white sand shone brightly in the day's afternoon sun. The beautiful, crystal-clear, blue water attracted Archie's eyes as he imagined sipping it to quench his intense thirst.

Archie looked down the beach to his left and to his right trying to spot his boat. There at the far end of the beach lay his boat still tied to the palm tree where he had left it. Thank the good Lord, praised Archie as he embraced the long, but victorious walk to his rowboat.

During the walk, he removed the purple and gold box from his jacket and looked upon it fondly. He inserted the key and the top popped open. Archie allowed a triumphant smile to spread across his face. One gold coin, one extraordinary ruby, diamond ring, and a matching, priceless necklace. He had done it. He was the proud owner of the most legendary treasure in the West Indies; excluding the ever-evasive Fountain of Youth. The victor smiled with pure glee as he pushed the rowboat into the waves and patiently rowed back to the mother vessel. He could not wait to present Olivia with these fine jewels. Of course that was pending her acceptance of his love for her. But Archie was confident Olivia still loved him or at least he could not accept the alternative at the moment. Archie rowed back to the alcove where the small vessel was nestled away and hidden.

As he approached Archie called out, "I'm back. Lower the ropes."

"Huzzah! Good to see yer smilin' face, Masta Rose. We'd wagers on whether or not we'd e'er see ye 'gain," Captain David yelled back from the railing.

"Capt'n, I hope you put your money on me."

The Captain chuckled, "Aye, I be the only one that done so. Ye returnin' has made me quite some gold."

Once Archie was back aboard the ship and the anchor had been raised, the ship embarked from Saint-Domingue and sailed back to Port Nassau. He was one step closer to making his envisioned return to Olivia a reality.

Archie slipped the purple and gold box into his personal belongings along with the key and fell fast asleep as soon as his head landed on the pillow.

• 28 •

Isabel and Archie boarded the *Magnus* early in the morning and Isabel was as giddy as a child on his or her birthday. Governor Raymond, Mrs. Raymond, and half of the mansions attendants and valets had escorted their baby girl, Isabel, to the docks to wish her the best on her honeymoon and a safe voyage across the world. Archie thought it was a tad excessive to have such an entourage of people send off Isabel, but he did not say anything and kept his peace. Isabel stood at the railing of the ship and waved goodbye to all her loved ones as the ship embarked from Port Nassau.

Archie placed a hand on her back and whispered in her ear, "Are you excited?"

Isabel turned to face him and through joyful sniffles, "Yes I am, just scared of what might happen."

Archie nodded and allowed her fears to be acknowledged. If he had his way, Isabel was right, things would happen, and she would be returning to Port Nassau without a husband. It was cruel and Archie's heart was wretched with guilt and the shame of having used

Isabel's love to save his life. When he made it to the pearly, white gates, he doubted he would be granted entry; until then, he would judge his own actions and nothing was more important to him than being with his beloved Olivia, the love of his life.

"Oh, darling. Once we get to England, you will have such a lovely time. London and Paris. Plus, all of the good food and shopping will make time fly by. You will be hugging your father and mother and sleeping in your own bed before you know it," Archie finally replied.

"I know, it's just it does not make leaving them any easier."

"I can understand that," Archie said as he remembered how scared of the unknown he had been when he first left Brighton for the New World.

Fear of the unknown or fear of change is a universal human emotion. After all the unknowns and events Archie had experienced and endured, a gentle passage across the world seemed like a walk in the park. Perspective, pondered Archie, is everything when it came to handling life's difficulties and challenges.

The journey to England took four weeks. On the last day of the trip, Archie was up bright and early to greet his dear, English homeland. The brisk, morning, dawn air and tangerine orange, baby blue horizon set up a beautiful welcome home setting for Archie. England's coastline was visible in the distance and Archie could not hide his excitement and anticipation of having finally arrived after all his trials and tribulations. As the landmass crept closer and closer, Archie's mind began to race on all the possibilities that were about to unfold.

He did not know exactly where to start his search for Olivia, but he figured that a decent starting place would be in Brighton. Nearly everyone knew Olivia in Brighton, especially his parents, and it would be the surest way to answer the most important questions first: was Olivia married, and did she still love Archie?

The *Magnus* pulled into the Portsmouth harbor and Archie was the first person off the ship onto the English soil. Archie stood beaming and looking around the docks as the morning sun warmed his face. He had defied all odds; he was back. Archie and Isabel did not spend much time in Portsmouth as they loaded their trunks onto their awaiting carriage and started their journey on the road to Brighton.

The half-day carriage ride was a pleasant trip and Archie answered all of Isabel's questions, as she wanted to know more and more about his past as they approached his home.

"I cannot believe you have been away from your home and your parents for such a long time. How long has it been again? Do you know if they are still alive?" Isabel asked.

"It's been four, almost five years. And honestly, I don't know if they are still alive or live in Brighton. I don't think they will have moved though. So, I cannot wait to see my parents."

"They will be excited to see you."

"Yes, yes, I imagine they will be," Archie said smiling as he spotted his house down the road. "There it is. Look Isabel, that one's my home."

Isabel looked out the window and gasped. "It's…it's so small. Pardon my shock, but that's where you live?"

Archie chuckled, "Not everyone can live in mansions. It is quite cozy for the three of us. It's home and there's no place that will ever replace it."

Archie and Isabel climbed out of the carriage, once it had stopped in front of the picturesque cottage, and the driver began to remove the trunks from the top of the carriage. A nervous excitement tingled through Archie's body as his knuckles rapped against the cottage door.

Archie's mother gasped as she opened the door, "Archie!"

"Hi-ya mum," he smiled giving her an enormous hug. When they parted, he continued, "It's so good to see you. I would like you to meet my wife, Isabel."

"Hello, Isabel. It's a pleasure to meet you my dear. I'm Joy," Archie's mother said addressing Isabel, but still in shock by the presence of her son.

"Hello, Mrs. Rose. The honor is all mine," responded Isabel smiling as she hugged Joy affectionately.

Joy called back into the house, "Richard, Richard. You won't believe this. Archie is back. Come say hello to him and his wife."

"Right, be down in a second, love," Archie's father, Richard called back from within the house.

Joy ushered her son and Isabel into the house and to the kitchen. Richard and Archie immediately hugged each other without needing to exchange any words to express the feelings between them.

"Dad, I'd like you to meet my wife, Isabel. Isabel, this is my father, Richard."

"Hi Isabel, it's nice to meet you," Richard replied. Then Richard turned back to Archie and whispered, "Son, you found a beautiful woman."

Joy smacked Richard's arm and Archie laughed. Archie was overjoyed to be home, see his parents' smiles, and be in a familiar, safe setting. His mother's cooking and the aroma wafting throughout the kitchen brought back incredible childhood memories.

"Tell us all about the Caribbean. What's it like? How did you and Isabel meet?" inquired Richard full of questions.

"I have so much to tell you both. The adventure I've been on, well, it's hard to believe, but I can honestly say that I am just happy to be alive," Archie said.

"Tell us over dinner, won't you dear?" Joy said. "That way you can have our full attention. I still have dinner to prepare. And, Richard, will you show Isabel to Archie's room? Archie, assist the kind driver with your and Isabel's trunks. Do not forget that you are still our son and not a guest in this house."

"Yes mum," Archie responded as he smiled. "I can see nothing has changed in my absence."

Archie thought to himself as he carried his and Isabel's trunks inside the cottage: The family was back together; albeit, one person was missing. He would ask his parents at a more discreet time if there was any word on Olivia's situation and her whereabouts. This might be the last time he ever sees his parents if his ultimate plan came to fruition. He would try and enjoy the next week without worrying about the future.

At dinner, Archie relived his adventure to the West Indies. His parents and Isabel, who until now had not heard the full story herself, listened to his every word. They hung on the edge of their seats as Archie recounted The Great Merchant's death and his inheritance of the Hollis Plantation and Company. How Archie's fateful partnership with Thomas lead to his capture at the hands of the infamous pirate Captain Rémi Montre. Archie decided to leave out his murderous acts of shooting Captain Jasper and Thomas, but he did show them the "d'Or" tattoo, which dominated his forearm. Richard ran his fingers over the ink embedded in Archie's skin. His mother merely stared at the "d'Or" tattoo in disbelief. Archie concluded his adventure as he was standing on the hangman's platform begging Governor Raymond for pardon.

Isabel jumped into the story and interjected, "Yes, as Archie was standing there staring at me, I recognized him and shouted out to my father to not hang Archie."

Archie picked up the story, "At the pleading of dear Isabel, I survived the noose and was pardoned of the charges of piracy against me. Isabel and I were married in Port Nassau shortly thereafter."

Isabel and Archie kissed each other.

"I will speak for both of us," Richard said looking at his wife. "Both of us are extremely thankful to the Lord, He has delivered you back to us."

———

Over the next week, Archie took Isabel around Brighton and showed her all the places he frequented growing up. Seeing each place—the seashore, the rolling green hills, and the numerous secret spots in town—was a painful reminder of his time spent with Olivia. The warm summer days and cool autumn nights, wrapped in each other arms, talking about the future reaffirmed his yearning to be with Olivia.

On the last night in Brighton, Archie found himself a moment alone with his mother. He took advantage of his chance and asked frankly, "Hi ma, is there any word on what happened to Olivia? I didn't see her at all this week in town."

Joy looked at her son thoughtfully, "Olivia married a couple years back to a banker from London. I'm sorry Archie. I know how much she meant to you, but you appear to have married a lovely woman yourself."

The words hit Archie hard rendering him speechless. She did not wait. Why had he thought she would? He had been away for years.

"Are you ok Archie?" Joy asked concerned.

"Ya," mustered Archie, shocked and stunned. He took a long sip of ale. Archie had believed that love was the key to keeping Olivia's heart, but she must have changed the lock. "I was just curious. Do you know if she is living in London at the moment?" he managed.

"I believe she is. Just be careful, won't you? I don't want you to bring her or yourself any more heartache. If you see her with her husband and she sees you with Isabel, well," Joy paused, "it just won't be the same as it was before you left."

"I'll be careful mum. Thank you."

Archie remained quiet for the remaining time as he helped his mother prepare the dinner's rabbit and potatoes. Archie was deep in thought. Olivia was in London, and she was married. It would make the next step of his plan a little more complex, but at least she was still close by. If she had moved North to Manchester or Liverpool, then it would have been nearly impossible to convince Isabel to make a trip to either of those two cities.

———

Archie watched as his house vanished from sight. It would be the last time he ever saw his parents and his heart ached at the thought. But if he wanted to be with the woman he had loved for as long as he could remember, then it was a necessary reality he must accept.

"Did you have a nice time?" asked Isabel gazing at her man. "Seeing your parents and hometown?"

"I did. Although, it was somewhat surreal. I can't believe how many years have passed. I will miss them," Archie answered, as he somberly looked out the carriage window watching his childhood and all his fondest memories flash past his eyes. Archie turned his gaze to Isabel, smiling, "You eager to see London?"

Isabel returned his smile. "I most certainly am. What should we do first?"

Archie thought briefly, "Let's go to the theater and then go for a nice meal in the city."

"Sounds marvelous," Isabel responded with sheer giddiness.

The journey to London took the entire day, and they arrived at their London hotel early in the evening. Archie and Isabel walked to the local theater and saw a performance of, "A Midsummer Night's Dream." The show amused them and they continued on to dinner, enjoying a delicious meal at The Fresh Catch Seafood Restaurant.

Archie scoured the restaurant half expecting, half hoping to see Olivia. With each woman that entered the restaurant, he glanced up from his meal and would see Olivia. Upon a second viewing, Archie would realize how wrong he was and desperate he was.

Isabel noticed him fidgeting and questioned him, "You alright love? Is something the matter?"

Archie caught off-guard from the question, "Yes...well no. No, of course not. I am fine. I think I am just tired from the long journey today. Some rest will do me good."

"Ok, dear. Tomorrow, I am going to go shopping all day and try on some new dresses. Would you like to accompany me?"

"I will pass, if that's ok, Isabel. I will join you the day after. Tomorrow, I am going to try and meet up with an old friend who is living in the city."

Archie began his search for Olivia early the next day. In the morning, he kissed Isabel goodbye and wandered the London streets considering where he should start his search. His mother had mentioned that Olivia's husband was a banker, so he elected to start with banks and bank offices and inquire about Olivia without raising suspicion. He realized it was going to be searching for a needle in a haystack, but he must start somewhere.

Archie checked at three separate banks, but none knew of an Olivia Hunt from Brighton. Frustrated, Archie realized this was going to take a lot longer than he had originally expected and he could not waste all day asking clueless bankers. Archie switched tactics and began asking at women's clothing stores, but his afternoon's efforts proved to be just as uneventful and uninformative.

Tired from all the walking across the city, Archie returned to the hotel and plopped down on the bed. Archie poured himself a glass of wine and let his mind wander off to thoughts of love, poetry, and loneliness. Isabel entered a little while later and saw her husband slumped on the bed.

"How was seeing your friend?" Isabel called out as she placed her boxes down beside the night table.

"Didn't see them today. I'll give it another go sometime this week. Would you like a glass of wine? And how was your day?"

"I'd love a glass," then Isabel continued on to recount her full, fruitful day of shopping.

Archie poured Isabel a glass of wine, as he half-heartedly listened to her droll on. She told him of the latest fashion trends starting to shape up in London, since the winter season was going to be upon them. Archie nodded politely and pretended to listen. His mind floated off to his next approach in searching for Olivia. The bank offices proved to be useless, as were the women's storeowners and he could not go knocking door to door on every home and apartment in London.

Isabel said something that snapped his train of thought.

"What was that dear? Say that again?"

"Which part?"

"You said something about all the women in London being invited to an event."

"Oh yes. Isn't that grand? And we will be in London for the opening. All the women in London have been invited to the new store opening of Roger and Stone Apparel. They sell premier women's clothing apparently, and they are having a grand opening sale to promote their new fashions. The promotional sale will last a week and is the current talk of London."

Archie tuned out Isabel, as his mind began actively thinking again.

Isabel continued, "Mr. Roger is from Ireland and he has the vision of an artist. Mr. Stone is a mysterious man, but he is apparently a distant descendent of Marco Polo."

"When are we going to the grand opening darling?" Archie asked formulating his plan, not listening to Isabel's background chatter.

"It's next week. So I thought we'd go for a couple of days, unless you had something else in mind."

"No, that sounds outstanding. We will make a grand time of it."

"Splendid," Isabel said warmly as she picked up her first box. "Would you like to see what I've purchased today?"

"Of course I would," Archie replied.

Isabel began undressing and making suggestive movements with her body; however, Archie's mind was not focused on his wife's naked body in front of him. The grand opening was going to be Archie's golden opportunity to run into Olivia, especially if all the women in London were going to be caravanning to the fashion store. Archie remembered how Olivia loved the newest fashion and knew at the very least, she would surely make a brief appearance at the event one time during the week.

The following week Archie accompanied Isabel to the Roger and Stone store and their fashion event. Archie was shocked by how busy it was and how many people had taken off work on Friday to preview and attend the grand opening day. The store was enormous. Archie reckoned that it must be the largest clothing store in London.

On this particular opening morning, it was packed full of perspective buyers and nosey onlookers. Archie thought to himself: Goodness, it will be a miracle if I spot Olivia in here.

Archie shadowed Isabel as they weaved in and out of people and around the store. Isabel would occasionally stop at certain items and try them on or ask Archie his opinion. Archie would respond cordially, but his eyes darted around the room searching.

"This is the last dress I'm going to buy, and then we can go," Isabel said as she was whisked away by the eager salesman.

"I'll meet you outside then," Archie replied absent-mindedly.

Archie was migrating toward the front door, glad to be finally getting some fresh air, when he spotted her. He stopped dead in his tracks and stared hopefully at the woman in question. She looked in Archie's direction and the two of them locked eyes. The woman was holding the hand of a child, who looked to be no older than three years old. Archie stood motionless and so did the woman. Already knowing whom it was, he strode purposefully over to her.

Archie whispered gently, "Olivia."

"Archie," she replied, still looking him directly in the eyes.

"Yes," Archie replied barely audible. Words had left him.

Archie wanted to bend over and kiss her on the lips. He fought the urge to act rashly in such a public setting.

"I can't spend too much time with you right now. Are you free tomorrow to meet?" Archie said briefly.

"Yes," Olivia responded equally motivated to kiss Archie, but wanting to do so in a more private location. "Meet me at the central park at nine in the morning. We will be able to have privacy there."

"See you then," Archie said smiling.

Before leaving, Archie took hold of her free hand and squeezed it tightly; then he continued onward and left through the store's front door. Olivia watched as Archie disappeared amongst the people in the street not sure whether she had seen Archie or an apparition.

Archie stood outside and waited for his wife to join him. He watched the men and women stroll up and down the streets meandering into and out of stores and cafes. He was thrilled and could not believe his luck. He had found her. He was in England and they were to finally meet after so many years apart, after all the promises, after all the tragedy, and after all the hopelessness. Archie could enjoy this lovely autumn day and he was filled with such elation he felt quite dizzy.

Isabel found Archie on the street looking cheerful and she playfully teased, "You seem to have perked up now that we are leaving?"

"Well, as much as I love shopping, I am glad to be back outside. Also, I've been thinking about where we ought to dine this evening," lied Archie.

Archie and Isabel chatted away and ambled around London for the remainder of the day stopping at cafes and shops, those which Isabel wished to see and experience. As the couple dined that evening, Archie's mind was calmed. He was going to see Olivia! For the first time in three years, Archie allowed peace and tranquility to flow through his veins and shower his heart.

• 29 •

The Cathedral bells chimed eleven times as people hustled and bustled around Archie. He looked solemnly around at all the faces and people as he waited patiently for Olivia to arrive. His mind twisted in flux: had she forgot about their meeting or did she decide she did not want to see him anymore? His mother's words echoed in his head: *I don't want you to bring her or yourself any more heartache.* Had his mother been right? Maybe Olivia had moved on. But why then would she have suggested meeting with him? Or Olivia had seen him leave with Isabel and had on second thought decided to not come. The endless string of question whirled around Archie's mind as he stood eyeing the gloomy and overcast sky. The grey clouds and frigid, morning wind did not lighten or improve his melancholy thoughts.

Archie spun around when he felt a sudden tap on his shoulder and there standing before him was Olivia and a little boy.

"Hi," she said. "You still love me. You waited just like you used to up on that hill." She paused and smiled at him before continuing, "I had to make sure you would wait. I would not have considered speaking with you or seeing you ever again if you had left earlier. I need to make sure you still loved me and this was not a fleeting quest."

"I've missed you," Archie replied allowing the elation of her presence to sweep over him. "I have waited a long time for this moment. I would have waited all day or all year, if it had been necessary. Shall we walk to the park?"

"Yes, but first, I'd like you to met my son, Charles."

The little boy hiding behind Olivia's dress slowly peeked a head out and looked up at the tall man. Charles retreated upon making eye contact with Archie and buried his face back into his mother's dress.

"You will have to tell me all that has happened since I've been away," said Archie, as cheerfully as possible, downcast to find that Olivia already had a son.

Archie would not pursue the idea of Olivia and him running away together if she was happily married and in love with another man, or if Olivia had a family. His only wish forever, was for Olivia to be happy always. He would reluctantly concede her to another if that was what she desired. He had to be realistic; it was obvious the reality of the current situation was far from his daydreams in the Caribbean.

Olivia and Archie walked in a relaxed silence as they both contemplated what should be said and what stories and questions were most pertinent to ask. The two sat down at a bench deep within the park, and Charles was released from his mother's grasp to frolic in the autumn leaves.

Archie broke the reticence by offering, "He is a beautiful child. You must be a proud mother."

"I am," Olivia responded as she watched Charles pick up and drop the same leaves over and over again with the same enthusiasm. Before continuing, Olivia turned her head and faced Archie, "Why did you not come back sooner? What happened? I don't understand. Your letter, rather, your letters did not explain anything?" Olivia's voice quivered as the anger and sadness spread throughout her body, "I waited but you...you never returned."

Archie sincerely stared back and said, "Please forgive me Olivia."

"I have forgiven you. If I hadn't, I wouldn't be here, believe me. But I want to know why you didn't come back sooner."

"I had every intention to, just as I had promised in my original letter. It's a long story."

"Well make it short. Please, I need answers."

"Did you get my last letter? The most recent one I sent you this summer?"

"I did, and it meant the world to me. I loved your poem, Archie. It touched my heart. I've missed you dearly."

"So have I. I will explain briefly for you what my letter could not. I was captured by the d'Or pirates, because my friend, Thomas who I mentioned in my first few letters, was heavily indebted to these pirates. And I know it's hard to believe, but they used me as insurance for his debt. In the end, I was held against my will for two years. I was imprisoned in their ranks unable to write, flee, or move without a bullet going through my head." Archie stopped and took hold of Olivia's hands. "Your poem was the one thing that kept me going. I memorized it and sang it every day. It gave me the courage and fortitude I needed in those hard times when hopelessness devoured my spirit. Your words gave me hope. Your words let me know you loved me and that there was a purpose to keep fighting, to keep living."

Archie could not stop himself. He leaned in close stopping shy of Olivia's lips. His lips hovered there waiting. His eyes were closed. Olivia kissed his lips gently. A tingling sensation ran down Archie's spine. Their lips locked together with feelings of love, longing, and warmth.

Archie withdrew and whispered, "Run away with me. Just the two of us, or rather three. I want to spend the rest of my days with you by my side. I cannot imagine a life without you in it."

Olivia looked fondly at Archie, "I'd love to be with you Archie, but where would we go? I am married, although it's been awfully lonely. The companionship has been terrible. Not initially. James was a marvelous catch. But over the years, it's only become worse. I'd go with you in a heartbeat."

"I am married too," Archie confessed, "but it was how I was able to stay alive. We will leave our spouses and be with each other. It was meant to be. We could go to Italy, Spain, anywhere warm," Archie ventured.

"James will kill me if he finds out I am leaving."

"Not if I kill him first," Archie responded seriously.

"Honestly Archie, how do you see us possibly being with each other? Since, we are both married."

"We would need to make plans for our journey soon and coordinate our escape. I am only in London for a week longer before going to Paris. When we return from Paris, we will have two weeks or so before I am back in the Caribbean forever. And I am not going back, unless you want to stay in England with James for the rest of your life. If that is what you want, please speak now or my heart will try endlessly to pursue a reality where you and I can be with each other, kiss, make love, and drink wine while you sing your poems to me."

Olivia turned her gaze back to Charles. She and Archie sat in silence for several minutes, while Olivia pondered her options.

Finally, Olivia sliced the stillness and said, "I like the sound of Italy."

"Do you?" Archie replied upbeat and excited.

"I do," smiled Olivia and she squeezed Archie's hand.

"I've been daydreaming. I can start a little fishing or merchant store at one of the town's docks. I have a small fortune with me from Port Royal that I managed to hide before leaving. It will be plenty for us to get started in a nice home on the water as well. Plus I have a gift for you. Something no other man could obtain."

"What is it?"

"Once we leave together, I will properly present it," Archie winked and continued on talking, "First, we must decide where we will go and I will make the necessary arrangements."

"Italy," daydreamed Olivia.

"Italy, it is." Archie kissed Olivia. "I love you."

"I love you, Archie. Thank you for finally coming home to me. And I want to hear all about the Caribbean and what it's like."

"You will my love, once we are on the sunny shores of Italia."

Archie's mind had already sprung into motion to plan an escape trip to Italy. They would need to board a ship to France and then ride a carriage from France to Italy. On top of all the logistical planning, they would both need to trick their spouses and evade suspicion during the next several weeks.

Olivia spoke in detail about her routine and her husband's weekly routine. Archie asked more in-depth questions and began to formulate an outline for the best course for escaping together. Archie reasoned if they could manage to leave when James was away on business, they would have eliminated one major obstacle. It would significantly improve their chances because they would be able to make it to France before James returned home and raised the alarm that his wife had run off.

Archie was confident in his abilities to conjure a fable and spin it to Isabel. He was not too concerned in lying about a last minute overnight trip to see a friend. This would allow him the time he needed to escape with Olivia. And before either spouse knew what had happened, Archie and Olivia and Charles would be happily situated on an Italian coastline.

Archie and Olivia walked Charles around the park for a little longer as they exchanged some short stories. Archie showed Olivia his tattoo and shared the awful experience of having to kill Thomas and Captain Jasper to save his neck. He told her about the fear he experienced being led to the hangman's noose and how the Governor made him a proposition that forced his hand in marriage.

Olivia told her tales about the day Charles was born and the awful drunken states James would get in after he had been sacked from his senior position at the bank.

Upon concluding their stroll, they found themselves at the entrance of the park.

Archie said, "This is it. Are you ready?"

"If we could leave today, I would want to."

Archie and Olivia kissed and held each other closely as Charles looked on indifferently. For Archie, kissing Olivia in this moment was something he had dreamed about ever since Captain Rémi Montre had captured him. Survive and return to England, return to Olivia—this had been his mantra. The euphoric emotions running through his heart and soul would have inspired the angels and cherubs in heaven to start singing. Olivia's soft lips pressed against his and Archie could smell her beautiful scent. The longing Archie and Olivia had endured, the pain and separation, the obstacles and challenges, and the walls built up for emotional protection were all washed away. The joy, the hope, the love, and the sensual passion exuded between them replaced the bleak void that had once consumed both their hearts. Time stood still while they kissed. Archie's and Olivia's tongues caressed each other and craved similar urges—both desiring more. Archie knew he was making the right choice. This was the woman he had longed for so long ago and these were the feelings, the passions, and the love he had fought so vigorously for.

As they parted, Olivia stood on her tiptoes and whispered in Archie's ear, "Now and forever." She then took Charles' hand and left the park.

As Archie watched Olivia and Charles walk out of his sight, he thought to himself how close and yet how far he was from ultimately being able to hold Olivia as his own.

Archie scanned the park before leaving himself. Momentarily, he caught a glimpse, or at least he thought he had, of an old man with wispy, white hair and a white beard walking out of the park. Before Archie could get a clear look, the old gentleman had disappeared.

Archie stood frozen in thought. He had seen the man before and he racked his memory to remember where and when it had been. *The man with the wise blue eyes and long, white hair...Louis*, Archie recalled. *From...from? Saint-Domingue. Quite impossible! How could it be? That had been a dream. How was Louis in England?*

216

During his walk back to the hotel, Archie allowed his memory to try and solve this peculiar dream and appearance of the old gentleman Louis; but unfortunately, he was unable to come up with anything concrete. He could not remember if it was real, a dream, or just his subconscious making him see apparitions.

For the remaining days in London, Archie spent his time gathering information on ships destined for the French coastline and searching for possible drivers that would provide them the necessary and arduous journey to the Italian countryside. It took him four days to find a ship that would be setting sail in a month's time from Dover, which was south of London, and arriving in Northern France.

On the last day before leaving for Paris, Archie finally found a French driver that would be able to make the drive from France to Milan. Archie bartered and haggled with the man over price, and eventually they were able to negotiate a fair deal. Archie explained the plan to the man: "Olivia, Charles, and I will meet you in London by the carriage hub on the first Friday in November. We will travel by carriage to Dover, then on a boat from Dover to France. From France to Milan, by way of Switzerland, via your carriage, which is currently awaiting us in France. Once in Milan, you will journey back to Paris with an Italian couple and never mention us to anyone." More importantly, thought Archie, my party and I will find a new driver, who will transport us to La Spezia—our new home.

The French driver nodded his head in agreement, as Archie traced his finger along the proposed route.

La Spezia, which was located just west of Florence along the western Italian coast, was an ideal location, reasoned Archie. It would be secluded from questioning eyes but also allow him to pursue his trade as a merchant since it was close enough to Genoa, a major port.

Archie and the French drive shook hands as Archie agreed to pay half at the beginning of the trip and half at the end.

With the deal struck, Archie proudly basked in his splendid ability to navigate and plan such a difficult journey in such little time. As Archie strolled around London taking in as much as possible, he allowed his mind to daydream: he would never set eyes on England again, but he had the fortune of looking forward to a new life and new start.

————

The following day, Isabel and Archie left London early for the tiresome journey to Paris. Isabel was ecstatic to be headed to Paris and could not wait to tell all her friends and family in Port Nassau. Despite everything going on in Archie's head regarding his other trip with Olivia, he found himself excited to see Paris and experience the French mainland. After all the time he had spent in Saint-Domingue, he fancied the French culture and was certainly looking forward to appreciate it without being a prisoner in Captain Montre's crew.

For the next three weeks while Isabel and Archie were enjoying their romantic honeymoon in Paris by drinking fine wines and soaking up the French culture, Olivia was slowly preparing herself and Charles for the biggest adventure of their lives. Olivia discreetly maneuvered her precious belongings and items into her trunk, while James was away on business.

On the last Friday in October, James left as he was scheduled, but unfortunately returned to the house unexpectedly. Olivia was in the bedroom preparing the finally arrangements in her trunk and Charles' trunk. James entered the house and dropped his case at the front door before walking up the stairs to the bedroom.

"Liv, darling, will you make me some lunch? The trip to Reading has been cancelled at the last minute."

James' footsteps could be heard on each step as he made his way to the bedroom. Frozen in place and scared, Olivia questioned herself, how was she going to explain the trunks full of clothes? Her only response was to slam the bedroom door shut.

"James, I'll be out in a minute, I'm just changing, if you don't mind?"

"Like hell you're going to lock me out of my own bedroom.

You're my wife, I've see you naked before."

James opened the door and Olivia shrieked. James surveyed the scene in front of him. He saw the traveling trunks and Olivia's belongings carefully organized ready to be packed.

"What the bloody hell is going on? Why are the trunks full of clothes? Are you trying to run off with my son? How dare you!"

Before Olivia could respond, James used the back of his hand and slapped Olivia across the face sending her to the floor. Olivia's face stung and immediately tears formed in her eyes as she cowered beneath her husband's raised fist. James walked over to Charles' trunk and emptied the contents onto the floor and began kicking them around the room before throwing the trunk against the far wall. He proceeded to the bed and similarly emptied Olivia's clothes all over the bed. He picked up her garments and dresses and threw them at her with impunity.

"You are not going anywhere, you bitch. I am disgraced by how ungrateful you are. Do you know what I have sacrificed for this family? What I have provided for this family? I put food on the table and a roof over your head. How do you repay me? How? You are going to run out and be a whore on the streets and on top of it, take my son with you. I will not have the mother of my child be a tavern tramp, and you will not shame my name by running away. You will respect me. You hear me? I said, did you hear me?" James was yelling at the top of his voice by the end of his rant as he continued to hurl clothes around the room.

His complexion was ruddy and it was obvious he had started drinking before returning home from the cancelled trip.

Olivia did not move as she remained on the floor covered in her clothes. She looked at James and an overwhelming sadness overcame her. How am I ever going to leave now, she thought. If James suspected her motives to leave him, he would never trust her; he would never let her out of his sight.

"Now," James said as he viciously grabbed Olivia's face with his hand covering her mouth. He then forced her face upward so they were looking eye to eye: "I don't ever want to see those trunks packed again. Ever!" He released Olivia's face, stood up straight, and patted his suit wrinkle free. "I will be down stairs awaiting lunch. Afterwards, I expect this room to be cleaned and spotless."

With that, James left the bedroom and Olivia heard the stairs creak under James' weight. Olivia cried silently and let the tears roll down her cheeks as she gingerly felt the left side of her face. Her left cheekbone was tender to the touch and she could feel her heartbeat in her face. Olivia slowly rose to her feet and descended the stairwell wondering if the nightmare was ever going to come to an end.

Olivia watched the rain pitter-patter on the window as she sat in silence and watched James eat his lunch. She did not try to make conversation and neither did he. He merely peered at the morning's paper and munched away. Olivia wondered how on earth she was going to tell Archie when she had to tell him their plan was ruined.

• 30 •

On the first Friday of November, Archie awoke nervous and frightfully eager. He gazed out the window at the early morning dawn, and then he rolled over and looked upon his wife, who was sleeping peacefully beside him. Today, Archie's life would change. He quietly climbed out of bed and began dressing. Through his routine, he ran his plan through his head over and over until he knew he could pull it off flawlessly.

Yesterday, he had informed Isabel he wanted to visit a friend for a day or so in Canterbury and would be back on Sunday evening. Isabel granted Archie his last minute trip, as he had given her nonstop attention in Paris. She was ready for some alone time for herself and it would be a pleasant change for a couple days. Archie double-checked his travel belongings in the small bag—clothes, pistol, gold, and the Queen's Jewels.

As Archie was preparing to leave, Isabel came up from behind him and squeezed him around the waist. "Travel safe, my love. I love you."

"Thank you, darling. You know I will. I hope you can find entertainment in London without me," replied Archie not trying to say anything he would regret.

"I might," Isabel winked, "but it certainly will not be the same without you. You make everything more," she paused thinking for the best word, "fun. Everything feels right with you."

Archie bent down and kissed his wife on the lips for what he anticipated would be the last time. "I will take care my dear. You do the same."

Archie closed his bag, but before he could leave, Isabel placed her hands in his.

"You love me, don't you Archie?" she asked innocently.

Archie hesitated slightly and his heart cringed as he lied, "Yes, Isabel, I love you."

She pulled in and kissed him passionately. "See you soon," she whispered.

Guilt flowed through his heart and into his soul, as he could not bring himself to say the identical sentiment. His conscience wept, as Archie continued to the task at hand, as he picked up his small bag and left. Archie forced himself to walk out of the room and shut the door on such a wonderful woman and loyal wife. He knew he could not break his promise to Olivia. Neither did he want to. However, Archie's sympathetic heart caused him to feel sick as he walked to Olivia's house. He was going to break Isabel's heart and he had used her so ruthlessly for his own gain.

Archie did not consider himself to be a selfish or mean person. But as he considered everything, he had to admit he had been a terrible man and husband to Isabel. Their entire relationship had been based on a lie, a falsehood, and he would have to live with the black shame staining his conscience. I have come too far to give it all up now, thought Archie, but if I want to I can still call it off.

Archie stopped at a cafe a block away from Olivia's home and purchased a tea and biscuit. He sat down near the window, as Archie would wait for James' departure before sweeping Olivia off her feet.

As Archie eyed the London pedestrians, horses, and carriages moving outside, a young girl and her mother accompanied Archie at the same table.

"Good day ma'am," Archie said as he nodded at the mother.

"Good morning, Sir," responded the mother. "Do you mind if we join you?"

"Not at all, please," Archie replied pointing to the chair across from him.

"Thank you. How has your morning been so far?"

"Honestly, I am nervous. I am moving away from England forever."

"Oh, heavens. What would ever compel you to leave forever?"

"For love," Archie said distantly, as he looked out toward the street again.

"Are you married, or going to be married?"

Archie paused and looked at the mother sharply.

"Sorry, Sir, I did not mean to over step my bounds. I apologize."

"It's alright. May I ask you a question?"

"Surely, just one second."

The mother tore her little girl's croissant into small pieces and fed them to her. "So, what is your question?"

Archie took a deep breath and started, "At what cost should one pursue love?"

The woman absorbed the question and they sat in silence as she contemplated it.

She broke the extensive quiet by saying, "Love is something special. True love only comes around once, sometimes twice, in a lifetime. So what is the cost of love? I would say it is invaluable. Have you ever read John Lyle's novel, *Euphues: The Anatomy of Wit?*"

"I have not. Why?"

"It's a story of a young man and his romantic adventures. But there is a part that applies to your question. In the novel, it says: 'The rules of fair play do not apply in love and war.' Therefore in my opinion, for love, you should do all that is necessary to acquire it or preserve it, just as one would do everything and anything in a war to achieve victory."

Archie pondered the words; but before he could continue the discussion, the woman stood and took her daughter's hand.

"I hope that helps you with your question. I must be headed off for the day. It was a pleasure meeting you."

"Take care and thank you ma'am" Archie responded as the woman and her child left.

Archie sipped on his warm tea and enjoyed his biscuit as he tried to push Isabel from his mind. His guilt, her sadness, and her future heartbreak weighed heavily on his conscience. Only the woman's words helped to console him. He knew it would take a long time before he ever truly forgave himself for using her and her love for his own selfish means. He would have a stain upon his conscience forever. Were all actions fair in the pursuit of love? It seemed as if this mentality were a extremely selfish and sinful evaluation of love.

As planned, Olivia said James was typically out of the house by ten o'clock for his weekend trip. Archie assumed if he waited until eleven o'clock then it would be completely safe to pick up Olivia and Charles before making the ride to Dover for the remainder of the day.

Thus, Olivia heard a knock on her front door at eleven o'clock. Olivia peered out from the upstairs window more scared than she had ever been in her life, at what was about to unfold. She prayed Archie was armed, or else she might lose the love of her life.

Archie stood motionless at the door wondering what was taking such a long time. When the door swung opened, Archie was stunned to find himself looking down the barrel of a pistol. Archie did not hesitate and reacted swiftly. His survival instincts had been honed in the Caribbean and he swung his small bag upward at the pistol.

Before James could fire, Archie's bag struck James' shooting arm and sent the gun flying back into the house. Archie took advantage of his opponent's loss of balance and lowered his shoulder and tackled James back into the door's entryway. The force of the blow knocked the wind out of James. Archie, who had been in life-threatening situations before, handled this one as he would any other—survive at all costs. Archie intuitively scrambled off James reaching for the gun laying only meters away. He grabbed it and spun around. James struggled to his feet and lunged at Archie tackling him into the adjacent room. The two fought and grappled for the gun as the two men rolled across the floor exchanging punches and blows. Finally James was able to grab hold of Archie's wrist and forced the gun toward Archie's head.

Exhausted, Archie swung hard and punch James in the side of the head, which momentarily stunned James and he released Archie's wrist. Archie tried to wriggle free from underneath James but was unsuccessful. James retaliated viciously and landed several punches, which sent Archie into a dazed state.

The fight became a blur of commotion and noise. Suddenly there was a loud bang and black smoke erupted around James and Archie. Somewhere in the background, Archie heard a scream. His ears were ringing and he blinked unsure of what had just occurred, as he lay sprawled beside James.

Olivia came flying down the stairs and yelled petrified, "Archie...James!"

Archie turned his head glancing up from the floor as Olivia rushed down the stairs. Olivia stopped at the bottom of the stairs and looked at Archie pleadingly. Archie immediately noticed the black and blue bruises on her throat and her swollen left check, which was now a horrid looking yellow and purple color.

Olivia raced over to James' motionless body and fell to her knees. Archie looked down at his body examining it, before he gingerly rose to his feet. He watched Olivia as she held up James' head and body in her lap. James was grasping his side in agony, while he slowly closed and opened his eyes as blood streamed from his abdomen soaking his clothes maroon. His eyes were staring up at the blank space above him. His blood began to trickle upon wooden floor drop by drop.

"Archie," whispered Olivia without removing her eyes from James, "what have you done?"

Archie remained silent unable to respond. Archie picked up the gun and placed it down on a nearby table next to an empty bottle of brandy as he contemplated what to do. His survival instinct kicked in and told him to run, and run like hell, as far away from everything and everyone as rapidly as possible.

Archie said in a hoarse voice, "I think it's time to go Olivia. We should leave now."

He watched as Olivia laid James softly down and stood up before retreated up the stairs. Archie stood motionless above James. He contemplated what to do with the gravely injured man.

"Olivia," he called out.

No answer.

"Olivia," he tried again as he stepped on the first stair. But as he looked up, standing there at the top of the stairs was Olivia with Charles in her arms with no trunks or baggage.

"We couldn't pack. James found out I was leaving, and he wouldn't let me out of his sight," explained Olivia. "He choked me until I told him our entire plan. He would have killed me otherwise."

"He was a vile man. Look at what he's put you through—your pretty face bruised and your throat. He deserved exactly what he got—a bullet."

"I cannot possible leave without my things," Olivia frantically continued, shocked at the sight of her dead husband in the middle of the hall.

Suddenly, there was a knock on the open front door followed by a female's voice, "Olivia. James. Are you both all right in there? We heard a gunshot? Everything ok? May I come in?"

"Com…," James started weakly, but Archie punched James hard in the chest silencing him.

"Hurry," Archie hissed in a low voice up the stairs at Olivia.

Olivia stifled her rebuttal and moved back into the bedroom to pack up her and Charles' belongings as quickly as possible.

Archie spun around and dragged James out of the front room into the back kitchen. James moaned loudly at the harsh and sudden movement.

"You'll hang for this. You'll hang for everything you've done, you miserable bastard. I pray to God that I live to see you swing," James mustered through gritted teeth and labored breathing.

Archie ignored James.

Archie grabbed a small rug from under a side table and threw it on top of the pool of blood that had coagulated in the front room between the stairs and the door.

Archie took a deep breath and strode into the hallway approaching the neighbor, who had begun to knock on the door again. The woman at the door gasped, as she was not expecting to see a man she did not know answer her knocking.

"Where...where is Olivia?" the woman stammered.

"Olivia is just upstairs now changing Charles," Archie replied coolly. "Let me not be rude. Allow me to introduce myself: I am Mr. Trent Kingsley. I am a distant relative of Olivia's from up North."

"How do you do Mr. Kingsley? I am Rebecca Hughes. I am Olivia's neighbor. And when I heard such a ruckus, then a gunshot, I had to check and make sure nothing was the matter."

Rebecca was trying her best to peer around Archie into the front hallway without overtly showing her intentions or being obviously nosey.

"Please, call me Trent," Archie replied trying to sound casual, calm, and collected.

"You're sure everything is quite alright?"

"Quite."

"Then will you get Olivia or James for me? I'd like to say hello and see if they will be available for tea this afternoon. And you, may join us too if you'd like."

"I will pass the invitation to Olivia."

Archie then realized Mrs. Hughes was buying herself time to investigate the situation because Mrs. Hughes was no longer looking at

Archie, but over his shoulder into the hallway.

"Oh and today's weather is perfect. Maybe we will have a picnic in the park?" Ms. Hughes continuing to shift her eyes beyond Archie to catch a glimpse of anything unusual inside.

Archie hastily proceeded on, "I assure you, all is well. I will tell Olivia of your tea invitation and we will notify you as soon as our day's plans are set."

Archie began closing the door, trying to end the conversation, when Rebecca cried out in terror and pointed into the hallway. Archie whirled around as a tingling sensation ran down his spine to his fingertips and toes. As he looked at the sight before him, he realized why Rebecca had screamed so loudly. There, at the bottom of the stairs, stood Olivia and Charles with their trunks; however, Olivia had forgotten one major detail in her frantic rush to pack. She had forgotten to change her blood soaked clothes. The bottom of her dress from her knees down was spotted and marked with fresh, crimson red blood, and the cuffs of her sleeves had stains of fresh blood where she had held her husband.

Olivia looked down at her clothes upon seeing Rebecca's face of sheer horror and Archie's look of bewilderment and confusion.

Archie was paralyzed, and before he could apprehend Rebecca, she was tearing down the street screaming bloody murder. Archie continued to look at Olivia and she looked back at him. Both Archie and Olivia stood frozen in time. Their worlds were headed for utter destruction and neither felt capable of stopping their demise.

Archie spoke slowly, suddenly fatigued and exhausted, "I…I do not know what to do. But if you want, you should stay here with Charles, and blame this," he pointed to the other room indicating where James' body lay, "on me. Or they will certainly hang us both for shooting him and running away. This is entirely my fault. I'm so sorry Olivia."

Olivia could not speak; she was speechless herself. She felt like there was a lump of hot coal lodged in her throat and her face became flushed and rosy red. Unable to stop the impending emotions flooding her body, she broke down in tears as the shock and fear and anxiety consumed her.

Archie did not try and console her with words or speech, for there was nothing he could possibly say to relieve the shock. Only time and comfort could do that. He walked over to Olivia and gently wrapped both his hands around her.

He kissed her on the forehead and then looked beseechingly into her eyes, "I love you, always have, and always will. You need to decide what you want to do. Will you flee with me, or will you stay?"

Archie's words hung in the air mercilessly. "Time is of the essence Olivia."

Olivia's body quivered. Her eyes were glazed over, but she came too and looked down at her son Charles. Charles looked up confused with all the commotion. She returned Archie's blue-eyed gaze.

"Archie, I'll…I'll," Olivia hesitated.

"Olivia," Archie repeated, "are you coming?"

"Yes, I just…" Olivia started.

But as soon as Archie heard "Yes" he did not even bother listening to the remaining of Olivia's statement. He sprinted into action. He rushed over to his small bag and grabbed his pistol, his gold, and the small purple and gold box. He tucked the pistol into his pants and placed the gold and the treasure box into Olivia's trunk.

Then Archie riffled through Olivia's trunk and pulled out a beautiful, blue colored dress and handed it to her saying, "Probably best to change before we leave."

Olivia took the blue dress in her hands. It was the same one so many years ago she had purchased to wear when Archie had returned. Olivia stripped as expeditiously as she could and put on the glamorous, blue dress.

"You look stunning," Archie said as he glanced at Olivia.

Olivia blushed, happy for the precious moment regardless of the circumstances.

Archie glanced once more around the room as he ran through a mental checklist. He decided to leave Charles' luggage. Archie thought to himself, Charles could have all new clothes and, well, whatever else his little heart desired if they made it out of this mess alive.

"Let's go," Archie commanded as he led Olivia and Charles out the back of the house and to the back alley.

As they rushed out of the back of the house to the back alley, James could be heard cussing and yelling incoherently at Archie and Olivia. Archie could only hope they escaped the city before Rebecca and James could tell the police everything.

As they made their escape, Archie wondered, could this really be happening again? Again he was going to be a wanted man, or was this just a dark, twisted dream?

As Archie, Olivia, and Charles continued down the back alleys of London farther from the house, they could hear yells and shouts in the distance. Archie did not say anything, but it was evident, Rebecca's screaming had finally arisen the attention of the police. They would be storming the house within minutes to find the crime scene and the severely injured Mr. Towns. Rebecca would relish spilling her rumors and theories of a suspicious Mr. Kingsley and the blood stained Olivia to anyone willing to listen. And of course, if James survived, he would no doubt relieve Archie's true identity, and Olivia would be condemned to hang too. Archie, Charles, and Olivia had just become the foxes of the hunt.

Archie shook his head as he thought to himself, how could he be so close to his dream and have done something so foolish. He glanced at Olivia walking besides him, and winced at the bruises on her neck and face. Olivia was one of the strongest women he had ever met. Her resolve had allowed her to survive the abuse and drunken tirades James had bombarded her beautiful soul and body with. James would serve his penance in hell one day, Archie reckoned.

The trio continued on their way to the rendezvous point where Archie had previously arranged to meet their French, carriage driver. Archie would glance around corners before entering the main streets and he continuously looked over his shoulder to make sure they were not being followed or chased. Amazingly, they made it to the rendezvous location safely and ducked into a nearby alleyway, which had an advantageous vantage point while keeping the trio hidden. They waited patiently for their French driver.

"Where is he?" Olivia asked crouched behind Archie out of sight.

"I'm not sure. Hopefully he arrives soon, the French are known to be notoriously late and untimely as it is," explained Archie trying to give any reason to instill calmness in both Olivia and himself.

The three waited patiently, with each passing minute feeling like an eternity. Finally Archie spotted their driver, walking casually along as if he was not twenty minutes late. Archie waited until the French driver strolled closer, before letting out a low, strong whistle to grab his attention. The French driver looked over and Archie waved, motioning him toward them. The French driver approached the hidden group looking around warily, immediately recognizing that something was amiss.

"About time," mumbled Archie clearly irritated at the man. "Why are you so late?"

"Why are you hidden?" shot back the French driver.

"Never mind that, are we all set to go?"

"Oui, we can go to the carriage and take off whenever you're ready."

"Excellent, we must not waste any time getting out of London."

The French man joined the group, and the four members slowly emerged into the street and made their way toward the carriage station at a quick brisk walk. The French man, motivated by Archie's gentle shoves in the back, walked at a brisk tempo leading the group to the hired carriage. During the walk along the River Thames, Archie was keeping his head on a swivel. He continuously scanned from left to right, as his eyes darted to evaluate all the people surrounding them. The last thing he wanted was a police constable to recognize them by Rebecca Hughes' description.

Thankfully, they made it to the carriage without any problems or incidents. Archie let out a sigh of relief as he placed the trunk on top of the carriage and took a seat inside. Archie closed his eyes and took a moment to slow down his heart rate. Olivia climbed in behind Charles and sat down next to Archie and took his hand.

"Archie?" she ventured.

"Yes," Archie replied not opening his eyes, but squeezing her hand to indicate he was listening to her attentively.

"Something has been on my mind and I wanted to ask you before we leave."

"What is it?" Archie said opening his eyes and giving Olivia his full attention fearful she was having second thoughts.

"Will you love Charles like he was your son, even though he is not."

Olivia looked expectantly at Archie hoping for his approval of her child.

"I will," Archie said nodding, despite his mixed emotions.

Archie had no desire to elaborate further. He hated that evil man—James Towns—for what he had put Olivia through and Charles was his offspring, with the same, cursed blood. Alas, as Archie now recognized, his priority was to be the best husband for Olivia and if that meant loving her son, he would do so.

He turned his attention to the French driver and yelled out the window, "Let's go."

"Certainly," called back the French driver.

The carriage began with a jolt and the horses trotted down the street.

Archie watched as London drifted by. This would be the last time he was ever in England. He squeezed Olivia's hand to get her attention.

She looked at him with tired eyes and said, "What is it?"

"I love you." Archie leaned over and pecked her on the lips. "I'm glad we are finally together once again. So much time has passed, yet not a day has gone by without my heart yearning for you."

"I love you too," Olivia said smiling at him and squeezing his hand back. "You are my King of Hearts."

"You are my Queen of Hearts, so what we have never parts," recited Archie.

Olivia nestled her head into Archie's chest as he wrapped his arm around her shoulders.

Both Olivia and Archie then looked at Charles, who had already snuggled and curled up on the cushion seat preparing himself for the long journey to La Spezia.

• 31 •

A new dawn was just beginning along the Italian coast. La Spezia's sunrise was magnificently illuminating the sky in bright, cheerful colors of pinks, oranges, blues, and yellows. Archie sat on the balcony of their new home with the purple and gold box in his lap and watched as the bright fireball inched over the horizon. At long last, he was going to properly propose to Olivia and place the Queen's necklace around her neck and the Queen's ring on her finger. The gold and purple box glinted in the sunlight as Archie held it up and opened it. Inside, the rubies and diamonds were flawless and shone brilliantly as rays of sunlight shot through them. Archie's eyes widened every time he looked at the jewels. They were truly a sight to behold.

Archie closed the box and set it back in his lap as he appreciated how amazing it was that he was sitting in Italy with the Queen's Jewels in his lap. After miraculously escaping with his life from d'Or, the noose, and the Caribbean, he had been able to find Olivia, free her from her abusive husband, and transport their new family safely to Italy. He was the proud owner of a little, Italian maritime business and shipping company, and they lived in a beautiful home overlooking the Mediterranean Sea. He had done it against all odds. He was with the woman of his dreams and they could live together happily as he had always intended.

Olivia came out onto the balcony, once the sun had peeked through the window and woke her. She saw Archie sitting overlooking the water and walked over to him.

"What's in the box?" she inquired curiously.

"What I promised you a long time ago," Archie said looking up at her excitedly. "Olivia, there's something that you deserved from the moment I met you, but I did not have it." Archie knelt down on one knee. "I asked you once long ago, if you would be my wife. I went across the world and survived every obstacle Death threw my way. I survived; rather, I lived because of you. Because in my heart, I knew I needed to ask you this one question again. This time I have exactly what I promised you on the night before I left—a ring only deserving for a queen. I love you with all my heart and could not allow another day to pass without you forever by my side. Will you marry me?"

Archie opened the box and removed the ring, holding it out in front of Olivia.

"Yes, yes, yes," Olivia joyfully exclaimed as tears began to form in her eyes and a radiant smile spread across her face. Her hands where covering her mouth as she processed everything at once.

Archie stood up, took her hand, and placed the ring on her finger. The diamonds fired brightly around the large, gleaming ruby. As Olivia was admiring her new ring, Archie removed the matching necklace and wrapped it around Olivia's neck.

"It's a matching set," explained Archie.

"It's so beautiful. Words cannot describe how happy I am."

Olivia jumped into Archie's arms and she started kissing him nonstop. Archie kissed her back passionately, allowing all the love he had for her to seep out of him and into this moment they shared. He held her tightly as the two lovers kissed like there was no tomorrow.

The warm sun shone brightly in the background as Archie and

Olivia made their way back into the bedroom. Archie laid Olivia on the bed as his hands caressed her body. Archie let his hands feel Olivia's soft skin and supple breasts, while Olivia's hands maneuvered down Archie's stomach to his inner thighs. The two moved in sexual, rhythmic motion together.

Olivia's heart was beating fast as her loving man graced and pleasured her body with all his love and attention. She had unknowingly craved this moment forever. Archie pressed against her softly and let the ecstasy capture both of them. Olivia moaned softly and gripped Archie's back, while Archie gently but passionately made love with her.

Afterwards, Archie lay on the bed and stroked Olivia's hair and massaged her head as she lay there in a state of blissful relaxation and happiness. The two allowed the warm sun to splash across their naked bodies as they basked in the beauty of their lives together. The two lovers would never be separated again.

Archie and Olivia were married in a small chapel in La Spezia. The newly wedded couple savored the glorious day and set their eyes on the future, a clear and fresh start for the family. Olivia proudly wore her Queen's Jewels, which sparkled brightly and complimented her ivory colored satin wedding gown.

As Archie admired his wife standing in her wedding dress, he fondly recalled the day when he had first met Olivia: tumbling down the hill, sweaty, dirty, and brazen. Back then, times were simpler. Dirt could be washed away, but he could not wash away the blood from his hands or cleanse his conscience of his sins, which cumulatively had allowed him to have this day with Olivia. The blood he spilt and sins would be with him for the rest of his life. Olivia standing in her wedding dress next to him, this end result, was worth all the horrific tribulations he had had to endure. No experience had changed his heart or worn away his love for the girl he had laid eyes on crossing that field. Olivia had experienced tragedy and heartache too. Both of them carried emotional scars, but they were about to face all the challenges together, as one, as a team.

Now it was their time for a new beginning. Archie held Olivia's hand and Olivia held Charles'. As the three of them walked back to their house from the peaceful Church, Archie considered himself a lucky man. He knew what he had was rare. The love of your life is someone incredibly special. Other people will come into and out of your life, whom you may think you love, but it is only a fleeting attraction. The first time you truly love, that individual will always hold a piece of you. That person holds the very first piece of yourself you ever gave away. When you give your heart to someone, it is a beautiful, leap-of-faith moment when you realize you are truly alive. It is a moment when you comprehend what it means to be selfless and to sacrifice for another person without needing or desiring anything in return. In love, you can experience feelings of happiness, hope, and passion that were unattainable before.

Archie smiled to himself and he concluded his thoughts: That is the type of love to die for; the type of love that is magnanimous and unconditional.

Epilogue

A pioneering, young boy, with striking blue eyes, was meandering down the beach looking for a coconut at the bottom of the palm trees. At periodic intervals, when he spotted a potentially good one, he would sprint down to the coconut to inspect it. He finally approached one that had uncompromising promise. It was unbroken and had a perfect ripeness about it. He picked it up and shook it vigorously next to his ear, to hear the sloshing of the milk inside. Pleased with his find, he withdrew his knife and cut an opening in the hard coconut shell.

As he was walking back through town to find his mother, he noticed a soldier putting up a fresh wanted poster on the town wall over an old, tattered one. Curious, as all boys are, he sauntered over and observed the Royal soldier as he put up the poster.

Once the soldier finished, he stepped away to admire his work, revealing the bold, black title: *Wanted Dead or Alive: Archie Rose.* The rest of the poster continued in smaller print:

Alias Trent Kingsley. Last seen in London. Crimes against

the Crown and Church of England: murder, kidnapping, piracy, treason, false identity, and perjury. Report any information or whereabouts to proper British authorities.

There was a sketch of Archie's face and the illustration made him look like a mean and vicious criminal.

The soldier glanced down at the boy studying the wanted poster. "He's been on the loose for over eight years now. Some say he has vanished in the night like a ghost, but your grandfather will stop at nothing to make sure this pirate is caught. Over the years, I have lost my belief that this pirate will ever be found. For all we know, he is already dead in some corner of the world."

The courageous boy heard the solider but continued to study the face. "I will catch him," the boy said confidently as he mused of vanquishing the pirate.

"We will see about that lad," the solider chuckled as he turned and walked off.

The young boy fantasized about the day he would conquer Archie Rose and be able to claim the hand of any beautiful lass, as the hero of Port Nassau. As the boy continued to stand there sipping on the coconut milk and daydreaming how he would avenge the Crown, his mother placed a hand on her son's shoulder.

"Hi ya mum," the boy said looking up at his mother standing by his side.

His mother did not respond or look down at her son. Her eyes gazed upon the familiar face in the poster staring back at her. No tears fell for this man any more. She would not shed another tear in her life over the lying scoundrel who had betrayed her. She would cheer and clap in jubilation on the day he was hanged by the neck.

Finally peering down at her son, Isabel maliciously said, "Take a good look Sinclair. Remember that face. If you ever meet that man, you have my permission to put a dagger through his vile heart."

The venomous statement made Sinclair shiver as an icy sensation ran down his spine. He had only known his mother to be loving and generous and this outburst made him fearful. Sinclair did not respond, as he obediently eyed the sketch of Archie, memorizing in every detail so he would never forget the face.

Isabel's cold heart and eyes softened slightly as she led her son away from the poster. She thought to herself, as she had myriad times before: Why Archie? What did I do to you to deserve such abandonment?

───────────

A crocodile's eyes barely visible above the Everglade water watched silently as Rémi Montre rowed his small wooden boat nonchalantly in the blazing afternoon sun. A crocodile will stay hidden, swimming slowly, concealing itself beneath the water long enough to sneak up on its prey, then at the last moment when life seems so peaceful and serene, the crocodile uses its speed and strength to capture its prey in its powerful, deadly jaws. The prey does not stand a chance. Helplessly, the animal will struggle and fight for life, but it is a futile pursuit for the omnipotent beast has already won.

Rémi tied up his boat at the small dock jetting from the bank. He walked down the main road in the small town and stepped into El Sol Saloon and Lodge. Rémi checked into the lodge and then went strolling through the town to familiarize himself with his new home.

The Florida territory had become Rémi's hiding place since his miraculous escape from the Battle of Nassau. Rémi moved often, never staying in one place for over too long, because he did not want to become friends with anyone. He did not want to be found or recognized. He used Florida and it's expansive undeveloped Everglades as his hiding place, just as a crocodile does. Being clandestine allowed Rémi the control to quietly scheme his methods to return to authority and power without the invasive eyes of the British.

In addition, Rémi desired nothing more than to avenge himself against Archie and once again become the most notorious and feared man in the Caribbean waters. However, Rémi had lost everything—his ships, his men, his gold, and his influence. But most importantly, he had not lost his life. He was alive and he could still fight for his vengeance.

Through the years in saloons and other illicit establishments, Rémi had heard stories of a French pirate marrying the daughter of an English governor. The tale, as Rémi had heard it, was about a d'Or pirate who somehow defied death in the Battle of Nassau and then miraculously wooed the Governor's daughter while he was hanging from the noose. The noose neither broke his neck nor seemed to cut off his air. The pirate could not be killed.

As he swung there in mid-air with the noose was tight around his neck and his feet were dangling helplessly, the pirate sang to the young woman's heart. His song cast a spell over her, which saved his life, because she fell in love with him and the two were married within the week. The Governor pardoned this pirate of all his crimes and made him a full member of British society.

Rémi did not correct the man's version of the tale or the numerous other fabricated versions, but he was able to piece together a more factual account of what occurred after that dreadful Battle of Nassau. Rémi knew Archie had double-crossed him and somehow had set him up by alerting Governor Raymond of d'Or's arrival. The wrath toward Archie had boiled inside Rémi ever since he learned that Archie had survived, escaped, and married the Governor's daughter.

One lazy, hot, humid, Florida afternoon at El Sol, Rémi was lying in his bed, eyes closed, but not asleep when someone began knocking gently on his door.

"Señor Rémi? Señor Rémi?" called out the lodge manager.

"Oui, what is it?" Rémi replied irritated.

"You have a visitor?"

Rémi, who had not had a visitor in eight years, removed his hat from over his eyes and face and sat up straight. He immediately began looking around the room for his best route of escape. Rémi cautiously called back, "Who is it?"

"Señorita Saphir."

Rémi paused. He was suddenly extremely curious as to why a

French woman would be visiting him. "Bring 'er in."

The door creaked open and Le Saphir emerged into Rémi's humble room.

Standing before Rémi Montre was the most exotic creature he had ever set eyes on. He had seen many beautiful women on his travels, but none as enticing as this one. The woman was dressed from head to toe in a cerulean blue dress with the same colored shoes. Her deeply tanned face was offset by almond shaped eyes, the color of coffee and her full sensual ruby red lips were slightly parted, revealing even white teeth. Her hair, as black as a raven's wing, tumbled over her shoulders in a mass of unruly curls.

"Close the door and take a seat." Rémi indicated to a chair beside his bed.

Le Saphir closed the door and sat down, before beginning, "Capitaine Montre, you're not an easy man to find. It has taken many years for me to finally be having this conversation with you."

"Call me Rémi. I am not deserving of that title until I have a ship and a crew. Tell me, who are you?"

"Fine, Rémi. I am your second chance and your best chance at getting out of this" Le Saphir looked around the room, "Spanish pigsty and back on top."

Rémi looked astonished by her rudeness. "Says who? I don't need your help."

Le Saphir carried on brushing off Rémi's comment, "I have information about your English pet, Archie. He lied to you. He was a traitor to you and the d'Or crew. He was working with Governor Raymond the entire time. He set you up."

"I know."

Le Saphir continued, "What you don't know is after the Battle of Nassau, a few months later, Archie showed up in Saint-Domingue after your treasure and the Queen's Jewels. He escaped with the Queen's Jewels, but not your gold or treasure."

"And how do you know this?" asked Rémi suspiciously.

"I was there. I stole your treasure."

Rémi glared at Le Saphir wanting to slit her throat on the spot. "If you 'ave all my riches, then why are you here," growled Rémi.

"Settle down Rémi. I am here to make a deal with you. I don't want your gold. I want the Queen's Jewels. That is what I really care about. The Queen's Jewels for me are the one thing so precious that all the gold in the world can't buy it."

"Oui," Rémi began then paused. "You want my help to retrieve the Jewels?"

"Oui. I will finance everything...."

"With my gold," interrupted Rémi.

Le Saphir repeated, "I will finance everything. Whatever we need, wherever we need to go."

"What's in it for me?"

"You can have all your gold and treasure back once I have the Queen's Jewels. Plus, you have the added pleasure of killing Archie."

Rémi considered Le Saphir's proposal. He wanted his revenge more than he wanted his gold. "I am intrigued. When do you want to leave?"

"Today," Le Saphir said extending her hand outwards.

Rémi shook Le Saphir's hand saying, "Where are we headed?"

"Europe." Then without another word, Le Saphir turned and left the room.

Rémi quickly grabbed his captain's hat and pistol before sprinting out of the room to seek his vengeance.

◊

Retrouvailles (n.) | *French* – the happiness of meeting or finding someone again after a long separation

Proof

Made in the USA
Charleston, SC
30 June 2016